THE SHAMAN'S HOUSE

By CHRISTOFFER PETERSEN

Published by Aarluuk Press

ISBN: 978-1-980379-85-0

www.christoffer-petersen.com

strictly I am judged
but I will Endure;
oh, they who have pressed
to have convicted
to See: who I fabricated
amid all my musing.

Author's translation from
ISBLINK
by
LUDVIG MYLIUS-ERICHSEN (1872-1907)

de dømmer mig strængt
men giver mig Styrke;
o, de har trængt
til at faa sigtet sig …
Se: jeg har digtet dig
alt, jeg har tænkt.

AUTHOR'S NOTE

The settlement of Nuugaatsiaq in the Uummannaq fjord region of Greenland was all but washed away by a tsunami during the night of June 20th, 2017. The settlement was devastated, buildings and homes were destroyed, lives were lost, and the community relocated.

I spent a memorable weekend in Nuugaatsiaq at the end of the summer of 2008. Even though I lived in the area for four years, I never returned, but the memory of the people and the spirit of their ancestors buried in cairns on the mountain has remained with me always.

I chose to return to Nuugaatsiaq in the pages of *The Shaman's House* long before the tragedy struck in the summer of 2017. I hope, therefore, that the descriptions of Nuugaatsiaq within the pages of this book, serve in some small way to preserve the memory of a very special place, and a very special community.

The Shaman's House is written in British English and makes use of several Danish and Greenlandic words.

Chris
December 2017
Denmark

The Settlement

NUUGAATSIAQ, GREENLAND

Chapter 1

NUUGAATSIAQ, GREENLAND

At the first crunch of gravel outside his house, the shaman hid the tupilaq in the top drawer of his work desk. He closed the drawer with his thumbs and brushed the loose hair, fur, bone, and seaweed to one side. He picked the last of the stubborn dog hair from the front of his cornflower-blue smock, twisted it between his palms into a long strand, and hid it in his trouser pocket. The visitors knocked at the door just a few seconds later. The shaman walked to the door, opened it, and welcomed his guests into the kitchen. He stood to one side as they jostled up the three wooden steps and inside the house, rubbing the straps of their deflated lifejackets against the walls as they made space for their guide, a middle-aged Australian, twice the shaman's height, half his age, three times as loud. The guide cleared his throat to get the group's attention and gestured at the shaman.

"This is Tulugaq, a good friend of mine," the guide said. The shaman shook the guide's hand just as he had been briefed. The guests – passengers or *PAX* from the adventure cruise ship in the fjord – smiled and greeted the shaman. "Tulugaq means raven in Greenlandic." The guide smiled and waited for the shaman to nod. He placed one hand on the Greenlander's shoulder and gestured with the other at the shelves covering the walls of the tiny kitchen. They were lined with figures carved in bone, each one more gruesome than the next. The figures leered at the PAX with assorted bulbous eyes, sharp teeth, exquisite fingers, and typically large phalluses. Some of the younger PAX giggled, the older ones stared, sizing up each figure for the display case in their dens back home in North America, Western Europe, and Australasia. "I've made a deal with Tulugaq," the guide said. "He has agreed to a buy two, get one free arrangement, but remember to buy only the tupilaq that are legal under the CITES agreement. So, only buy those that are…"

"Made from reindeer bone," said a large passenger as he crossed the kitchen floor to study a particular figure that had caught his eye. "It's a shame," he said as he inspected a small figurine polished to the colour of cream. "The narwhal figures are so intricate."

"And illegal to export," said the guide.

"I know, but…"

The shaman slipped into the living room and stood by his desk. Two of the PAX followed him, beckoning to the guide to take their picture with Tulugaq.

"Do you mind?" they asked.

The shaman shook his head. He posed between the two women as the guide took photos with their digital cameras and iPhones. The shaman waited for the cameras to be returned, took a step backward and paused as a tall man entered the kitchen. The shaman's brow furrowed as he studied the man, noting that he wore no lifejacket, and that his jacket was black, unlike the red and yellow cruise ship jackets provided for all PAX. The man caught the shaman's eye at the same time that the guide noticed him.

"Sorry, mate, this is a private viewing," the guide said. "If you wouldn't mind waiting outside until we're finished."

"I can wait," the man said. He removed his glasses and wiped them with a cloth from his pocket.

"Outside, if you please."

The PAX paused to listen as the man cleared his throat, nodded at the shaman, and said, "I'll be outside."

"Thank you," the guide said as the man left. The shaman walked to a window and watched the man as he walked across the gravel to stand beside two tall men dressed in black fatigues. The men wore pistols in holsters clipped to broad belts. "Do you know them?" the guide said, as he leaned around the shaman.

"*Naamik*," the shaman said.

"Ah, and that means?"

"No. I don't know them."

The guide stepped back to answer queries from several of the PAX. There were twelve of them, and they spilled out of the kitchen and into the lounge. The shaman posed for more photos, and received handfuls of Danish kroner, as the PAX bought all of the figures made from the antlers, bones, and skulls of the reindeer. Once the shelves had been stripped of tupilaq fit for export, the PAX and their guide left, and the shaman was alone for the time it took them to walk back to the zodiac inflatables waiting to take them back to the ship. He stuffed the money in a second drawer in his desk and stared at the men outside, until the man with the glasses walked up to the kitchen door, knocked and entered.

"Tea?" the man said in Danish.

"Just for you?"

"For you and me. My men will wait outside."

The shaman filled a pan of water from a plastic

container and put it on the stove to boil. The man studied the remaining figures on the shelves.

"Do you use a drill?" he said.

"Sometimes."

"So, that's how you get them so smooth." The man lifted a figure made of narwhal. He rubbed his thumb across the surface.

"Are you a collector?"

"Me? No." He laughed. "At least not these. I am only interested in tupilaq."

"These are tupilaq," the shaman said. He frowned through the steam as the water boiled.

"They might think so," said the man, with a nod to the retreating blight of yellow and red PAX as they boarded the zodiacs. "But I think you and I know the difference. Don't we?"

The shaman put a tea bag inside a dirty mug, added the water, and a generous helping of sugar. He removed the bag and handed the mug to the man.

"Thank you."

"You're welcome," the shaman said, as he prepared another mug of tea.

"Now," said the man, "how about you show me the real tupilaq. The ones you don't find in display cases, nooks, and dens. Eh?" He took a step into the living room. "Are they in here?"

"Wait," said the shaman. He left his mug on the kitchen counter and followed the man. He stopped as the man put his mug on the desk and picked at the loose strands of fur and seaweed on the work surface. The shaman watched as the man sorted them with his fingers, plucking a hair from the tangled mess and holding it up to the light.

"Human?"

"*Aap.*"

"Female?" The man teased the hair into one strand the length of his arm.

The shaman raised his eyebrows, *yes.*

"Whose?"

"I cannot say."

"Fair enough," the man said, as he laid the hair back on the desk. "But you use it to bind the tupilaq. Am I right?"

"*Aap.*"

"Show me."

The man stepped to one side as the shaman opened the drawer in his desk. He curled his fingers around a rough figure and held it in the light. The man nodded as the shaman opened his palm.

"Yes," he said. "Just as I thought. You have used the woman's hair to bind the seaweed around the bone." He cocked his head to one side. "A human bone?"

"*Tuttu.* Reindeer."

"And this?" The man used the nail of his little finger to tease the arms of the figure.

"Wood, from the sea."

"Of course," he said, and lowered his hand, "and when it is finished, will you cum on it?" The shaman frowned, and the man made a jerking motion with his hand. "Will you cum on it?"

"*Aap.*"

"I read that somewhere. But why?"

The shaman placed the figure back in the drawer and said, "For energy. For the magic."

"Ah, magic," the man said. He picked up the mug of tea and walked across the floor to the couch, the cushions sighed as he sat down. "I know a thing or two about magic."

The shaman turned the chair at his desk to face the man and sat down. They stared at each other as the man sipped his tea.

"Do you want to buy a tupilaq?" the shaman said. "A real one?"

"Perhaps." The man leaned forward to place his mug on the floor. "Tell me," he said, "what can it do? What can *that* one do?"

"That one will keep a child safe."

"How?"

"I will throw it in the sea."

"After you have charged it with your energy?"

"*Aap.*"

"Why?"

"There is a girl travelling to Uummannaq. She is going alone. Her mother wants her to be safe."

"And so she paid you to make a tupilaq?"

"*Aap.*"

"I see," the man said. He stood up and walked over to the wall. He stopped in front of a photo and tapped his finger on the frame. "Is this your family?"

The shaman nodded. He rested his hands in his lap. He waited.

"And where are they?"

"Nuuk."

"Why?"

The shaman wrinkled his nose and shrugged. "They don't like Nuugaatsiaq."

"They don't like this village?" The man removed his glasses and cleaned them. "That's strange," he said. "It's such a beautiful place."

"No jobs."

"That's true," he said and stuffed the cloth in his

pocket. He put on his glasses and gestured in the direction of the cruise ship. "But you do all right."

"In the summer."

"And the rest of the year?"

"I hunt." The shaman pointed his thumb at his desk. "I help people."

"Yes," the man said, "about that." He crossed the floor and stood next to the shaman, "I want you to help me."

"You want me to make a tupilaq?"

"Yes."

"It can be dangerous."

"How?"

The shaman took the figure from the drawer. He pointed at the different elements as he explained. "If the girl finds this, she can take the magic. She can ruin it, turn it against herself."

"I don't understand."

"This tupilaq will guard her from the sea. If she takes it from the sea, it cannot help her." He paused. "She might drown."

The man looked out of the window, and waved at the two armed men waiting outside the house. The taller of the two tapped his watch, and the man nodded. He looked at the shaman. "Go on."

"This tupilaq is made to protect a person, but if I make a tupilaq to hurt someone the opposite is true. If I put something of a person inside and that person finds it, they can use it against you, if their magic is stronger than yours."

The man frowned. "How do you know I want to use a tupilaq against a person?"

"Them," the shaman said and pointed at the men outside the house.

"Alright. Suppose I do." The man reached inside his pocket and removed a length of black hair twisted around a pencil stub. "I want you to use this."

The shaman took the hair and held it closer to the window. He turned the stub in his fingers and rubbed a loose end of the hair. He sniffed it and said, "This is not real?"

"The hair is real."

"But the colour."

"No," the man said, "she has a habit of changing that." He leaned against the wall. "Can you still use it?"

"*Aap*. But maybe it will lose some power."

"Then maybe you will have to charge it twice," the man said. He shook his head as he laughed. "The very thought."

"You laugh."

"Yes."

"But this is not funny."

"No," the man said. The smile on his lips faded. "It is deadly serious."

"What should your tupilaq do?"

"It must kill." The man held the shaman's gaze and said, "Can you do that?"

"*Aap*," he whispered. "I can do that. But the hair…"

"I will settle for wounding or maiming the girl."

"Girl?"

"In her twenties. She is quite resourceful."

"And she is coming here?"

The man pushed off the wall, walked around the small living room and stopped at the window. He wiped a smear of grime from the glass with his thumb, leaned close to the clean spot of window and stared at the oil tank to the right of the general store. It was cordoned with a chain link fence, but the door was open, and the man smiled. Beyond the tank was a narrow beach leading to the water. The sand was littered with clumps and boulders of ice, debris from the icebergs in the fjord. He turned to the shaman and nodded.

"Yes," he said, "she will come here, eventually."

"When?"

"Oh, I don't know. Perhaps at the beginning of winter?" He moved away from the window. "Which reminds me," he said, "I am going to need your house." He waved at the men outside and waited as they hurried to the door and into the kitchen. The shaman stood as they entered the living room.

"Don't move, grandpa," said the tall one. His hand strayed to the pistol at his hip. His partner moved into the room and took a position by the side of the couch.

"Who are you?" the shaman said. He looked at the man.

"You can call me Vestergaard, or you can call me *the Magician*. A lot of people do."

The shaman flicked his gaze from one face to the next, returning to the man in the middle of the room, the one calling himself a magician. "Then you know magic?" he said.

"I can make things happen, or people disappear, in my own way, yes."

"Then you don't need me," the shaman said and moved to throw the pencil stub of hair into the middle of the room. He stopped when Vestergaard raised his hand.

"You will make me a tupilaq, the most powerful

you have ever made," he said, "and you will allow me to use your house, as and when I need to."

"What if I don't want to?"

Vestergaard clicked his fingers and pointed at the picture on the wall. The tall man walked to the wall and tugged the picture from beneath the tacks pinning it in place. The corners ripped and the shaman twitched, fists clenched.

"Careful, grandpa," the tall man said. He took a long look at the photo before folding it in half and stuffing it inside his jacket.

"You will do what I say, because I have friends in Nuuk," said Vestergaard.

"I have no choice?"

"None."

The shaman relaxed his fingers and smoothed his palms on his thighs. "I need a name," he said. "A real one."

"Why?"

"For the tupilaq."

"Alright." Vestergaard sat down on the couch. He leaned back and crossed his legs. "Her name is Konstabel Fenna Brongaard."

"Konstabel?"

"She was in the Sirius Patrol," Vestergaard said. He waved a hand in the air. "It's not important, but she still uses the title."

"Boss," said the tall man. "Should you be telling him all this?"

Vestergaard looked at the shaman. Studied him for a moment, and then said, "It's alright. I believe we understand one another." The shaman raised his eyebrows in agreement and waited for Vestergaard to continue. "Besides, it might come to nothing. We still don't know if our favourite Konstabel will complete her mission."

"And if she does, boss?"

"Then she will need a safe house," Vestergaard said and looked at the shaman. "This one."

The Mountain

NORTH CASCADES, WASHINGTON, USA

Chapter 2

SEATTLE TACOMA AIRPORT, WASHINGTON, USA

It should have been simple, but like most conversations Konstabel Fenna Brongaard had with men in uniform, it quickly turned into an interrogation, and then the border patrol officer called his supervisor. Fenna saw his hand as he slid it under the table and pressed what she imagined to be the emergency button, signalling that he required assistance. Burwardsley, she noticed, had been processed through the Seattle Tacoma Airport without any problems. *What is it about me,* she wondered, *that makes everything so complicated?* The supervisor approached the desk and stared at Fenna before signalling to his colleague to join him for a moment. Fenna watched as they whispered back and forth. She tapped her fingers on the counter. She stopped when she saw her nails. There was blood in the corners, the stubborn kind that soap could not remove. She traced the small scratches and tiny scars from her nails to her knuckles, shrugged and smiled as she decided that maybe the customs guy had a point. She saw her reflection in the glass of the booth and dipped her head so that her fringe might hide the bruising on her cheek, the graze beneath her eye.

"Yeah," she whispered. "I guess I was crazy to think this might work." She stopped speaking as the supervisor approached the glass and sat down, the officer stood behind him, and Fenna noticed his hand resting on the grip of the Beretta at his hip.

"Fenna Brongaard?" the supervisor said.

"Yes."

"Arriving from?"

"Reykjavik," she said. "Originally, anyway. There was a layover..."

"In Amsterdam. Yes, we have you there too."

"What does that mean?"

The supervisor studied her passport, giving Fenna a moment to take stock of the security crowding the entrance to the United States of America. She looked up when he started to speak.

"You're aware of the situation in America right now? You heard about the assassination?"

"Yes." Fenna held her breath for a moment, and thought, *more than you think.*

"Then you can appreciate us being interested in a young woman of your height, hair colour," he paused, his eyes lingering over Fenna's face, "facial description."

"You're saying you are looking for someone matching my description?"

"It was all over the news," the man said and stared at Fenna. "You must have seen the pictures?"

"Sure." Fenna frowned. "But if that's all this is..."

"It's a pretty big deal."

"I understand, but if I was that person, do you really think I would be trying to get *into* the country? You don't think I'd be trying to get out?" The supervisor stiffened, and the officer curled his finger around the grip of his pistol. "Sorry," Fenna said and raised her hands for a moment. "I'm just tired after the flight. I am sure the situation is tense." She glanced at the security officers as they talked into their microphones. "Very tense," she said.

The supervisor stood and gestured for his colleague to sit in the chair. He gave the officer

Fenna's passport as the man sat down. "You're right, the situation is tense. We need to be thorough." He tapped the officer on the shoulder. "You filed ESTA, a tourist VISA. My co-worker will process you now." He took a step backward, lingering just a metre from the glass.

"What's the purpose of your visit, Miss?" the officer asked.

"Recreation."

"Specifically?"

"Backpacking."

The officer lifted his head and peered over the counter. Fenna smiled as he scrutinised her trekking trousers and hiking boots.

"The rest of my gear was in the hold," she said.

"You're hiking alone?"

"I can take care of myself." Fenna held her breath as the man shifted his gaze to her face. She tried a smile, but he ignored her.

"Just process her, Richard," the supervisor said. He nodded at the line behind Fenna as the officer looked at him."It's going to be a long day. We can't hold her just because she looks like someone – regardless of the circumstances."

The officer handed Fenna her passport, pinching it in his grip as she took it.

"What?" she said.

"Just one more thing. Where will you be staying?"

"Motels and camping."

"No contacts in Seattle?"

"Maybe."

"Who?"

Fenna thought about the hour she spent with an American at Heathrow Airport. "Solomon Owens," she said. "He's a friend of the family."

"Richard," the supervisor said.

"Alright," said the officer. He let go of Fenna's passport. "We're done here."

Fenna waited for a moment, tucked her passport into the pocket of her hiking jacket and looked from one man to the other. She walked away as the supervisor turned his back to her. *Don't push it, Fenna.* She nodded at the officer and walked through the border inspection area, following the signage to the baggage reclaim section of Arrivals.

Burwardsley met her at the conveyor belt for the flight from Amsterdam, as he did his best to blend in with the shorter travellers – mostly Chinese – waiting for their luggage. He stood close to Fenna, but, from a distance, observers would have struggled to connect the two.

"You took your time," he whispered.

"Mistaken identity," she said, her voice low, lips hardly moving.

"I'll pick up the car. Meet me out front."

Burwardsley walked to the belt and picked up his military Bergan. He slung it over one shoulder and walked toward the exit. Fenna waited for her backpack to roll around the belt before grabbing it. She used the bathroom, and then walked through the exit, orientating herself with a quick glance at the signs.

It had taken the best part of a week to set up what Fenna considered the rescue operation, to find Alice – America's most wanted – and to get her out of the country. The young assassin was going to be the world's greatest bargaining chip, and Fenna had sold her to the highest bidder. *I know where she is*, she had said to Vestergaard when he had cornered her at the end of the road just north of the landing strip of Nuuk International Airport in Greenland's capital. Now, the million-dollar question was if she had been right.

When Fenna met Alice on the military base in Yuma, Arizona, they had bonded, in secret, as the only women on a base populated by arrogant A-type special forces soldiers. *Men with more testosterone than sense*, she remembered. *Apart from the smart ones, and they were the most dangerous. Men like Burwardsley.* Fenna looked up as a Jeep rumbled past. It looked like the kind of car he would hire, and she wondered at just how much trust she had placed in him – *the man who had my partner killed.* She hadn't slept on the flight, not least for the conflicting thoughts battling in her mind, thoughts that included her closest ally, who, just a few months earlier, had not only been responsible for ending her Sirius partner's life, but had done his best to end hers too. *And yet, he's the one with the contacts all of a sudden.* She sighed. *I need him.*

A string of cars stopped in front of the entrance, loading and unloading travellers, friends, and loved ones. Fenna waited, long enough for drivers in the next line of cars to switch on their lights as the twilight became dusk. She blinked as the driver of a small Prius flashed its lights. Fenna shouldered her pack and walked over to it. The driver popped the trunk as she reached the car, and Fenna dumped her pack before opening the passenger door and sliding onto the seat.

"You took your time," she said.

"Tell me about it," Burwardsley said. He waited for Fenna to fasten her seatbelt before pulling away and into the stream of traffic heading toward the city.

"This is cosy," she said, looking around the interior of the car.

"But less conspicuous."

Fenna looked at Burwardsley hunched behind the steering wheel and laughed. "Yeah, about that."

"You want to drive?"

"I don't know where we're going."

"Exactly," he said and accelerated onto the highway. "So shut the fuck up."

"Touchy."

"Just tired." Burwardsley took one hand off the wheel and pressed his thumbnail into one of his fingers, just beneath the nail.

"Still can't feel anything, eh?"

"Just tingling. But better than before."

Fenna remembered pulling Burwardsley out of the refrigerated container on the building site in Nuuk – a convenient Black Site, operated by one of several likely agencies. *But which one?*

"How about you?" he said. "Tired?"

"A little. But we have to keep going, right?"

"Right. Just one stop, to pick up some gear, guns, and ammo." Burwardsley smiled. "Any preferences?"

Fenna leaned back, lifted her foot onto the edge of the seat and tugged off one hiking boot, and then the other. She bent her knees to her chest, squirmed her toes on the dashboard, and said, "I can shoot, but I don't really give a shit what I shoot with."

"You should," Burwardsley said and slapped at her feet.

"What?" Fenna sneered as she lowered her feet to the foot well.

"They smell."

"They've smelled worse," she said, and then, "*I've* smelled worse."

"I know."

"Yeah, I tend to forget that." Fenna chewed at her lip for a moment, glancing at Burwardsley when she thought his attention was focused on the road. "We never talked about it," she said, as he slipped the Prius into the outer lane. "When you and that Nepali bastard..."

"Bahadur."

"Right, when you had me stretched between you, when you sliced my clothes off with that fucking sword of his."

"Fenna..."

"How far were you going to go?"

"Come on, Konstabel."

"How far?"

Burwardsley looked at Fenna, held her gaze for a second, and then said, "As far as I needed to."

Fenna nodded and looked away. "I thought so."

"I'm a professional, Fenna. We both are. Right now we are on a job – your job. So, wind your neck in, and get with the programme."

"Right."

"I mean it," he said and slowed as they approached an off ramp. "Now, what preference do you have?" He slowed the car to a stop at the end of the ramp.

"Short-stock carbine. Can your friend do that?"

"Sure. What else?"

"Nine millimetre back-up."

"Glock? I'm not sure he can do Austrian."

"No preference. Just small, with a large mag."

Fenna looked out of the passenger window. The

street lights and neon signage reflected on her cheeks and caught in her eyes. She saw her reflection in the side mirror and smiled at the thought of what a little colour could do to her cheeks, how she had used it on a ship and at a conference, to grab the attention of her mark, her assignment, usually some bastard who would die shortly after meeting her. *I'm getting good at this. Perhaps too good.* She nodded when Burwardsley said they should have a couple of grenades each.

The neon sign of the *Subway* at the junction caught Fenna's attention. She sat up and said, "Wait."

"What?"

"Food."

Burwardsley pulled into the parking lot of the *Subway* once the lights changed. Fenna tugged on her boots and they got out. She lifted her chin and flicked her eyes at the police patrol car parked outside and Burwardsley nodded.

"Won't be a problem. We're not on any watch list."

"No?" she said. "Why do you think it took me so long at passport control?"

Burwardsley stopped at the door, his massive frame blocked the light from the restaurant, throwing Fenna into shadow.

"Hey, I can't help it if I look like her."

"You look like Alice?"

"A few years older, otherwise..."

"Great," he said and pulled open the door. Fenna followed him inside. He nodded at the policeman eating at a table by the window, and approached the counter. The young Chinese man behind the counter pulled on a fresh pair of plastic gloves and waited for their order. Burwardsley ordered for both of them.

Fenna said nothing.

"Go sit down," he whispered. "I'll bring it over."

Fenna sat at the table closest to the counter, her back to the policeman. She saw his image reflected in the glass, he was staring at her back. Burwardsley sat down and handed her a wrapped sandwich.

"We're eating here?" she said.

"Still waiting on my sandwich."

Fenna leaned across the table. "Fine," she said. "But it looks like you're dining with public enemy number one."

"Something you failed to mention back in Greenland," he said and stared at her.

"They had guns, you fuck. It was the end of the line."

Burwardsley's lips parted, and a barely-suppressed tremor rippled across his shoulders.

"You think this is funny?"

"No," he said, and laughed.

"We haven't even been in the States for more than..." she looked at her watch.

"A couple of hours, and we're about to be busted by Policeman Plod over there."

"What?" Fenna glanced over her shoulder. "Shit. He's coming over."

"Just relax."

Burwardsley shuffled his seat away from the table and placed his hands on his thighs. Fenna took a breath and followed his lead. She leaned back in her seat and placed her sandwich on the table. She closed her eyes for a moment and pictured the layout of the restaurant — the counter with the Chinese man preparing their food, the policeman, and no other guests. *He can take cover behind the counter*, she thought with a glance at the young Chinese man. She caught Burwardsley's eye. *He'll take out the cop while I get the car.* Fenna willed her hands to be still, and, with a quick plan in place, she felt that familiar calm that came just before the storm of action. She was ready, not for the first time, and definitely not the last. The policeman stopped at their table, his thumbs tucked into the front of his belt, just behind the buckle.

"Evening," he said.

"Hi," said Burwardsley. Fenna smiled. "Can we help you?"

"Maybe," the policeman said. "Your accent? British?"

"You got me there. It's a difficult one to hide, especially over here."

"It sure is. And what about you, Miss?" he said. "Where are you from?"

"Denmark," Fenna said, grateful all of a sudden for her own accent. She added a little more for effect. "West coast. I'm from Esbjerg."

"Really?" The policeman relaxed his grip on his belt, and Fenna imagined she saw the tension ease out of the man's shoulders. "My family is from Norway, originally."

"Really? Have you visited?"

"On my pay?" the man laughed. Fenna smiled, noticing for the first time his grey moustache and the wrinkles around his eyes. "Maybe as a retirement gift, for me and the wife."

"Norway's beautiful," Fenna said. "You agree, Mike?"

"Oh yes," Burwardsley said and smiled. He looked up as the Chinese man brought his sandwich. "And we'd better be going," he said and stood up.

"Nice to meet you," Fenna said. She picked up her sandwich and the two drinks from the tray. The policeman took a step back for her to pass and she followed Burwardsley to the exit.

The policeman coughed and called out just as she reached the door. "Just a second, Miss," he said and pulled his mobile from his belt.

Fenna glanced at Burwardsley, caught the slight shake of his head. She turned to the policeman and waited.

"Something wrong?"

"Well, you might be from Denmark, and I don't doubt your friend here is from England..."

"But?"

"But... you look real familiar." He held up his mobile and turned the screen toward them. "See what I mean?" he said and let his free hand slide to his gun.

"Yeah," Fenna said. "I see what you mean."

Chapter 3

Burwardsley let go of the door and it closed with a quiet snick. He nudged Fenna and took the drinks and sandwich from her hands, leaning in close to whisper in her ear, "He's all yours."

The policeman turned the Smartphone in his hand and studied the screen, flicking his eyes from Fenna to the mobile and back again. The young man retreated from the counter, edging his way to the storage room opposite the cash register. Fenna followed his movement before turning back to the policeman. She felt the second kick of adrenaline since entering the restaurant, flexed her fingers, and curbed the rush of energy. She gauged the distance between them, made the calculations, factoring in the policeman's height, reach, build, age, his likely speed, his dexterity. She lifted her chin and took a step forward. The policeman tightened his grip around the pistol. He lowered the mobile.

"What are the odds," Fenna said, "of you catching the President's assassin?"

"Then you know who that is?"

"Yes," she said and sighed. "This is the second time today I've been stopped because of her."

"And the first time?"

"At the airport."

"And they let you in." He let his hand slide from the pistol.

Fenna waited. The hum of the air conditioning unit filled the space between them, with a steady drone punctuated suddenly by a loud slurp. She turned as Burwardsley swallowed and let the drinking straw slip from his lips.

"What?" he said.

"You're enjoying this?" Fenna whispered.

"We're on holiday." Burwardsley looked at the policeman. "A vacation. We've been planning this for months." He shrugged. "It's not every day your girlfriend gets mistaken for an assassin."

"I guess not," the policeman said. He shrugged at Fenna. "Sorry, Miss, but the whole country is pretty keyed-up right now."

"So," she said, "maybe I should wear a hat?"

"Maybe."

Fenna laughed. She could feel the adrenaline flushing out of her system. She relaxed, looked the policeman in the eye and said, "Did you just agree that I should wear a disguise?"

"I guess I did," he said and slipped the mobile into his trouser pocket.

Burwardsley took another slurp of cola. The *Subway* employee stepped out of the storage room and shuffled a selection of cookies onto the counter.

"They're on me," he said.

"Thanks." Burwardsley pressed his cola into Fenna's hand and grabbed the cookies from the counter. He winked at the policeman and walked to the door. "Time to hit the road, baby," he said and walked out of the restaurant. Fenna smiled at the policeman and followed Burwardsley into the parking lot. The light from the restaurant reflected on the rain beading on the car.

"Baby?" she said. "Really?" Fenna licked at a drop of rain on her lip.

"It seemed like the thing to say," Burwardsley said. He placed the food on the roof of the car and opened the door. Fenna did the same. They looked at each other for a moment, laughing as they picked up the food and slipped inside.

"We don't need that again," Fenna said and pressed the drinks into the plastic holders.

"Maybe you should buy a hat?" Burwardsley said, backing the car out of the parking space, as Fenna pulled on her seatbelt.

Fenna curled a fist into his ribs and suppressed a smile. "Just drive," she said.

Burwardsley pulled out of the parking lot and followed the road east, beyond a row of cheap motels and into a small industrial area. There was an open lot with a small concrete building framed by trash cans and dumpsters on either side. Burwardsley pulled around the back of the building, stopped the car and turned off the engine.

"Eat your sandwich," he said. "I'll let my guy know we are here."

Fenna ate as she watched Burwardsley climb out from behind the wheel and walk over to the building. There was a metal box screwed into the concrete wall by the side of a rusted metal door. Burwardsley opened the box and pulled out a handset. He held it to his ear and waited. Fenna heard him grunt a few words before he returned to the car, squeezed his massive frame into the driver's seat and unwrapped his sandwich. He left the door open and hooked his left leg out of the car.

"We just wait?" Fenna said, taking the last bite of hers and wiping her hands on her trousers.

"We do," he said.

She opened the glove compartment and shuffled through the papers until her fingers caught on something a little sturdier. "*Rand McNally*," she said and pulled out a map of the State. "Totally old school." Fenna unfolded the map on her lap and traced a route to the North Cascades Mountain Range to the east, close to the Canadian Border.

"So why did the girl…"

"Alice."

"Right," Burwardsley said. "Why did she choose this particular cabin?" He pressed the empty sandwich wrapper into a ball and tossed it onto the back seat.

"It's personal," Fenna said.

"How?"

She looked at Burwardsley. "It's the last place she and her dad visited, before he died."

"The lookout cabin?"

"He was a climber," Fenna said.

Burwardsley sipped at the cola. He pulled his leg inside the car as the rain increased, spreading from beads to damp patches on his cargo trousers.

"My old man was a banker. An arrogant sod at that. We didn't talk much, and he parcelled me off to boarding school when my mother got sick. We haven't talked since she died."

Fenna turned her head. "Not at all?"

"Nope." Burwardsley finished the cola and tossed the empty cup into the back. "It was my aunt who came to both my graduations – school and the Marines. She's the only link to my old man, and his money."

"Any brothers? Sisters?"

"Nope. Just my aunt."

Fenna thought of her sister looking after their alcoholic mother in Esbjerg. She stifled a pang of guilt, consoling herself with the thought that their lives were so far removed, they wouldn't have anything to talk about, nothing to connect them, not since her father died.

"What about you?" Burwardsley said. "What about your old man?"

"He was in the Jægerkorps, killed in Afghanistan."

"Hunter Force? Yeah, I know them. They're about the only unit that can give us a run for our money. How did he die?"

Fenna took a breath. "I don't know."

"Classified?"

"Maybe. I never asked, and no-one told me." *Perhaps one day*, she thought.

Burwardsley slapped Fenna's arm, as a taxi stopped on the street and an African American woman got out. She walked around the cab, tottering as she found her balance. Her high heels, Fenna noticed as the woman approached, were like meat skewers, pressed into thick ankles.

"I thought you said it was a guy?"

"Just wait," Burwardsley said, a grin spreading across his face.

The woman stopped at the door to the building, nodded at Burwardsley, and then unlocked it with a key attached to a long chain. There was a metal tube dangling from the end. It reminded Fenna of a policeman's nightstick, just shorter.

"Let's go," Burwardsley said, as the woman opened the door. Fenna followed him out of the car. They picked their way between the trash until they stepped inside a dark space, the size of a closet, just wide enough for them to stand side by side. Burwardsley's upper arm pressed against Fenna's shoulder, and he cocked his head to one side of a naked bulb screwed into a plastic light fitting in the ceiling. They blinked as it was switched on, revealing a small armoury that filled the building space beyond the thick metal grille. Burwardsley squeezed around Fenna to close and lock the door behind them. He pressed against her as he turned to face the woman leaning against the counter behind the grille. Fenna looked at the stiletto heels the woman placed on the counter, and caught her eye.

"Them fuckers gonna kill me," the woman said. Fenna frowned at the deep boom of her voice. She looked at Burwardsley and said, "What you want, babe? What you need?"

"Two M4 carbines," he said. The woman pulled two purple tickets from a wire suspended beneath the counter. She placed them on the surface, tapping them with thick nails glued onto stubby scarred fingers.

"And?"

"Couple of pistols. One 9 mil."

"American?"

"Austrian," said Fenna. "If you've got one?"

"Listen child," she said and put a green ticket beside the purple ones. "There ain't nothing I don't got." She cocked her head and stared at Fenna. "What kind of Glock?"

"I don't mind."

"You should, child. How about a 20?"

"Sure. Why not?" Fenna caught herself from commenting as the woman sighed.

"And you, B? You don't want some Austrian shit, do you."

"You know what I want, Charlie."

"Yeah, babe," Charlie said. She flashed her white

teeth at Burwardsley and placed a thick brown ticket on the counter. "A Browning Fighting Pistol," she said, forcing a mock shiver from her shoulders to her large, masculine behind. "Such a sexy weapon for my sexy friend."

"Alright, Charlie," Burwardsley said. "Take it down a notch."

"But, babe..."

"I mean it."

Fenna caught the edge in Burwardsley's voice. She glanced at his face and saw the steel in his eyes. She had seen it before. From Charlie's reaction, she had too. *Before or after he became a she?* Fenna wondered. Charlie placed her palms on the counter and lowered her eyes. Fenna studied her nails, broken, chipped, false. The rest of Charlie's ensemble was just as cheap, and yet, Fenna was beginning to see the merits of such a disguise, if that was what it was, for what must be the most well-stocked illegal arms store in Washington State. She nodded, and risked a smile for Charlie.

"What?" she said.

"Nothing. I'm just impressed. That's all."

Charlie stared at Fenna and then laughed. "Sure, honey. Be impressed. I don't mind. Charlie has the best stock..."

"In the wettest State of America," said Burwardsley. "I know, but we are on a tight schedule. We need to get going."

Charlie smoothed her hands off the counter and plucked at the plastic tickets suspended from the rail. "Okay, B. I'm all yours. Ready and ..." She closed her mouth at another look from Burwardsley.

"Eight grenades."

"HE or my friend, William Peter?"

"What's that?" said Fenna.

"White phosphorous," said Burwardsley. He waved a hand around the store. "There's a lot Vietnam surplus here."

"And white phosphorous?"

"Sticks on the skin and burns, child," said Charlie.

"It could be useful," Burwardsley said. "They certainly won't expect it. Okay," he said and nodded. "Add another M4 and one more Glock. As back-up," he said, when Fenna frowned.

Charlie swept the tickets off the counter into her large palm. She closed her fist around the tickets and said, "How many rounds?"

"Five magazines each for the carbines. Another three for the pistols."

Charlie nodded and walked away from the counter. She stopped when Burwardsley called out her name.

"You forget something, B?"

"No, but maybe you did." He took a step closer to the grille and said, "My special order?"

"Right," Charlie said and nodded. "For our mutual friend."

"That's right," Burwardsley said. He leaned against the grille as Charlie weaved her way between the racks of weapons, piling them into a shopping trolley as if she was picking groceries from the aisles in the local Kmart.

"What's that about?" said Fenna. "What special order? Who's the mutual friend?"

"You don't need to know everything, Konstabel."

"I think I do. It's my op."

"No," Burwardsley said. "It's Vestergaard's, for as long as we let him think it is. But if we are going to get out of this alive, we need to play an ace or two. I have an ace, and I intend to play it."

"You going to tell me what it is?"

"I won't need to. You'll find out soon enough." Burwardsley turned around as Charlie bumped the trolley full of guns and ammunition into the counter.

"It's all reconditioned, with the serials sanded off. Apart from the grenades. But," she said and laughed, "they're so old, no-one is ever going to trace them."

"It's all good, Charlie. Thanks."

"Don't thank me before you paid for it, honey."

"PayPal?"

"You know it."

Fenna pressed her hand on Burwardsley's arm. "How are we paying?"

"PayPal," Burwardsley said. He laughed at Fenna's wrinkled brow and said, "Don't worry about it. Charlie sends a mail to another mutual friend, and we make a transaction. See," he said and pointed at Charlie as she tapped the tip of a broken nail on the keypad on her Smartphone.

"Okay," Fenna said. "That answers that, but the other thing... the special order?"

Charlie slipped her Smartphone onto the counter and reached into the shopping trolley. Wedged between the crate of grenades and wooden box of magazines for the carbines and pistols, was a long blade wrapped in a leather cloth. Fenna's breath caught in her throat as she recognised the handle, and the curve of the blade as Charlie pulled it out of the cloth and flashed it in front of them. She made swooshing noises as the blade caught the light. Fenna felt her skin contract into bumps on her arms, as she followed the arc of the kukri blade, back and forth, followed by one false swoosh after another. She forgot about the mission. She was no longer wedged into a cubicle inside a secret arms store. Fenna was back on the ice, outside a cabin in Greenland's Northeast National Park, as a small Nepali man in Arctic camouflage pressed her Glock to the back of her partner's head and pulled the trigger.

"That's a Gurkha blade," she said, the words whispering over her lips as Charlie brought the blade to a stop, at the end of a mock attack aimed at Fenna's head.

"It sure is, child. You seen one before?"

"Yes," Fenna whispered. "I have." She looked at Burwardsley, glared at him as she clenched her fists to her sides. She pressed her knuckles into her trousers. She imagined the red marks beneath blooming on her skin stretched over tight muscle. Fenna opened her mouth to speak, but Burwardsley shushed her.

"You want to get the girl?"

"Yes," she breathed.

"And you want to live?"

"Yes."

"Then we need an ace."

"But not him." Fenna shook her head, "not the Nepali."

Chapter 4

Fenna forgot all about Charlie's eccentricities and barely registered the scrape and clang of the heavy iron door in the concrete wall beneath the counter, as Burwardsley received the weapons, followed by the crate of grenades, pistols, and ammunition. The kukri was in the crate. Fenna was consumed by the thought of it as she carried the carbines into the night, stashing them to one side of the trunk of the Prius, as Burwardsley found space for the crate. She got into the car without a word or a backward glance at Charlie's covert arms store. She was aware that Burwardsley was gone for a moment, aware that he closed the rusty door, crossed in front of the car, and climbed in behind the wheel. Fenna felt the car rock as he shut the door, she even answered him when he confirmed the road they wanted. It led north and east, out of the city, into the wilds, into the mountains. *Where he is*, she thought. *The Nepali*.

It was irrational, Fenna knew, to project her combined fear and hate onto a tiny man from the Himalayas. He was only following orders. Burwardsley's orders. But there was something about the Nepali's cold professionalism that was ingrained in Fenna's mind. The man was a killer, just like Burwardsley, but there was something more. Where Burwardsley was tall, muscular, the epitome of a Lieutenant in the British Royal Marines, his Gurkha partner seemed oddly built to be a killer, *and that's what frightens me*.

"You need to understand something about Bahadur," Burwardsley said, as he pulled out of the industrial lot and onto the road. "Where he comes

35

from, his village in Nepal, it's a matter of honour to be recruited for the Gurkhas. The men that don't get selected – boys really – a lot of them don't go home. They throw themselves from the first bridge out of the village selected to host the recruiters. Better that than face the shame of returning to their home village."

Fenna listened to Burwardsley, but she didn't respond. The lights of the highway washed over the windscreen in waves, and she let the rhythm lull her into a kind of trance. The white light became a reflection from the ice, and the occasional thump of the tyres as Burwardsley changed lanes was a pistol shot, the same one each time, followed by the last sigh of Oversergent Mikael Gregersen's body as his body slumped onto the snow in front of the cabin. The only consolation she could find, was that he died in the terrain that he loved, in the country that he had adopted as his own, much like Fenna had done. *But I went one step further, I fell in love with the people too.*

It was the people, the Greenlanders, who helped Fenna forgive Burwardsley for his part in Mikael's death, for she knew he loved them too. *Love – too strong, perhaps.* He respected them, respected their harsh way of life in a wholly unforgiving environment. She had first noticed it aboard *The Ice Star*, before she had stabbed one of the men truly responsible for Mikael's death in the ear, on the bathroom floor. Burwardsley had ignored the fat lawyer's bloody ear and pitiful moans, focused as he was on Fenna. But in the hold, where the lawyer's partner, Richard Humble, had kept Dina like a filthy pet, naked in the bowels of the ship – it was there that Fenna had seen that even the consummate professional, the gun thug that was Burwardsley, had a human streak. He actually felt responsible for Dina in the end, as she twisted beneath the eaves of the cabin in Uummannatsiaq, a length of dog whip cinched around her neck. It was the death of the young Greenlandic woman that had driven Burwardsley to find the man truly responsible for everything that had happened on the ice, and it was the life of another young woman that had put Fenna and him in the same car heading north east to the North Cascades of Washington State.

"We're going into the mountains," Burwardsley said. "We need a man who understands them."

"And it has to be him?"

"I trust him with my life."

Fenna looked at Burwardsley, the corners of her eyes narrowing as she said, "But I don't."

"That, Konstabel, is something you are going to have to deal with."

"The back-up weapons. They're for him, aren't they?"

"Yep."

Fenna turned away, leaned back in her seat, and forced herself to focus on the plan. *Plan*, she laughed, *it's a hare-brained scheme at best.* She needed Alice, America's most-wanted assassin, as a bargaining chip. The girl was the only thing keeping Fenna and Burwardsley alive. Fenna laughed again.

"Something funny?" Burwardsley said as he fidgeted behind the steering wheel. "Or is the thought of Bad so unbearable you have opted for insanity?"

"Bad?"

"Sergeant Bahadur. Your mate."

"Fuck off, Burwardsley."

"Sometimes, love, I really wish I could. But one way or another, you and I are going to see this through to the end."

"It was the thought that we have a plan that made me laugh."

"Tell me about it."

Fenna leaned her head against the window and ignored him.

"I mean it, Fenna." Burwardsley yawned. "It's been a long trip. I need you to talk. Need you to keep me awake. Tell me about the plan."

"Okay," Fenna said. She pushed herself into a more upright position. She reached for the *Subway* cup and took a sip of cola. "If Alice is in the cabin..."

"She is."

"What?" Fenna's hair caught in her eyelashes as she flicked her head around and stared at Burwardsley. "You know she's there?"

"Listen, love, you think I would fly all this way, shove a load of guns and ammo into the back of a pissy little Prius and head into the hills on a hunch? I put Bad on the case."

"He's with Alice?"

"Relax, Konstabel. He knows nothing more than he needs to. I gave him the location of the cabin, and told him to keep an eye on it, and to keep me updated."

"You mean he just scrambles up and down the mountain with a situation report?"

"You've never been to the Himalayas, have you?"

"No."

"Well," Burwardsley shrugged, "there's a reason the British hand pick Gurkhas from the mountains."

"You never thought to share this information?"

"You never asked. You've been pretty cagey with any information up to now, pretty quiet too – preoccupied is another word for it. I just took over."

Fenna slumped into her seat. She pushed the cup into the drinks holder and nodded. "You're right. I've been preoccupied."

"And I've been busy."

"Yes."

"Hey, Konstabel." Burwardsley thumped Fenna's thigh. "We want the same thing, and we're working toward it."

"Vestergaard."

"Right. And this girl, she's our ticket. He wants her, and we are going to give her to him. And that's what you're struggling with."

"Yes."

"Well stop, 'cos we're not going to let anything happen to her. We need her."

"To kill him?"

"As leverage, yes. Then we send that motherfucker into oblivion." Burwardsley gripped the wheel and accelerated. Fenna glanced around the road. She spotted a police car in the distance and pointed at it. Burwardsley lifted his foot off the accelerator and slowed the Prius to within the speed limit. "Tell me more about the plan," he said. "I've just made the preparations, it's time you give me more to work with."

"There's a flight out of Iqaluit."

"Nunavut? Okay," he said. "So we're going to Canada."

"The flight is chartered. It's an evangelical flight direct to Qaanaaq."

"Greenland."

"Yes."

"And we're on that flight? With a load of evangelicals?"

"We will be. Provided we can get to it."

"And how do you think we are going to do that? How are we even going to get across the border into Canada?"

"That's where Vestergaard comes in. He wants Alice, alive. He needs her for whatever leverage he is trying to create with the Americans. His name will get us across the border. I just don't know how. Not yet."

Burwardsley yawned and held out his hand for Fenna's cola. She gave it to him, waited until he had finished it, and then pushed it back into the drinks holder. He scratched his head, yawned a second time and pressed the button to roll the window down a few centimetres.

"There's a good chance he is following our every move," he said.

"I'm counting on it."

"Then what's to stop him taking the girl any time from now until Greenland?"

"He won't."

"No? You're sure about that?"

"Vestergaard wants us as much as he wants the girl. And he wants us in a country he can control. There are too many variables in the US and Canada. Too many actors and agencies. No," she said, and ran a hand through her hair, "he wants us in Greenland. He wants to finish things there."

"Finish us you mean."

"Yes."

"But until then?"

"We keep her alive. At all costs."

Burwardsley rolled the window up and tapped the steering wheel. He snorted and said, "You're projecting an awful lot of Dina onto this girl..."

"Alice."

"Right. You know that, don't you."

"Alice is alive. You said it yourself. Dina's gone. We can't bring back the dead."

"But this girl – Alice – she is toxic. America wants her head on a plate."

"And it was America – some Deep State at least – that created her."

"And yet, you feel responsible?"

It was Fenna's turn to snort. "You wouldn't understand."

"Whatever it is, I am about to die for it, so try me."

"You're not a woman."

"No, love, I'm not."

"Until you can put yourself in my shoes, you'll never understand."

"Charlie tried," Burwardsley said and laughed. "And you saw where that got him."

"Yes." Fenna shook her head. She felt her cheeks dimple and she allowed herself a smile. "But a gun-dealing drag queen isn't quite the same."

"I never said it was."

"No. You didn't." Fenna closed her eyes. *There's no place for equality in the world of men*, she thought. *At least not this world, the world of guns, death, and power. Not unless you carve that place for yourself.* She pictured the kukri in the crate in the trunk of the car. *It's time to make this happen. It's time to even the odds. And,* she realised, *the Nepali might just be the ace that we need.*

Burwardsley slowed as he pulled onto an off-ramp. Fenna focused on her thoughts as he stopped at a tank station. He turned off the engine and switched off the lights.

"Coffee?" he said.

"No."

"Okay."

"Wait," she said, as Burwardsley opened the door. "I've thought about it. I understand why we need him. Why we need the Nepali."

Burwardsley nodded. "That's good."

"But I don't have to like it."

"I never said anything about that."

"Then you'll keep him away from me?"

"Jesus, Fenna. He killed your partner. Believe it or not, he said the same thing to me." Burwardsley shrugged and got out of the car. Fenna heard him mutter, "It's like I'm some kind of god-damned nursery teacher." He shut the door and Fenna smiled.

The plan then. Fenna pulled the map out of the glove compartment and studied the approach to the National Park. Once they were in she figured they would abandon the car, maybe even before the parking area and campsites. They would hike in under the cover of night, find somewhere to wait until the following evening, and then make the climb – mostly exposed ladders – and then get Alice out of the cabin, off the mountain, and into Canada. She took some solace in the fact that Bahadur had been keeping an eye on Alice, and that he would do whatever Burwardsley ordered him to. Loyalty, she realised, was going to be crucial to the success of the mission. Beyond getting Alice off the mountain, Fenna also realised that the plan was raw and full of holes. First they needed to get to Iqaluit, the Inuit governed territory of Canada, then Qaanaaq, in Greenland, then south from there. Fenna knew their ultimate destination. Vestergaard had even hinted at the location of a safe house — the shaman's house, in a tiny settlement ringed by glaciers. They would get there, of course, but the how and when were just a little obscure.

She forgot all about the details when she saw Burwardsley stride out of the tank station, two cups of coffee in a paper tray in one hand, his mobile in the other. He tripped before the car, and Fenna would have laughed if it wasn't for the look on his face.

"We have to go," he said, as he got in the car and thrust the coffees at Fenna.

"What's going on?"

"Text from Bad. There's movement on the mountain."

"Movement?"

"A team, well, he says it's a team."

"How many?"

"Two for the moment. A couple, posing as hikers."

"How does he know they're not actual hikers?"

Burwardsley started the car. He backed out of the parking space and accelerated out of the lot and onto the highway. The rain had lifted, and the first grey of dawn was stretching across the horizon. He held out his hand for a coffee.

"Tell me what you know?" Fenna said and pressed the paper cup into his hand. Burwardsley took a sip, stared straight ahead, as if willing the miles to be shorter, the distance less. There was an urgency in his grip, his frostbite long forgotten, and the look of imminent action that Fenna recognised.

"Bad recognised the guy. An Australian named Rhys Thomas. We've done some jobs together in the past. There's no way he's on the mountain for any other reason than Alice."

"No coincidence?"

"None."

Fenna took the lid off the coffee. She pictured dawn breaking between the peaks. A blood red dawn, and a very frightened young woman – *a girl*, she reminded herself. *A girl I am responsible for.* She looked at Burwardsley. *For better or worse, this is the mission.* She took a sip of coffee, squashed the lid around the rim, and stared straight ahead. Burwardsley steered, sipped, and stared in the same direction, toward the mountains, where there was no such thing as coincidence.

"Just so we are straight," he said, as he handed Fenna his empty cup. "We are about to mix it up with foreign nationals in what could be a pretty good gunfight."

"We're clear on that."

"Good," he said. "Because the consequences..."

"We're clear," Fenna said. "Now just get us there. We'll figure things out along the way."

"That's a bad habit, you know?"

"Yeah, and a hard one to break." Fenna sipped at her coffee, occupied, all of a sudden, with angles of attack, high rates of rounds per minute, and the shadow of gun battles, on and off the ice. She nodded and whispered through the steam of coffee, "Just hold on, Alice. We're coming."

Chapter 5

NORTH CASCADES NATIONAL PARK, WASHINGTON, USA

Fenna didn't say a word until they passed Everett and Burwardsley drove off I5 and onto the Mountain Loop Highway, heading east into the North Cascades National Park. He pulled his mobile from his pocket and tossed it into her lap.

"You must be the only twenty-something I know that doesn't have a Smartphone."

"Twenty-four, single and friendless," she said. Fenna swiped the screen and waited for Burwardsley to give her the pin code. The screen glowed with a limited number of apps and no history that Fenna could see. "Besides, it's not like you are drowning in social engagements." Fenna turned the screen toward Burwardsley and he shrugged at the lack of messages in the feed.

"It's a registered with a fake account." He slowed as they passed a tank station, turned around and stopped beside one of four empty pumps. The grey light of dawn lit the sky like pale smoke. Burwardsley turned off the engine. "Time to fill the tank. Do a search for this lookout of yours. Bad said something about turning off the highway and onto a forest road."

Fenna nodded as Burwardsley got out of the car. He left the door open and the smell of gasoline tugged at her nostrils. She curled a finger through her hair and teased the ends between her fingertips as she searched. Burwardsley leaned into the car and held out his hand for the trash.

"Want anything?" he said.

"We need food for a few days at least."

"My Bergan is full of MREs – meals ready to eat. We have plenty of food. I'm talking about snacks and coffee."

"Sure. Whatever you find."

"Alright."

Fenna finished her search, as Burwardsley paid. She enlarged the map on the screen and showed it to Burwardsley when he got back in the car.

"There," she said. "That's where we leave the highway. About forty minutes' drive."

Burwardsley looked at the mobile and nodded. He handed Fenna a coffee and a bag of doughnuts and then shut the door. "It's light now. We want to be on the trail as soon as possible, before any hikers."

"It's not that kind of hike," Fenna said. "It's not that popular – too strenuous for the casual hiker. We'll need to rope up before the climb to the lookout, depending on the conditions."

"I have rope." Burwardsley started the car and pulled onto the highway. "We have to decide what to do with the car. Depending on your girl, our best bet is to yomp over the border."

"Yomp?"

"Royal Marine for carrying heavy shit a long way. Heard it a lot when they talked about the Falklands."

"Okay, that's the second thing I have no clue about. The Falklands?"

"The war in 1982."

Fenna looked at Burwardsley and frowned. "Not your war?"

"Fuck off," he said. "How old do you think I am?"

"Thirty-five, single ..."

"… and friendless. Yep, I get it. Burwardsley no-mates. We're a fine pair, Konstabel."

Fenna said nothing, concentrating instead on the twinge of her lips at the corners of her mouth. The mountain was forgotten for a moment, along with the mission, the girl, even Bahadur and the wicked curve of his kukri. She waited for Burwardsley to turn his head and said, "So? How old?"

"Thirty-seven," he said. Fenna's lips twitched and he continued, "I've been knocked about a bit, seen some shit, done a whole lot more."

"And yet," Fenna said, as she lost the battle over her smile. "You've aged so well."

"Jesus wept." Burwardsley sighed and gripped the wheel. He looked at Fenna, rolled his eyes, and stared at the road ahead. "I'm not forty yet, love. Still got a full head of blond hair."

"Mixed with a bit of grey," she said and reached out to tease at the short-cropped hair on the side of Burwardsley's head. He slapped at her hand and she giggled, laughed, and choked for the better part of a kilometre.

"Don't die, Konstabel. I'm not doing this alone."

"I won't," she said. "Not yet. But it's good to laugh. It's been a long time." She turned sideways in her seat and looked at Burwardsley. "Since I applied to Sirius, my life…"

"Hasn't been your own? I know. Been there. I joined at eighteen, direct entry to officer training after A levels. That's the same as gymnasium in your country." Burwardsley smiled.

"High school in America."

"Right."

"And then you went to war?" Fenna blew a

strand of hair from her lips and tucked it behind her ear.

"The first time, yep. That's where I met Bad. We were fighting alongside the Gurkhas."

Fenna felt her stomach churn as Burwardsley reminded her of the Nepali, but then the words tumbled from his mouth, as if he needed to speak all of a sudden, and the mission was lost once again as Fenna listened and Burwardsley drove.

We met on the ice, she mused as he spoke, *tried to kill each other, and yet, this man is about the only friend I have.* The image of Nicklas Fischer – the RCMP Inspector turned double agent – and the time they spent together at the Desert Training Center in Yuma, flashed before her, and then it was gone – *he* was gone, faded and dead, just as Jarnvig had said. *Dead, like Jarnvig.* Fenna turned back to the living, listened to Burwardsley's deep voice as he opened up, sharing from his past. She almost stopped him, almost reached out to touch his arm and shake her head. *The more he tells me,* she realised, *the more I might actually begin to care about him, despite our past, and because of it.* Instead, she clasped her hand between her thighs and listened, swapping images of snow for dirt, ice for dust, lots of dust, caked in the pores of Burwardsley's skin, crusting the bloody wounds on his body.

"We were trapped in the open, between these fucking lines of chalk in the dirt."

"Chalk?"

"Marking a path clear of Improvised Explosive Devices," Burwardsley said. "Of course, some bastard Taliban with a detonator triggered an IED just as we walked past. Cunningham, a corpsman, caught most of it in the chest. Saved the rest of the squad. At least to begin with." He paused for a sip of coffee. Fenna waited. "That was the first of three remote detonations. I was losing men left and right, the TACP was busy, so many contacts in the area, he was put on hold, like we could just wait. That's when the Taliban opened up with AKs and a .50 in the scrub, and from the compounds. We were surrounded. There was shit kicking off all around us," he said and waved a hand in the air. "This one kid, Nicholls – I think his name was, he was on the GPMG, it jammed, he screamed, and then lost his head from a burst of fire from the bushes. We were going to die there. I knew it. The TACP said he had an A10 circling above, ready to let rip with thirty millimetre. You've never heard the like, until you have, if you know what I mean, love."

Fenna shifted position as Burwardsley took another sip of coffee. He didn't look at her, just stared at the road, steered, followed the curves of the Mountain Loop Highway, but his thoughts, she knew, were in a field of dirt, under fire, near death.

"I told the TACP to call it, to put those rounds in Danger Close, right on fucking top of us. This big fucking beauty of a bird screams in and lets rip with a burr of bullets – big fucking bullets – and the ground, ahead of us, right? It's like it's pulverized into some kind of dirt cloud, and I'm up, kicking the guys up, and we're running. There's another rip, more clouds, more dirt, thick in your teeth. That's when this fucking trigger man detonates another IED, and the guy I'm dragging goes down. We both do."

Burwardsley slowed to a stop, bumping the Prius onto a patch of dirt on the side of the highway, letting the engine idle until it stalled, and it was quiet. Fenna unbuckled her seatbelt. She placed her hand on Burwardsley's arm, turned and listened.

"There was so much shit in the air," he said. "Dust so thick. You couldn't see anything. But I looked down, and there's these fucking lines in the dirt. Chalk lines, and I'm on the wrong side of them. I just lie there, right. Nicholls – I think it was him – he's half over the line. His legs are gone, and his blood is all over me. I thought it was mine. And then I hear them. Once the A10 has fucked off, and the field is quiet, orange with dust. I'm in this cloud and I can hear the fucking Taliban creeping toward me, all sides, and I ... Fuck, Fenna, I thought that was it."

"But it wasn't."

"No," Burwardsley said and shook his head. "This one guy – a rag around his head and mouth – he comes out of the cloud and sticks his AK in my face. That's when I heard chatter on one of our radios. Guys asking for help, calling in air support – Troops in Contact – all that shit. And these Taliban, they're just laughing. There were four of them. And that guy with the AK in my face, I just knew he was the trigger man, and I started screaming and yelling at him, and he just keeps on laughing. Laughing and pointing, right up to the moment when his chest explodes and I have to turn away for all the blood that spatters across my face. Then there's more rounds, full auto, and this tiny little fuck in full British battle gear, he comes charging out of the dust, and I remember shouting at him to watch those chalk lines, and he just grins at me, fires his SA80 from the hip until the mag is empty, reaches behind his back and pulls out this fucking sword. He leaps over me, goes to work on the last of the Taliban, and then he comes back, grabs my webbing and pulls me to my feet. The little fuck carried me across the field to a compound we had secured. He dumps me against the wall, rocks back onto his heels, cracks a cheesy grin and hands me a bottle of water. Never saw anything like it." Burwardsley looked at Fenna and she leaned back. She squeezed his arm and Burwardsley shrugged. "Bahadur was just following orders," he said. "He got the order to rescue me, and he did it. I gave him the order to kill your partner, and he did it. If I tell him to get the girl onto the plane to Greenland ..."

"He'll do it," Fenna said. She swallowed. "I know he will."

"That's good, love, because in about twenty minutes from now, you're gonna have to face him, and I just want you to know, I need you to know, that he's not a threat to you, and neither am I. Not anymore."

"We have a common enemy," she said and slipped back onto the passenger seat.

"And the enemy of the enemy is..."

"My friend. I understand." Fenna reached for the bag of doughnuts. "Breakfast," she said and handed him the bag.

They ate in silence and the light changed from grey to cream, the cloud base low, beneath the peaks and high mountain trails of the Cascades. Fenna rinsed the sugar from her teeth with the last of her coffee. She leaned against the door, propping her feet on the side of Burwardsley's seat. *The memory drained him*, she realized, as she studied the Royal Marine's face. He looked old, all of a sudden, and yet there was a young man just beneath the surface, a man who had seen too much, and been asked to do too much, just like the young men before him, *and now*, thought Fenna, *young women too*. She had once met a Danish female Tactical Air Control Party called Ida – embedded with and coordinating air support for troops on the ground, serving in the Danish Army. They had swapped stories over drinks, stories about training and men. Both of them single and serving in demanding environments, typically reserved for men. Fenna remembered being in awe of what Ida was required to do. She smiled at the memory of Ida's comments about what Fenna and her partner would be forced to do to while away the hours on patrol in the middle of nowhere.

"It won't be like that." Fenna had assured her.

"Right."

"Seriously."

And it wasn't. It had been nothing like that. Whatever Fenna might have felt for Mikael, whatever thoughts they might have entertained, they were just thoughts, and now he was dead, and his death had not been the last.

"I'm going to drive," Fenna said. She swung her feet into the foot well and tied her laces.

"Alright." Burwardsley got out of the car and Fenna clambered over the handbrake to sit behind the wheel. She reached beneath the seat and slid it forward so that she could reach the pedals. Burwardsley paused to open the trunk. When he got into the car, Fenna saw he was carrying two pistols.

"If Bad is right about Thomas," he said, "then we may as well get tooled-up before we get out of the car."

"And ditch it at the end of the fire road?"

"We have to." Burwardsley slid a magazine into

Fenna's Glock and handed it to her. She tucked it beneath her thigh. "Bad knows we are coming. He'll meet us at the end of the road. We'll hear what he has to say, and decide whether or not to go for the lookout today, or once it gets dark."

Fenna started the car. She shut the driver door and pulled onto the highway. Burwardsley fiddled with the large Browning pistol he favoured, and Fenna let her thoughts drift to think of Alice. She was five years younger than Fenna, not even twenty, and she had been recruited to assassinate the hardest possible target: the President of the United States. Somehow, she had done it. Somehow, she had survived. *They let her go*, Fenna realised. To create chaos, a distraction, to allow them, the Deep State, to avoid attention, and to begin the work of influencing and rebuilding the government in a time of uncertainty, suspicion, and grief. *Shock tactics*, straight from the shock doctrine playbook.

Fenna pulled off the highway and onto Forest Road 41, two large telephone poles placed close together marked the turn. Burwardsley pointed them out. Grit from the road peppered the sides of the Prius as Fenna accelerated up each incline and steered around the bends. Burwardsley tapped the dashboard and pointed as they neared a bridge.

"It's damaged," he said. "According to a local trails site. We'll leave the car here."

Fenna pulled into the side of the road and stopped. She turned off the engine and got out, grabbing the Glock from the seat and tucking it into the waistband of her hiking trousers.

"You going to call him?" she said, the words masking the churning in her stomach.

"No need," Burwardsley said and waved in the direction of the bridge. "There he is."

The low cloud beaded their clothes with spots of rain, but it was the sight of the tiny Nepali man that bumped the skin on Fenna's arms. She forced herself to look at him, realised that they needed him, and focused instead on Alice.

He'll get you on the plane to Greenland, she thought as Burwardsley and the Gurkha embraced in an awkward man-hug made difficult by the extreme difference in height between the two British soldiers. "But if he makes one wrong move," she muttered, nodding at Bahadur when he looked at her, "I'll kill him."

Chapter 6

Fenna spread the *Rand McNally* road map on the bonnet of the Prius and pointed at their location with the tip of a folding knife. Bahadur leaned over the map and used the end of a twig to show the location of the lookout hut, followed by the location of Thomas' tent. A quick look at Burwardsley's mobile showed that the tent was above the tree line, pitched on a ridge in a meadow called Goat Flats, before the trail continued to Tin Can Gap. Fenna allowed herself to smile at the names. It helped ease the tension between her and Bahadur. They hadn't spoken, choosing instead to communicate through Burwardsley.

"You're sure it's him, Bad? Sure it's Thomas?"

"Yes, *Saheb.*"

Burwardsley grunted. "And he's got a woman with him?"

"Yes."

"Long weapons?"

"No weapons. Maybe pistols in backpacks. I not see." Bahadur glanced at Fenna. He tapped the map with the twig when she looked up. "Your friend in cabin. All safe."

"For how long?" said Burwardsley.

"I see her one week. But maybe she be there longer. I only be here one week."

Bahadur ran his hand over his head releasing a shower of rain from his thick black hair. *Like a Greenlander's,* Fenna thought. She forced a smile and said, "Thanks."

"No problem," he said, and then, "she look like you."

"We know," Burwardsley said.

"Maybe not so tough," Bahadur said and then he punched Burwardsley on the arm. "You got my present, Mike?"

"Maybe."

"Maybe? What *maybe*?" Bahadur's face creased and he stared at Burwardsley. "I been on fucking mountain, one fucking week, *Saheb*. All rain. All fucking days."

"Calm down, you little runt," Burwardsley said. He grinned as Fenna looked from one man to the other.

"Rice and rain, all fucking days. I want a burger. Want my present. Special order you say."

"I might have."

"No fucking might. You say *special order*. I special. I want present."

While the thought of reuniting the Gurkha with his kukri gave Fenna the chills, she couldn't help but smile at Bahadur's vocabulary. *Endearing, almost*, she thought. If it wasn't for the fact that he was a stone-cold killer. *And*, she realised, *shorter than me*.

Burwardsley pushed his mobile toward the centre of the map and stood up. He shoved his hands in his pockets and ignored Bahadur. "The Gurkhas usually have a British commanding officer."

"Usually?"

"Historically," Burwardsley said and shrugged. "Anyway, there was this Taliban leader we wanted. We knew where he was, the intel was good, we just needed a unit mad enough to go in and get him."

"No, Mike," Bahadur said. He crossed his arms over his chest. "That not me."

"So, we sent his lot. Partly 'cos we knew they

could get the job done, partly 'cos we knew they would scare the crap out of the Taliban." He paused to nod at Bahadur. "The CO wanted proof of death, once they took out the target."

"Not fair. Not me."

Burwardsley laughed. "They brought back the guy's head. It was all over the papers."

"Jesus," Fenna said. She looked at Bahadur, caught his eye. He was quiet for a moment before he cocked his head and shrugged.

"They wanted proof. They got proof."

Burwardsley reached for his mobile and waved it at Bahadur. "You could have taken a photo."

"Not me, I say."

The rain fell harder and Fenna shook the map before folding it. She tucked it into her jacket pocket as Burwardsley pointed at the Prius. "It's in the boot, Bad."

Bahadur nodded and jogged around Burwardsley. He opened the boot and pulled the kukri blade from the crate, tossing the leather wrap to one side as he twisted the grip within his hand. A second later it was gone, as he slipped it into an empty scabbard at the back of the broad belt around his waist. Fenna could see the change in the Nepali's demeanour, he seemed whole all of a sudden. Taller too. She noticed then the small pack on his back, the light grey fleece tube around his neck, and the jacket, cinched tight at the waist above trousers with cargo pockets bulging at the sides. His black boots came up above his ankles. They looked comfortable, as if they were painted onto his feet. Her own gear was bought, not customised. She was caught off-guard with a brief thought of how Bahadur might teach her a thing or too, but the

57

moment was gone as he pulled a Glock from the crate, felt the weight in his hand, and looked over the iron sight, pointing downwards, execution style. *It's the same man*, she reminded herself. *The one who killed Mikael. And yet...* She looked at Burwardsley, thought about how she had overcome the paralysis she felt when he had forced his way into her hotel room in Nuuk.

"The enemy of my enemy is my friend," she whispered. Fenna lifted her collar and zipped it to her chin. She ran her hands through her hair and tugged a hair band from her wrist to hold it in place. Her chestnut roots were pushing through, but she was still mostly black. She felt a few strands of hair fall onto her cheeks and ignored them. She took a breath and said, "We need a plan."

Burwardsley nodded at Bahadur as the Nepali checked the M4 carbines and slapped a magazine into each of them and then turned to Fenna. "You okay?"

She shrugged and said, "The stories help."

"Good."

"And he's been looking out for Alice."

"Yep."

"We need him."

"Glad you feel that way. Now," Burwardsley said and nodded at the grip of the Glock peeking out from beneath the hem of Fenna's jacket. "You're gonna have to stow that so it can't be seen. We'll sling the carbines over our backs and pull the packs over them. They should be hidden, from a distance at least."

"And when we get close to your friend?"

"Thomas? Yeah, I don't know what his game is."

"Is he connected? To Vestergaard, I mean."

"Shouldn't be. I knew him before I got the gig on

The Ice Star. But who the hell knows anymore."

Burwardsley looked up as Bahadur approached and handed them both an M4. He slung it over his shoulder and head so that it hung at an angle down his back. Bahadur took a step and adjusted the sling so that the carbine hung straight down, the muzzle pointing to the ground. He did the same for Fenna, and she bit her lip when she felt his fingers on her back. Then, as he moved away, she relaxed, thanked him, and looked at Burwardsley.

"Whatever Thomas' intentions, we may as well push on to the lookout," she said and looked up at the ridge. "We're close. I need to see her now."

"And we will." Burwardsley pointed at the boot of the car. "Share out the MREs, Bad, and pull out my rope. I'll sling it around my chest for the hike up."

"Yes, *Saheb*." Bahadur jogged to the car and Fenna turned to follow him. Burwardsley grabbed her arm.

"Listen…"

"What?"

"Thomas. Whatever his game is, we may need to take him out."

"I know."

"And, the woman with him."

"Yes?"

"Fenna…"

"Christ, it's like code or something." Fenna shook her arm out of Burwardsley's grip. "Every time some man calls me *Fenna* instead of *Konstabel*, they are preparing me for something difficult, as if killing Jarnvig, and the Gunnery Sergeant in the desert…"

"What Gunnery Sergeant?"

"My first test," she said, "and don't change the

subject." She pushed a knuckle into Burwardsley's chest. "When the time comes, I'll pull the trigger. You don't have to worry about that. Alright?"

"Sure. Okay," he said and stabbed his finger into her shoulder. "And if this is just a coincidence?" He stabbed again, rocking Fenna onto her heels. "Konstabel. If the woman is some young thing, his fiancé?" He stabbed her again. "Innocent." Stab. "Young." Stab. "If she's just…"

Fenna slapped Burwardsley's arm to one side and slammed her forearm into his collarbone, a blocking action. She curled her fist toward his head, over her arm, stopping just a few centimetres from his jawbone. Burwardsley flicked his eyes to her fist, and stepped backward.

"We off them, both of them," she said. "Innocent or not. They're just collateral."

"That's harsh, love."

"Life is harsh," she said and lowered her guard. Fenna turned at the sound of Bahadur closing the boot. She saw her backpack and pulled it on. The straps were too tight and she loosened them until the sharp angles of the carbine pressing into her back were bearable. She pulled the Glock out from her waistband, tucked it under her arm, and fastened the buckle above her belt. Her jacket had a map pocket on each side of the zip, and she zipped the Glock in the pocket on the left. Bahadur handed her two spare magazines and she stuffed them into the other pocket.

"Everything okay?" he said.

Fenna ignored him and marched in the direction of the bridge. As she passed Burwardsley she said, "I'll lead."

"Sure," he said and waited for her to walk past him. Fenna heard him say something to Bahadur about letting her cool down, which only made her angrier.

"I'll pull the fucking trigger myself," she said, her words low, edged, and laced with venom. Fenna spat, crossed the bridge damaged by flood water, and continued along the trail through the forest toward the meadow on the ridge. A glance over her shoulder confirmed that the two men were following her. Burwardsley was one hundred metres behind her, Bahadur brought up the rear.

Fenna's anger churned the muddy trail beneath her feet. She slipped in the mud, cursing until the trees thinned and the ridge loomed above her. The trail steepened, and Fenna felt the familiar shortness of breath and the tight tug of the muscles in her thighs, as her body adapted to the trail. She cursed the stab of the rifle in her back between breaths, cursed the two men behind her, and the world of men they belonged to. She thought of Alice, and, finally, the waves of anger receded. She pictured the girl hugging her knees beside a gas stove in a corner of the lookout, preparing for one more uncertain night, and the challenge of another sunrise where, despite the beauty above the clouds, there were no solutions, only the solace that this was her father's favourite place. As long as Alice was close to his spirit, Fenna imagined, as long as she could talk to him, then she might put off the only option she might have considered: getting off the peak without using the ladders.

"I won't let you do that," Fenna said, pausing as the trail levelled out before the meadow. "I'm here to give you an option, to give you a life, the one that

Dina can't have, that I couldn't give to her." She lifted her head and looked in the direction of Three Finger Lookout and said, "Just hang on, Alice. Just a little longer."

"Fenna."

She barely heard his whisper, but Fenna turned to see Burwardsley crouched by the side of the second row of trees inside the tree line. He waved her into a crouch, and she saw that his carbine was in his hands and his Bergan on the ground. Fenna searched for Bahadur, but could not see him. She moved slowly to the tree line and crouched beside Burwardsley.

"You didn't hear me?"

"When?" she said.

"Before the ridge."

"Been busy. Thinking. Cursing."

"Fuck, Fenna. Get it together."

Fenna shrugged out of her pack and peeled the rifle sling from her sweaty back. She wrapped the end of the sling closest to the muzzle twice around her left hand and held the carbine tight around the grip.

"Ready," she said.

Burwardsley nodded and pointed toward the beginning of the trail to Tin Can Gap. There was a small dome tent with a green flysheet tucked beneath rocky crags on the side of the trail.

"Bad is moving in from above. He'll let us know if anybody is home."

"Won't Thomas have thought of that?"

"Counter measures? Sure, he might have put in a few. If he has, then we'll know."

"What?"

"If this is a coincidence or if it's game on."

Fenna frowned, and said, "And if he deliberately

didn't, in order to make it look innocent?"

"Don't over think it, Konstabel."

Fenna stood up. She rested the carbine against a tree and pulled on her pack. Once she had buckled the belt she picked up the M4 and tucked it into a fighting position.

"What the fuck?"

"Either way," she said, "your old pal is a dead man walking. We may as well plug him and keep going."

"Wait a minute." Burwardsley stood up. "Is this how it's going to be? You charging in half-cocked, guns blazing?"

"No-one put you in charge. You don't like it. You can fuck off."

"Fenna," Burwardsley said. He shook his head as she scowled. "Konstabel, fuck ... whatever you want me to call you, just think. Just for a minute."

Fenna felt the rain pool into a blister above her hairline. When it was heavy enough the water bubbled through her hair and ran down her nose to slip onto her top lip. She let it roll into the crease between her lips. It seeped between them and she tasted the sweet water before she licked her lips and wiped more rain from her hair.

"Okay," she said. "Sorry."

"You're thinking now?"

"For a minute, sure. I'm thinking."

"Then we'll do this my way. We'll let Bad do a recce, and then we'll move in."

"Sure."

"Fenna?"

"Yes. We'll do it your way." She looked over her shoulder at the tent, and then dropped to one knee.

"Good," Burwardsley said. "Thank you."

"Don't mention it," Fenna whispered.

"What?"

"It's just we're close now, and there's always something or someone in the way."

"You thought it would be easy?"

"I hoped it would be easier. Just for once. Just for a change."

Burwardsley shifted into position behind a tree opposite Fenna. "It doesn't get easier, Fenna, never. You just stop caring how difficult it is."

Fenna thought about that, as the rain dripped from her hair and down her neck. She felt it merge with the sweat on her back and wished she wore a neckie like Bahadur's. The rain was slick on her hands, and she thought about wearing gloves. She thought about the things she could change, things that might make a difference, might make it easier. *To do what? To kill someone?*

Fenna ignored the questioning look Burwardsley cast, and pointed instead to the figure of a small man moving out of concealment and closer to the tent.

"Got him," Burwardsley said, switching the selector off the safety setting and into single shot mode. Fenna did the same.

A scream from inside the tent clipped its way across the meadow before the wind picked up and hurled it away, over the ridge and down to the plains below. The scream was followed by the sound of a tent zip opening and the curses of a man as he tumbled out of the tent wearing nothing more than a t-shirt.

"That's him," said Burwardsley with a grin. "I'd recognise those cheeks anywhere." He stood up and grabbed his Bergan, tossing it over one shoulder in anticipation of an easy stroll to the tent.

The pistol shots that followed the man's exit surprised both of them. Fenna and Burwardsley crouched on the trail as the flysheet was ripped to shreds by projectiles from a large calibre handgun.

"Fuck," Burwardsley said. "It's game on." He ditched his Bergan and ran down the trail. Fenna followed at an angle, increasing speed to cover more distance as the shooter inside the tent changed magazines.

Chapter 7

The rain splashed across Fenna's face as she pounded across the grassy surface, swerving around boulders and leaping over small rocky outcrops. She gripped the M4 in one hand as she unbuckled her waist belt and shrugged out of her pack. It thumped onto the ground behind her and she picked up the pace, gaining on the Australian and the white flash of his cheeks beneath his t-shirt. He glanced over his shoulder as she closed the distance to just a few metres, his eyes caught the dull outline of Fenna's carbine and he frowned for a second before increasing speed. Fenna might have admired his attempt to outrun her, if it wasn't for the spectacular way he twisted on a tuft of mountain grass and pitched forward onto his face. He sprawled on the grass, sliding for a metre or so until he stopped and tried to get back on his feet. That was when Fenna leaped, landing on his back, knees bent. She grabbed the back of his head and thrust his nose into the grass, pressed the muzzle of her M4 into his neck and yelled, "Keep your fucking head down."

"Alright, alright. I'm down."

"Thomas? Is that your name?"

"Do I know you?" He twisted his head. Fenna grabbed a handful of his hair, yanked his head up, and slammed his forehead into the ground.

"Is that your name?" she said, pausing between each word.

"Yes," he said, his voice grassy and muffled. She lifted his head, and he said, "Yeah, I'm Thomas."

"So, tell me, Thomas, what are you doing on the mountain?"

"Who wants to know?"

Fenna dug the muzzle of the carbine into his neck. She heard a scream, a curse from Burwardsley, and something like a cackle of laughter. *That's Bad*, she thought. She forced the image from her mind and focused on the Australian sprawled beneath her.

Perhaps it was the commotion at the tent that distracted her, or that she had underestimated Thomas, but he must have felt a change in the pressure of her knees, a shift in the muzzle pressed into his neck. Thomas bucked, freed one arm, and threw an elbow into Fenna's ribs, shoved his palm into her face. Fenna flinched and then he was on his feet, his penis dangling in front of her face, as he slammed a knee into her chest.

"Do I know you?" he shouted as Fenna slumped onto her back. She choked. Fumbled her grip on the carbine, caught the flat of Thomas' foot in a kick to her head. "I don't know you." He sidestepped around her. She turned, moved the carbine to grip it with both hands, but he kicked it out of her grasp.

Come on, Fenna. Fucking move.

Fenna took a second to focus. She caught a flicker of movement as Thomas opened up with another kick. She blocked it, twisted her arm around his ankle and gripped it beneath her armpit. Fenna yanked Thomas' leg toward her to slam a knuckle into his chest. She hit him again, her left hand pistoning back and forth into his breastbone, until he gasped and she kicked his leg out from beneath him, and they tumbled to the ground.

Fenna's hand got caught in Thomas' t-shirt and she fumbled it free. She released his leg, slapped at it and kneed him in the groin, pressing his penis beneath her knee as she hit him twice on the side of the head. Thomas groaned and tried to raise his hands. Fenna slapped at them, and punched his nose until it bled.

"Jesus," he said, blood spluttering from his mouth.

"Fenna," said a voice. It was distant. She ignored it, until she heard, "Konstabel." Closer this time, louder.

She looked up and saw Burwardsley striding toward her. He held his carbine in a loose grip around the magazine. She rolled off Thomas and stood up, scanning the ground for her own weapon. She found it, picked it up, and waited for Burwardsley. Thomas groaned at her feet.

Burwardsley chuckled as he crouched beside Thomas. He gripped the Australian under his arm and pulled him into a sitting position.

"Mike?" Thomas said, his voice gubby with blood. "S'that you?"

"Yep."

Thomas looked at Fenna. "Who's the fuckin' Pitbull?"

"That is Konstabel Fenna Brongaard."

"She with you?"

"'Fraid so."

Fenna said nothing, concentrating instead on her breathing, ratcheting her breaths into a steady rhythm.

"She's fucking insane, mate."

"She's passionate," said Burwardsley. "I'll give you that." He looked at Fenna, smiled and shook his head.

"What?" she said.

"Used to be me you looked at like that."

"And?"

Burwardsley kicked Thomas' leg. "I'm just pleased it's him. Pleased you've moved on."

Fenna said nothing. She checked the safety on the carbine, and glared at Thomas.

"What's going on at the tent?" she asked.

"Bad's on top of it, or on top of her. It seems Thomas' American squeeze didn't take too kindly to his advances," Burwardsley said and cocked his head to stare at Thomas. "Still can't shake those old perversions, eh, mate?"

"Fuck you, Mike."

"Anyway, Bad collapsed the tent with her inside it. He's got her pinned down. Literally. So, we," he said and stood up, "can have a more intimate chat with our friend, here."

Fenna looked up at the glacier. She could just make out the path leading up to the lookout tower.

"Just be quick about it," she said. "We have to move."

Burwardsley slung his carbine over his shoulder and pulled a knife from his belt. He opened it and locked the blade in place. Thomas watched him through bloody fingers. He gripped his nose and lifted his head up. *He should keep it down*, Fenna thought, *let it flow until it clots*. She smiled at the observation, then studied the Australian, the muscles on his calves, his bruised manhood, and the khaki camouflage shirt he wore over his muscled torso. There was a logo stencilled on the t-shirt above his left breast. He had the same logo tattooed on his forearm, a winged dagger.

"How's life, Rhys?" Burwardsley said and crouched beside Thomas.

"Peachy, mate. Yourself?"

"Bit hectic at the moment, to be honest." He pointed the tip of the blade at Fenna. "Pitbull over here drives like the devil."

"Thought you liked that kind of thing?"

"A few years ago, maybe. Getting on a bit now."

"Thinking of settling down then?"

"Like you and the missus?" Burwardsley nodded in the direction of the tent.

"I thought about it." Thomas looked at his hands. He pressed the length of his finger under his nose and checked for blood. He looked at Fenna. "You're a feisty one, that's for sure."

"You shouldn't have run."

"Hey, I didn't see you, alright? I was running from Sally. We had a disagreement. She found my pistol."

"And why do you have a pistol on you?" said Burwardsley. "I thought this was a romantic holiday."

"It is, and, well, old habits and that."

"So, you're not here for any other reason?" Fenna asked.

Thomas repositioned his legs, wincing as he moved them. "Nah, it's all good. I'm here for a little R&R. Nothing more."

"You just happened to be on this mountain, when we came along?" Burwardsley shuffled closer to Thomas. The blade flashed in his hand.

"Mike," Thomas said and sighed. "If you're gonna cut me, mate, stop fucking about and just... ow. Fuck." Thomas flinched as Burwardsley slashed the knife across his thigh.

"I don't believe in coincidences," Burwardsley said. He looked at Fenna. "What about you,

Konstabel?"

"I think," Fenna said, "with all that's going on in the States right now, the chances of an Aussie special forces operator just happening to be on the same mountain as us, are far from coincidental."

She nodded at Burwardsley and dropped onto her knees, pinning Thomas' ankles to the ground. Burwardsley shoved a massive palm into the Australian's chest, pushed his body to the ground and stabbed the blade of the knife into Thomas' thigh, all the way to the hilt. Thomas gritted his teeth and suppressed a scream. Blood leaked out of his nose, as his nostrils flared and he snorted for air. *What am I doing?* Fenna resisted the urge to stand up, to back off and let the man go. *But we need to know*, she thought, steeling herself. *For Alice, to keep her alive.* She looked at Burwardsley. He gripped the shaft of the knife between his finger and thumb, and twisted it.

"Fuck," Thomas shouted. He gulped air into his lungs, his neck muscles straining as he bit back the pain and glared at Burwardsley. "I'm on my own, for fuck's sake. This isn't an op."

"No?" Burwardsley said, as he twisted the knife again. He pressed his knee onto Thomas' chest. "If you're sure? Otherwise, I could just swap with Bad. Let him give you the old Gurkha treatment."

"Fuck, no," Thomas said.

"I didn't think so." Burwardsley moved his knee off Thomas and sat beside the man's thigh. He tapped bloody fingers on the knife shaft.

"Mate," Thomas said, as he sat up. "Please?"

Burwardsley let go of the knife. He slipped the carbine into his hands, and pointed the muzzle at Thomas. "We'll just leave the knife there for the moment, eh?"

"Sure," he said, and grimaced. "Whatever, mate. I'm not going anywhere." Thomas looked at Fenna. "What's so special about the mountain?"

Fenna wiped the rain from her face. It had lessened, but she could feel the patches on her jacket that needed waterproofing. Her shoulders were soaked.

"Nothing that need concern you," she said.

"Ha," Thomas said. He wiped a bloody palm across his mouth. "You're both in the shit, aren't you? This is some Hail Mary, some private op to even up the odds. Am I right, Mike?"

"Keep talking," Burwardsley said, he glanced at the knife in Thomas' thigh.

"Right, well, I don't know all that much," he said, "but I can tell you that there's another team in the woods back there."

"What?" Fenna lifted her head and stared at the trail leading to Tin Can Gap.

"You won't see them. They're dug in real well. Of course," he said, "then there's the girl in the cabin." Thomas' brow creased as he smiled. "Your sister? Maybe?" he said with a glance at Fenna. "Funny thing is, she looks just like the girl on TV. The one they say killed the President." Burwardsley reached for the knife, and Thomas waved his hands. "No, mate, wait. Let me speak."

"I think you probably should," Burwardsley said.

Thomas took a breath and rested his palms on the grass either side of his body. "There's a bounty on this girl's head," he said. "That's why I'm here."

"How did you know to come here?" Fenna said. "To this mountain?"

"Ah, that would be secret, wouldn't it?" Thomas stared at Burwardsley as he reached for the knife. "A secret I would be happy to share."

"Go on."

"Whoever trained the girl, set her up to be caught. Only, they wanted to be sure that the right people caught her. Not an American. So, they left a trail of breadcrumbs, see? Snippets of information here and there, including a tiny bit about her dad being a climber, and how close they were."

"And that led you here?" Fenna frowned.

"No, that led me to the climbing fraternity, of which Sally there is a member."

"And you just used your charm to ask where would-be assassins might hide in the mountains?" Burwardsley laughed. "Give me a break."

"You can laugh, mate, but those breadcrumbs included a bit of family information, including the girl's home state."

"Washington," Fenna said.

"Right."

Fenna listened with just half an ear as Thomas told Burwardsley how he had used some shared contacts to meet climbers in the area, how he had created a contact within the community, and how he had narrowed down the likely possibilities.

"I mean," he said, "she's found a well-defended position, with great visibility, and at a height that puts off most visitors. Not to mention a great view. The only problem is, she can't exactly leave, not once everyone figures out where she is. The only way she is getting off the mountain is if she jumps."

And I won't let that happen. Fenna stood up and nodded at the trees. "Who's in there?" she said.

"I've no idea."

"But you know there's a team in there. How?"

"They rotate at night."

"Are they guarding her, or waiting for her?" Burwardsley said.

"At a guess," Thomas said, "a bit of both."

Fenna walked around Thomas. She stared at the trail leading into the woods, idly fingering the selector switch from safe through full auto as she studied the terrain. *If there's a bounty*, she mused, *then someone is counting on people coming after Alice. But who, and why?* She clicked the switch to the centre position, semi-automatic. The rain intensified. She licked the drops from her lips, lifted her chin and nodded.

"Right," Burwardsley said. "Brace yourself." Thomas yelled as Burwardsley pulled the knife from the Australian's thigh and stood up. He tugged a bandage from his pocket, tossed it onto Thomas' lap, and walked over to Fenna.

"I've figured it out," she said. "There isn't a bounty on Alice's head."

"There isn't? That makes no sense."

"It does if you think about it."

"And you have?"

"Yes."

Burwardsley bent down to clean the knife on the mountain grass. He closed the blade and waited for Fenna to speak. When she didn't, he said, "You're going to have to enlighten me, love."

"The bounty is for us."

"Us?"

"Yes," she said and laughed.

"What's so funny?"

"You don't get it?"

"No."

"They're covering their tracks," she said. Fenna sighed at the confused look on Burwardsley's face. "Alice was the instrument they used to kill the President."

"Yes."

"So, why would you want to catch her?" Fenna didn't wait for Burwardsley to answer. She nodded, and said, "It's brilliant, really."

"What is?"

"They set us up." Fenna swore. "That team over there in the woods, and others like them, they're waiting to catch the team sent to pick up Alice. They'll try to kill us, of course. Then they'll parade our bodies on TV as the agents that orchestrated the assassination."

"That's pretty thin, Konstabel. They've got no proof. No way to tie us to the President."

"They won't need to. Once we're dead, they can tie us to anyone they want to. Shit, he's done it again."

"Who? Vestergaard?"

"Exactly. *The Magician* has been pulling strings again, and we're dangling at the end of them."

Chapter 8

The meadow was above the tree line. It was rocky and exposed, below the glacier, and with little cover suitable for an ambush. *So, they are more of a blocking force then*, Fenna thought as she considered the role the team was playing. *They'll take us on the way down, block our escape.* She scanned the terrain as Burwardsley pulled a second field dressing from his cargo pocket and dressed Thomas' wound. She looked in the direction of the tent and saw Bahadur wandering around it, the carbine held loosely in his grip.

"Done," Burwardsley said and stood up. "Let's get back to the tent."

"That's it?" Thomas said. "We're just going to wander back up the hill as if nothing has happened?"

"You've been played, mate," Burwardsley said. "The bounty notice was selective. You never thought to ask if anyone else was in the loop?"

"No." Thomas shrugged. "You know me, Mike. I'm a man of few talents. I don't see the bigger picture. I just track. That's what I'm good at."

"And that's what they used you for," Fenna said, as they walked toward the tent. "You sure about your girlfriend? Sure she's innocent?"

"Yeah," Thomas said. "Poor girl. I used her. That's all." He looked at Burwardsley. "Catch and release? Can we do that at least?"

Burwardsley nodded and said, "We left the keys to our hire car on the wheel. It's down by the bridge. She can drive it out."

"And what about me?" Thomas said. Fenna swapped a look with Burwardsley. She looked down at the tree line. Thomas saw the direction she was looking and said, "There's five of the bastards down there, and a sixth up at the cabin."

"Six men, eh?" said Burwardsley, as Fenna flicked her eyes to Thomas. Her grip tightened on the carbine.

"One of them is in the cabin?" she said.

"He walked up there early this morning."

"Did you see him? What did he look like?"

"Yeah, I saw him. Kind of athletic. Good looking fella."

Fenna didn't need any more details. She imagined she knew just what he looked like, how he walked, moved under fire, how he spoke, his touch, the taste of his lips. Jarnvig had shown her a file back in Nuuk, just before she had killed him. But, like everything else in this game, there were so many threads, so many loose ends, and those that were tied off, could easily be unravelled, if they had ever been tied at all. Fenna realised that Vestergaard would have to minimise the number of people in the know in order to protect himself. She knew who he trusted, and with Jarnvig gone, there was only one person left who could be trusted enough to deliver Fenna and Alice, and he was supposed to be dead.

"Fuck," she said. Fenna stopped walking, signalling to Burwardsley that they needed to talk.

"What's up, love?"

Fenna waited until Thomas was out of earshot and said, "I know who's in the cabin with Alice."

"Who?"

"Nicklas Fischer," she said and swallowed.

"Who is he?"

"He's one of Jarnvig's men, so he works for Vestergaard. He got me out of Toronto, tidied up after I shot Humble." Fenna paused to swear.

"And?"

"He was at Yuma, watching out for me – maybe for me and Alice. After I killed the sergeant in the desert, he got me out. Shit, I remember him saying something now, something about being on the same side as the men who picked me up."

"You're not making much sense, Konstabel. Who is this guy?"

"He's an Inspector with the RCMP."

"He's a cop? Fuck me," Burwardsley said and laughed.

"He's not just a cop, he's anti-terror." Fenna punched Burwardsley on the arm, as he laughed again. "He's an operator, like you. Like me."

"So, the Mountie is a threat. Is that what you are trying to tell me?"

"Yes."

Burwardsley shrugged. "Let's just add him to the list, eh? Come on." He tugged her arm and starting walking toward the tent. Fenna walked beside him, thoughts about Nicklas momentarily put on hold as she saw Bahadur pull the tent pegs out of the ground as a dark-haired woman flew out from beneath the flysheet like a pheasant from a coop. She ran past Bahadur and didn't stop to look back. Thomas called after her, something about a car, the keys, and an apology of sorts. Fenna paid little attention, and once the woman had disappeared out of sight, she forgot all about her. She stopped to one side of the tent as Thomas pulled at the flysheet to find his pants, trekking trousers, and gear. He dressed as Burwardsley teased Bahadur.

"Thomas says there's a team in the woods,"

Burwardsley said.

"I no see anyone."

"That's the point, Bad. You missed a whole fucking team."

"No fair, Mike. He fucking tracker," Bahadur said and pointed at Thomas. "Not me."

"Too fucking right, mate," Thomas said and winked at Fenna. Bahadur leaped across the collapsed tent skin and drew the kukri from his belt. Thomas raised his hands and stumbled, partly dressed, onto the ground. He clutched his leg and groaned, waving at Bahadur to stop with his free hand. "Easy, Bad. Easy. I was joking."

"You fucking joking? I carve you up, you joking. See who laugh, eh?" Bahadur raised the kukri above his head. Fenna tightened her grip on the carbine and moved the butt slowly into her shoulder.

"Stand down, Bad," Burwardsley said.

"He the tracker, sure," Bahadur said, as he took a step away from Thomas. "But he no fighter. Girl beat him," he said and pointed the tip of the blade at Fenna before sheathing it in the scabbard behind his back. Fenna lowered her carbine and flicked the selector switch to safe.

"Everyone alright?" Burwardsley said. He made a point of looking each of them in the eye. Fenna nodded, her thoughts racing. She flicked her eyes more than once in the direction of the glacier, and the lookout cabin she knew was perched on the rocky summit.

We have to move, she thought. *We don't have time for this.*

"Get dressed." Burwardsley tossed a pair of boots at the Australian's feet. Thomas pulled the socks out from inside each boot, and pulled them on. Burwardsley looked at Bad and said, "He is the tracker, you're right, Bad. And now he's working for us."

Thomas stopped lacing his boots and looked up. "I am?"

"Yep, just like old times."

"I'm confused, Mike," Thomas said. He grimaced as he stood up. "You stick a knife in me, chase my lady down the mountain, and expect me to just join your crew?"

"Pretty much." Burwardsley tugged the Browning from the waistband of his trousers. "Do you have a problem with that?"

"I guess not," Thomas said. He smiled and looked at Bahadur. "No hard feelings, Bad."

"You the tracker," Bahadur said. "Not me."

"Sure." Thomas looked at Fenna. "You don't say much."

Since landing in Seattle, driving the three hours into the mountains, and discovering that her one-time lover is still alive, and preparing to deliver her straight to Vestergaard – *all things considered*, she thought, *it's no wonder I'm lost for words.*

"You're a tracker," she said. "Can you avoid people, too?"

"Like those guys in the woods?"

Fenna shook her head. "Not them. We're going to kill them," she said and looked at Burwardsley for confirmation.

"Yep," he said.

"I need to know if you can get us around law enforcement, and get us across the border."

"The Canadian border, you mean?"

80

"Yes."

Thomas scratched behind his ear and said, "What's in it for me? Seeing as there's no bounty anymore."

The rain splashed on the tent fly, but not enough to disguise the click of the selector switch as Fenna shifted her grip on the carbine. "Do I need to say more?" she said.

"No, mate," Thomas said. "I think we're clear."

"Good." Fenna nodded at the tent. "Take what you need. Bahadur will give you your gun." She took a step away from the tent and turned her back on the three men. She heard Burwardsley approach, waited for him to speak. When he did, it was a whisper.

"Take a breath, love," he said. "You're holding on too tight."

Fenna lifted her chin, as she felt tears well in her eyes. She let the rain wash them down her cheeks. "I've been played from the start," she said. "Ever since Sirius."

"Yep, I guess you have."

"Jarnvig said as much. He told me, back then, that he recognised certain abilities that I had, gave me some bullshit story about having the qualities of an agent." Fenna waited for Burwardsley to speak, and then continued when he did little more than grunt in understanding. "They sent me to the desert to create a timeline, to put me in the right places at all the right times. Which makes me wonder," she said, as she looked at Burwardsley, "what's your role in all this? Are you really doing this for us, for Dina, for some sense of rough justice, or..." She stretched her finger across the trigger guard.

Burwardsley looked at her and nodded. "Yes," he

said, "for Dina."

"Really?"

"Yes."

Fenna tapped the trigger guard with her finger. "Can I trust you?"

"Yes," he said. He sighed and then shrugged his shoulders. "But, fuck, Fenna, I would understand if you didn't."

"What about him?" she said.

"Bahadur?"

"There's no question, he does what you do. I might not like him, but I know where I have him." She flicked her eyes at Thomas. "*Him*. The tracker."

Burwardsley smiled and said, "As far as the border, I would guess, no further."

"That far?"

"Hey, he needs to get out of the country just as much as we do."

Thomas caught Fenna's eye as he changed magazines in his pistol, and filled the empty one with rounds from a box in his pack. Fenna watched him until he looked away.

"And when that time comes, Mike, will you take care of him?"

"One way or the other, yes."

"Good." Fenna wiped the rain from her face and nodded in the direction of the trail they had walked in on. "I'll get my pack," she said and walked away.

The walk back for her pack gave Fenna the space and time she needed to think, to prepare for the coming action. She slung the carbine over her shoulder and smiled at the thought of how much she had changed. From the ice of Greenland, approaching the cabin door, heart thumping, Mikael covering her from afar with the bolt action rifle, before bursting in on Dina, scaring each other half to death with a cocktail of nerves and adrenaline. It had gotten easier. She had Burwardsley to thank for that. *And, I guess, Jarnvig and Vestergaard. Mikael. Nicklas.* All the men in Fenna's life, all the way back to her father, had encouraged her, trained, shaped, and forced her toward a life of action. *Dad,* she mused, *what the hell would you think of me now?* The thought had crossed her mind before, when her traitorous actions had likely caused her father to turn in his shallow grave, somewhere in Afghanistan. The casket they had buried in Denmark had been empty. She knew that. It hadn't bothered Fenna that her father's remains had remained on the battlefield, the location hostile, remote, classified; it was different for her sister. Fenna's acceptance of that fact had driven her sister and her apart. *And now she's caring for my mother, and I'm about to wage a private war in a foreign country. If I die,* she thought, *they probably won't even allow my body to be buried in Denmark.* The thought made her stop, and she saw her pack just a metre or so in the grass ahead of her. Fenna bent down to pick it up, wishing the traitorous thoughts out of her mind as she slung the pack over one shoulder.

She used the walk back to clear her mind, processing thoughts of each previous encounter through her mind as she settled on the one redeeming feature of her immediate and future actions: saving a life.

"I couldn't save Dina," she said aloud. "But I will save Alice." *Or die trying.*

Fenna heard the men talking as she approached, their words shivering on the chill wind blowing down from the glacier. They fell silent as she stopped in front of them. She suppressed a smile, as she studied them, Burwardsley towering above them all on the right, a climbing rope coiled around his chest, the carbine small in his large hands. Bahadur was tiny in the middle, his hair slick in the rain, the neckie loose around his thin neck. He had removed the sling from the carbine, wrapping it instead around the strap of his small pack, through which he stuffed a flashlight, the American kind with the lamp at right angles to the handle. Fenna recognised the type as surplus from the Vietnam war. She looked at Thomas last, surprised at his change in demeanour, and the professional care which he seemed to have taken over each tuck and crease of his gear. She doubted he would make any noise, there was nothing that could flap or twitch in even the strongest of winds.

"Ready, Konstabel?" Burwardsley asked.

Fenna leaned her carbine against her leg as she adjusted her pack and fastened the belt around her waist. She picked up the carbine and nodded.

"You're with Bad." Burwardsley paused, anticipating a reaction, but Fenna was silent. "Once we've engaged, he'll get you up the mountain, all the way to the lookout cabin. Thomas and I will keep the bastards busy, kill them all if possible."

"See, that's the part of the plan I'm less wild about, mate. You do realise, they know we're coming?"

"Yes."

"And that doesn't worry you?"

"No," said Burwardsley. "Should it?"

"Too bloody right it should, mate. There's six of them. All tooled up and spoiling for a chance to get it on."

"Five," said Burwardsley. "There's only five down here. That's what you said."

"I know, but that other fella, the one up top? He's the one you need to be worried about." Thomas looked at Fenna. "I might not have seen much in the way of features, but even in the gloom, and from a distance, anyone with an ounce of military training could see he was a fella who knows what he's doing. And we're sending her and Bad up to the cabin, alone, where he has a perfect field of fire. Christ, you won't get within a hundred yards before he fucks the both of you with a couple of high calibre bullets."

"That's why it has to be me that goes up there," Fenna said.

"And why is that?" Thomas said. He folded his arms across his chest and stared at her.

"Because the last person he fucked was me." Burwardsley laughed, as Fenna pushed past Thomas on her way to the head of the trail to Tin Can Gap. She saw shadows in the tree line and tightened her grip on the carbine. She took a deep breath. It was going to be a long day.

Chapter 9

They were good. Fenna knew as soon as they opened up with short suppressed bursts of 5.56mm rounds, shredding the trees with angles of fire that shepherded Burwardsley and Thomas into what appeared to be a prepared location. Burwardsley had just enough space to crouch, but not enough cover to fire without exposing himself to well-placed rounds, determined to pin him down and encourage him to surrender. Thomas hadn't fared much better. If he had been just a little taller, a little more muscular, he would have had difficulty taking cover at all.

They planned this from the start, Fenna realised. They obviously knew the direction Fenna and her team would arrive from, but the attention to detail surprised her. *Nicklas.* She knew it was him. *What other surprises has he prepared?*

Fenna fidgeted beside Bahadur. She tried to raise her body, to lift more than her head, but the Gurkha pressed her down with a small but firm hand on her back. She whispered, "Okay," and bit her lip as she watched the ambush unfold.

Each time Burwardsley tried to squirm into a better position, the blocking force opened up with another volley of lead. In the vacuum following each salvo, as the mountains absorbed the splinter of twigs and the chatter of bullets blasting through silenced assault rifles, Fenna heard Burwardsley curse. He was pissed off, she could see it in the hunch of his shoulders, the way he slapped the carbine on the carpet of pine needles beneath him.

"No," Bahadur said, as Fenna fidgeted one more time. "Wait and watch."

Fenna thought she heard the scratch of static and a series of clicks from a radio. She imagined the team to be radioing Nicklas with situation reports. She thought she could make out the voice of the leader in the trees, and words that might have been *affirmative* and *momentarily*, and a sentence that sounded like, *no sign of the girl yet.*

No, thought Fenna, *because the bloody Nepali won't let me join the fight.* She turned her head and gave Bahadur a hard stare. He ignored her.

A sudden shift in Bahadur's attention forced Fenna to look at Burwardsley. She heard him whistle to Thomas. He tossed a round object at the tracker, followed by one more. Burwardsley held up his hand, his fingers splayed, counting down, folding each finger over his thumb until there were none left. Thomas nodded, and the two men curled their fingers through the ring pull of the grenades in their hands and tossed them.

The shouts of alarm confirmed that the men in the trees had not expected grenades. At the first flash and shoosh of white hot phosphorous, the men broke out of cover, rolling out of range of the thermite explosions to the right and left of their position. Just as Burwardsley and Thomas had been herded into a specific spot, the two men did the same to the blocking force as they tossed two more grenades before rushing out of cover and emptying a magazine each in the direction of Nicklas' men. Thomas yelled, "Changing mag," and Fenna heard the loud bangs of Burwardsley's Browning as he covered the Australian. Then it was Thomas' turn to cover Burwardsley as he changed magazines. They threw two more grenades and moved forward.

"Now," Bahadur said and dragged Fenna to her feet. He raced toward the trailhead leading to Tin Can Gap and the glacier, Burwardsley's rope slung around his chest and bouncing on his knees as he ran. Fenna followed, amazed at the Gurkha's speed, and more than a little impressed at the way Burwardsley and Thomas had turned the ambush back on the blocking force, and given them the break they needed to push for the lookout tower.

They kept up the pace all the way to the edge of the glacier, the tongue extending into the valley far below them. Bahadur pulled off the rope as they caught their breath. Fenna felt the cold from the ice as she dragged it into her lungs. She smiled and allowed herself a brief laugh. On impulse, she slapped Bahadur on the arm.

"It's good to be back," she said and pointed at the ice. The rain had stopped, and the light in the sky was stronger, blue behind the grey clouds. They were going to climb in good weather, and Fenna felt her spirits lift. She smiled again and Bahadur nodded.

"Mountains and ice. Like home," he said.

"Like Greenland too."

"Greenland too flat," Bahadur said, his brow wrinkled.

"Flat?" Fenna shook her head, and then she remembered where the small man called home. "Yeah, okay. I understand," she said and tied the end of the rope around her waist. They had agreed that Bahadur would lead when they talked down in the meadow. The climb wasn't difficult, but it made sense to take precautions. *Besides*, she thought, *if Nicklas decides to make things interesting...* The thought tailed off as Fenna considered how Nicklas might react and what he might do.

Thoughts of Nicklas plagued her as they set out across the ice in the direction of the ladders that Bahadur had confirmed would lead them all the way to the lookout tower, over 2,000 metres above sea level. Fenna pushed any sentimental feelings she might once have had for Nicklas to the back of her mind. When Jarnvig had suggested Nicklas was dead, all traces connecting him to the operations he and Vestergaard were running cleaned away, she had buried those same thoughts, choosing to act instead. Killing Jarnvig and the guard outside the door, freeing Burwardsley and the chase that followed, had pushed any possibility of grieving to the back of her mind. Now she had to face the first man that had shown any kindness toward her since Bahadur had killed her partner. Fenna shook her head, tired of the threads twisting in her mind. *Remember the real villain*, she reminded herself, *the man who spins all these threads and pulls all the strings: the Magician. Vestergaard.* Fenna spat on the ice and kept going.

The ladders were fixed in place. The robust rungs were thick and square, the sides worn, smooth but fibrous to the touch. Fenna felt connected to the climbers and hikers who had scrambled up each rung before them, as she climbed up after Bahadur. He tugged the rope each time he was ready for her to follow, as the sunshine broke through the clouds, Fenna allowed herself to forget the firefight in the tree line below the glacier, to forget her hate for the man who killed her partner, and to enjoy the fresh air as it thinned, just a little, with each rung she climbed. She smiled the whole length of the second ladder from the top, stopping only when Bahadur placed his rough finger on her lips and nodded toward the last ladder, the shortest one yet, leading to the rounded summit and the Three Fingers Lookout Tower, the cabin with the greatest view of the Cascade Mountain Range.

"I stay here," Bahadur whispered. He held out his hand for Fenna's carbine, and exchanged it for two spare magazines for the Glock pistol she had in her jacket pocket.

"Where will you be?" Fenna asked.

"I go around," he said. He made a walking motion with two fingers.

Fenna looked in the direction he indicated and said, "But there's no ladder."

Bahadur grinned. "I am mountain man. Not some stupid tracker. I go around."

"Alright. But don't move in unless you need to."

"Why everyone think I am stupid?" Bahadur slapped his hand against Fenna's arm. "Go," he said, "before Mike call us on radio."

"What radio?"

"His," Bahadur said and nodded in the direction of the cabin. He flashed a smile at Fenna before scrabbling around the rock and out of sight.

Fenna untied the rope around her waist and looped it through the coil at the base of the ladder. She was stalling and she knew it, but she realised she wasn't prepared for what to expect in the cabin. It made no sense to keep Alice alive, and yet she hoped that was exactly what Nicklas had done. If Alice was dead, there would be nothing to stop Fenna killing him. *Nothing at all.*

The rungs on the last ladder were just as old and just as worn as the ladders below, but they felt tacky somehow, as if each successive rung was more difficult to let go of than the last. Fenna forced herself to reach for the next rung. She moved onward, upward, stopping only when she could see the roof of the cabin, the storm shutters clasped to each side of the window, and the glass, reflecting the sun, spoiling her view of the cabin's interior. Fenna finished her climb, raised her hands and shouted.

"Nicklas Fischer."

She kept her hands in the air as the light wind carried the sound of movement from inside the cabin to where she stood beside the top of the ladder. She saw him as he stood. Heard the scrape of something like a chair leg across a wood floor, as he walked to the window. Fenna held her breath, her hands trembling above her head, and then she laughed, a release, for there was Alice, beautiful Alice. She was alive, she seemed unhurt, and she was here, just four metres and one short-barrelled submachine gun away from Fenna. *It might as well be four kilometres*, she thought, as she stared at the weapon slung around Nicklas' chest and her smile faded. I'll never reach her. *Not before he can put an end to us both*. But then Nicklas did something that made Fenna at once hopeful and wary. He pulled the sling of the submachine gun over his head, removed the magazine, and rested the weapon in the corner of the window where Fenna could see it.

"I'm coming out," he shouted. And then, quieter, "Stay here, Alice."

Fenna lowered her hands as Nicklas opened the cabin door and stepped out. She glanced at Alice, and was relieved to see her smile. Alice pressed her hand against the window and splayed her fingers against the glass. Fenna took a breath and smiled. She turned back to Nicklas, and he stopped just two metres away.

"What now, Fenna? Shall we sit down?"

"Yes, okay," she said. He sat first, crossing his legs as he waited for Fenna to do the same.

"Not too cold for you?" he said.

"No."

He turned to look at the sun and said, "It finally cleared up. It's been rotten weather the past few days, I was thinking…"

"What do you want, Nicklas?"

"Want?" he said and looked at her.

"You want something. You wouldn't put a team in the woods for nothing."

"It's not me," he said, and Fenna thought she caught a flicker of sadness in his eyes. "I never wanted this. Never wanted the Yuma assignment."

"But you took it."

"I took it. Christ," he said and rubbed his hand across the stubble on his chin. Fenna waited. Nicklas rested his hands on his knees and said, "It's not like I had a choice. I was groomed from the start."

"There's always a choice," Fenna said.

"Really, Fenna. You of all people believe that?" Nicklas shook his head. "They teased me, you know? They had these intriguing stories, rumours of special operations, an elite fraternity, an exotic life." He paused to sigh, and Fenna noted the way he scratched at his knees with restless fingers. "It was exciting. I was fast-tracked into the RCMP anti-terror unit. Vestergaard came later. He recruited me with the full cooperation of my superiors. They could all see I had certain talents, and only one real flaw – I couldn't turn it off. I couldn't distract myself wholly from each assignment, had a tendency to get too engaged. Vestergaard said he could help. Promised he could fix me, and he did, to a point. Until you." Nicklas flattened his fingers against his thighs and looked at Fenna. He shrugged and looked away, blinking into the sun. "You were meant to be disposable, a patsy for the real assassin, the girl," he said and gestured at the cabin, "but you have real grit, Fenna, and I fell for that. I fell for the way you took a punch. Clean hair and make-up were furthest from your mind, but..." Nicklas looked at her and smiled. "I've seen the photos. You clean up good, but you'll always be that girl in the boxing ring for me. I can still smell your sweat, feel the grit beneath your fingers, the dust in your hair." He stared at her, and Fenna saw his eyes glaze, his pupils widen, just a little, despite the sun. "You were my assignment, Fenna, but not everything I did was for Vestergaard. Some things I did for me."

Fenna bit her lip, and said, "I was told you were dead."

"I probably should be."

"It was Jarnvig who told me. You were dead, the Gunney's team was dead – all of them, even the pole dancer they brought onto the base to teach Alice..."

"It's true. They are all dead."

"But not you."

"No." Nicklas ran his hand through his hair. "Would it be easier if I was?"

"Maybe," said Fenna. She unzipped her jacket pocket and pulled out the Glock. Nicklas just nodded as she pointed it at him. "I've come for Alice. She's all I want."

"I know," he said.

"Are you going to let me take her?" Fenna

glanced at the cabin, reassuring herself that Alice was free to move, that she wasn't chained to the wall. *Like I was once, back in the beginning.*

"I want to, Fenna. You believe me, don't you?"

She knew, as soon as he said it, that she didn't. Fenna curled her finger inside the trigger guard, and applied the first squeeze of pressure. She felt the centre blade of the safe action trigger beneath her finger, followed by the flood of adrenaline as she tried to clear her mind, to ignore what Nicklas had said, how he had said it. *I need to be clear. Focused. I can't let him confuse me. Can't let him play on any emotions — his or mine. This is about Alice, it's for Dina, it ends with Vestergaard. But it starts with him.* Fenna raised the pistol, controlled her breathing, cleared her mind of conflicts, until Nicklas lifted his hand and pointed at the breast pocket of his fleece.

"I have something in here. You'll want to see it. Before you pull that trigger."

"What is it?"

"You'll let me take it out?"

"Yes," Fenna said. She frowned as he slipped two fingers inside the pocket and pulled out a thin piece of plastic. "Is that a remote?"

"Yes."

"Fuck." Fenna shook her head and lowered the Glock. "It's wired. Isn't it?"

"The whole cabin," Nicklas said. "Yes. And," he said, turning the remote in his hands. Fenna could see two slim buttons. "The top button will trigger the detonator. And the second button…" Nicklas looked at his watch.

"Pauses the timer?" Fenna looked away, swearing under her breath.

"Exactly." Nicklas stood up. "It's a little cold out here. Will you come inside?" He waited for Fenna to stand, took the Glock from her hand and led her inside the cabin.

Chapter 10

The sun lanced through the clouds as Fenna stepped inside the lookout cabin. The floorboards creaked beneath her boots and she blinked in the sunlight, as Alice flung her arms around her neck. Fenna leaned into the younger woman's embrace, pulling her close to her body, ignoring Nicklas and the pistol he pressed into her back to push her further inside the cabin. Alice's tears were warm on Fenna's skin, her sobs muffled. Despite the situation, because of it even, Fenna smiled, choked, and cried, her own tears splashing on Alice's hair. The world shrank all of a sudden, and the combined cares and concerns of the two young women were forgotten. No longer were they alone in the world of men, for once they outnumbered them, in that tiny cabin in the Cascades.

"They want me dead," Alice said, her voice hoarse, the words splintered with tears.

"If they did, then you would already be dead," Fenna said. "I won't let that happen."

Alice looked up. She wiped the tears from her face with one hand, clung to Fenna with the other. Her eyes misted, her pupils widened, and she gripped Fenna's jacket with both hands. Fenna wrapped her arms around her and pulled her tight, so tight she heard Alice gasp, but she didn't let go.

"Us girls," she said, "We have to stick together."

"For sure," Alice said.

Nicklas moved around them. He scraped the legs of a chair along the floorboards and sat down. Fenna heard the dull thud of her Glock as he placed it on the table. She lifted her head and looked at him. The lines of stress on his face, small fractures in his skin highlighted by several days of exposure to the sun, were new. She studied them, studied him, searching for the old Nicklas, the one who had protected her in the desert, the one who might resurface in spite of his orders. *But he's not there*, she realised. *That Nicklas is buried deep.* He shifted, fidgeting under her gaze, reached for the pistol, let it go, stared back at her.

"I have my orders," he said. Fenna noticed the remote was still in his hand. "But I'm not a monster. No matter what you might think."

"I've met my fair share of monsters," Fenna said, as dark thoughts of a fetid hold in the bowels of *The Ice Star* pricked at her, the image sharp, painful.

"I know," he said.

"You helped me get rid of the last one," she said, and replaced the image of the hold with that of Humble bleeding in his Toronto office.

"I did."

"Then help me again."

Fenna felt Alice relax in her arms. She smoothed Alice's hair from her cheeks and guided her to a chair against the wall opposite Nicklas. The sun lit Alice's face and Fenna was relieved to see there were no scars, no visible signs of trauma or weakness. *Don't be fooled*, she chided herself. *Her pain will be on the inside, and will run deep.* Once Alice was seated she turned back to Nicklas, calculating the distance between them to be about a metre and a half. *Too far.* Nicklas placed the remote beside the Glock and pressed his palm flat on the table.

"What are you up to, Fenna? Why did you come here?"

"I didn't have much choice. Your boss had me surrounded."

"Vestergaard?"

"Who else?"

"Jarnvig was my handler."

"Jarnvig is dead."

Nicklas pinched the bridge of his nose and said, "I thought so."

"But you didn't know?"

"Vestergaard works on a need to know basis. He gave me this assignment personally. He didn't mention Jarnvig."

"But you figured it out?"

"I figured it would go one of two ways, and, if you were involved, well…" He snorted. "You have a knack for getting out of tight situations."

Fenna let that sink in for a moment. She smiled and dipped her head, using the movement to scan the cabin, taking in the bookshelf, the desk, the deep window sills, the guest book and pencil on the table by the Glock and the remote. She saw the shelves of tinned food, and the makeshift kitchen area that Alice and Nicklas had used. There was an empty mug stained with dregs of filter coffee. Fenna swallowed at the sight of it. *But where are the explosives? The walls are too thin*, and she didn't remember seeing anything in the space beneath the cabin, between the wooden supports and the bare rock. *He's bluffing.*

"You're going after Vestergaard," Nicklas said. "That's why you came for the girl?"

"That's one reason, but it seems he already knew where she would be."

"Yes," he said and glanced at Alice. "We knew everything."

"And you played me from day one."

"That depends on when you started counting."

"In Copenhagen, when I met Jarnvig."

Nicklas nodded. "That fits," he said, "pieces were being moved into position. You were one of them."

Fenna gestured at the wall to the right of Nicklas and took a step toward it. She rested her bottom on the lip of the window sill, and stuffed her hands in her jacket pockets. Alice watched her every move. So did Nicklas.

"Who?" she said.

"Who *what*?"

"Who moved…" She corrected herself with a sigh. "Who is *moving* the pieces? I don't believe it is just Vestergaard."

"Ah," Nicklas said, "you think there is a deep state at play in America?"

"You suggested as much, when you pulled me away from the special forces operators in Arizona."

"I did." Nicklas tapped his finger on the table and looked at Fenna. She recognised the look, it was the same one he had used before, just before disclosing mission-sensitive information. "What if I were to tell you that Vestergaard is a freelancer? Would you believe me?"

"To a point. Maybe." Fenna frowned.

"But you think it is unlikely. How can one man wield so much power without the resources of a state backing him?"

"Yes."

"And what country serves to gain from turmoil in the United States?"

Fenna laughed. "That's a long list."

"Narrow it down," he said.

"In light of recent events?" she said and shrugged her shoulders. "I don't know. China?"

"That's one for starters."

"You only asked for one."

"To make you think." Nicklas rested his elbows on his knees and leaned forward, his head less than a metre from Fenna. He looked at her, waited for her to speak.

"Okay, more than one country…"

"Operating independently? They've tried that."

"So they need to coordinate their efforts."

"They can't. They won't, not publicly, not face to face. We're talking about rogue states and countries that are tired of America's domination, its meddling."

"You're saying they need a broker?"

"Exactly."

"Vestergaard?"

"They wouldn't call him *the Magician* if he couldn't work a little magic."

"Coordinating the efforts of several countries at once…"

"Magic."

"…to destabilise the United States?"

Nicklas leaned back and Fenna realised she had missed her first opportunity to strike, that she would have to wait for another. *If he gives me the chance.*

"So, the deep state," she said, "is really more than one?"

"And each state thinking they are the only one."

"And if they were to find out?"

"They won't."

"But if they did?"

Nicklas picked up the remote. He smoothed his thumb lightly over the two buttons. "They won't," he said.

Fenna took a deep breath. She felt the sun warm

her face as she breathed out, her eyes on the remote, as she processed the information, coupled it together with what she knew of Nicklas, his professionalism. She wondered if Vestergaard had finally broken his Achilles heel, had taught Nicklas to overcome the flaw that prevented him from distancing himself completely from the mission. And then she understood that it was exactly that flaw Vestergaard was exploiting when he tasked Nicklas with the mission in the cabin at the top of the Cascades. *The blocking force*, she realised, *they're not just here for us, they're here for him too.*

Nicklas smoothed his thumb once more across the remote. He looked at Alice and said, "It'll be over soon."

"No," said Fenna, as Alice began to tremble. "You don't have to do this. I'm not alone. The men in the tree line… we've eliminated them."

"There's more than one team."

"Then we'll take care of them, too," she said and pulled her hands from her pockets.

"I'm too involved, Fenna. Vestergaard made sure of that."

"Then we'll work together. We'll change that."

"You don't understand."

"I do. Really." Fenna took a step toward Nicklas. He stood up and pushed her away. He raised the remote above his head.

"Stop," he said.

"You stop," she said. "We can stop this together."

"And do what? Tell the world? Forget it, Fenna. The world doesn't want it to be known. If we don't die here, we'll die somewhere else. We'll be pursued

until it's over. They'll send one team after another."
He pointed at Alice. "Ask her. She knows what it is
like to be America's most wanted. How about the
world's most wanted?"

"Not if we kill him first. Not if we stop him."

Nicklas shook his head. "You don't understand.
It's already begun. It's over, Fenna."

Alice screamed as the first bullet from the M4
carbine shattered the window, showering her in
shards of glass, as it tore through Nicklas' wrist. He
dropped the remote and Fenna lunged for it, kicking
at Nicklas' injured hand as he swore and scrabbled
after the remote. She heard the light pounding of
boots on the rock outside the cabin, followed by the
splinter of wood as Bahadur kicked at the door and
burst inside the cabin.

"No," she screamed, as Bahadur tucked the
carbine into his shoulder and punctured Nicklas'
chest with a burst of three rounds. Nicklas crumpled
to the floor, his blood pooling onto the floorboards
and seeping into Fenna's trousers and jacket as she
cradled his head on her knees and pressed her hands
on the entry wounds in his chest. He looked at her,
blood spilling from his lips as he raised his shattered
hand to her cheek.

"You were real for me," he said, his words wet
with blood. He spluttered, coughed, and said, "You
were real."

"I know," she said. Fenna pressed his hand to her
cheek, her tears mixing with his blood as they
splashed onto his fingers. He closed his eyes and she
felt his hand slip from hers. She held on, ignoring the
clump of the Gurkha's boots as he ordered Alice out
of the cabin. Fenna looked away from Nicklas' face

and saw the remote on the floor. She picked it up, considered, just for a moment, ending it all. *It would be so much easier*, she thought. *So simple. To end it here, on the mountaintop.* She recalled Nicklas' last words, about being wanted across the world, never being safe.

"Fenna?" Alice said. Her feet shuffled on the floorboards as she pushed past Bahadur and reached out to touch Fenna's shoulder. "This man says we should go. But I'm not leaving without you."

The remote was warm within Fenna's fingers. She traced the swell of the detonator button with her thumb, looked at Alice. *So simple.*

"Fenna? Won't you come?"

Nicklas' lungs expelled his last breath as his body slipped from Fenna's knees and onto the floor. She laid his hand across his chest, bent down to his face and kissed his lips. *He's gone.* She looked up, saw Alice by her side, Bahadur in the doorway. *And it's time we were gone too.* Fenna stood up. She took Alice's hand in hers and squeezed it.

"Give me a second."

"Sure," said Alice, "but only a second." Her body trembled. "The man…" she nodded at Bahadur, "he said we can't wait."

"I know. I just need…" Fenna let go of Alice. "I just need a second."

"Okay." Alice retreated to the door.

Fenna looked down at Nicklas. She held the remote in her palm, wiped the tears from her cheek with a bloody hand.

"You taught me to fight dirty," she said, choking on a laugh as she remembered the dancing lessons in the dusty boxing ring in the desert warehouse. "I won't forget. I'll never forget. How about that? Is that enough? I mean, can I just leave you here?" Fenna looked out of the window, squinting as the sun broke through another swathe of cloud and lit the cabin with a soft pink light. It filtered onto Nicklas' face, and then she realised that he was at peace. *Someone will find his body*, she thought. *And I have to go. He would want me to go.*

Fenna looked at the remote in her palm. She tapped the detonator button with her nail, and then pressed the button below it to pause the timer. She frowned, turned the remote between her fingers and slid the battery case from the back of the remote and swore. It was empty. Fenna bit her lip, pinching the skin between her teeth until she tasted the first drop of blood. She licked the blood from her lips and leaned down to slip the remote inside Nicklas' short pocket.

"Vestergaard never did erase that flaw, did he?" she said, wiping her tears from his cheek, her voice soft, a whisper. "I'll get him," she said. "I'll finish this." She smoothed Nicklas' hair from his brow and stood up.

Bahadur was waiting at the entrance to the cabin. Fenna picked up her Glock from the table and stuffed it inside her jacket pocket. She nodded at Bahadur, brushing past him as she walked out of the cabin to join Alice on the rock above the first ladder.

"He told me you would come," she said and took Fenna's hand. "I recognised him from the camp in the desert. He said you were friends."

"We were."

"He said you were tough, and that you would protect me."

"I will," Fenna said and looked at Alice, "if I

can."

"I believe you." Alice smiled.

"And do you trust me?"

Alice nodded. "Yes."

"Good. Because this isn't going to be easy."

Fenna fell quiet as Bahadur joined them He tied the end of the rope around Alice's waist and nodded for her to climb down the ladder. Alice hesitated. She gripped Fenna's hand.

"Come on," Bahadur said. "We go. Now."

"Fenna?"

"It's okay," Fenna said. "You can trust him."

Bahadur looked at Fenna, his brow wrinkled as he studied her face.

"Yes," she said. "I mean it. I trust you. I have to."

The Gurkha smiled and gripped the rope, feeding it through his small hands as Alice let go of Fenna and began to climb down the ladder. Fenna looked back at the cabin, took one step toward it and then stopped. There was a shout from the ice below the ladders. She ignored it. As the cold pinched her cheek she realised that Nicklas was at peace.

"And if I want the same," she said, "I am going to have to fight for it."

Fenna turned her back on the cabin and walked to the ladder. She waved down at Alice and lifted her arms as Bahadur tied a bight of rope around her waist. Fenna stepped onto the top rung of the ladder and climbed down it as Bahadur fed the rope between his fingers. Alice took a step away from the ladder and Fenna felt the rope tug at her body. *We're connected*, she thought, and smiled. *And we'll stay that way, all the way to the end.*

Chapter 11

Burwardsley was waiting at the foot of the last ladder when Fenna started her descent. He tugged her to one side as she stepped off the last rung and untied the bight of rope around her waist. Bahadur climbed down the ladder and Burwardsley handed him the rope to coil. Alice was already free of the rope. She reached out and Fenna clasped her hand for a moment before following Burwardsley to the boundary between rock and ice, the carbine slung across his chest. Fenna pointed at blood coming from a long cut across his brow.

"A branch," he said. "What about you? What happened up there?"

"We're all fine."

"I didn't ask about the others. I asked about you."

Fenna frowned at the tone in Burwardsley's voice. *He cares*, she thought.

"Yeah, okay, Konstabel. I care," he said and fiddled with the sling. "It's a weakness, apparently. But tell me, what happened up top?"

Fenna waited a second and then said, "Nicklas was there. He had Alice in the cabin, captive, one way or the other. I think he had been there several days. But she looks fine. Doesn't seem to be concerned about anything he might have done, only what she did."

"And what is that, exactly?"

"I don't know yet," Fenna said with a glance at Alice. The young woman waved before resuming her conversation with Bahadur. The Gurkha seemed to be on his best behaviour, and, she noticed, he had a winning smile that seemed to please Alice. "Nicklas suggested the cabin was wired."

"Suggested?" Burwardsley said. He reached out to touch Fenna's arm and she turned to face him.

"There were no batteries in the remote. But..."

"What?"

"Bahadur shot him anyway."

"Yeah, that's on me, love. I told him to be vigilant and fast."

"He was." Fenna took a breath. "Shit, Mike, he did what he had to do. I don't hold a grudge, and, truth be told, I think Nicklas wanted out, and that was the only way."

The sun disappeared behind a cloud and Burwardsley looked at his watch. He wiped a smear of blood and dirt from the face and tapped the glass above the hour hand.

"We have to move," he said. "We need to get off the glacier and back on the trail before dark, before more teams show up."

"They will," Fenna said. "Nicklas said there would be more. I think they intended to trap us all up in the cabin, him included."

"Vestergaard tidying up again, eh?"

"I think so," she said, and paused. "Mike?"

"Yep?"

"How did you get involved with Vestergaard?"

"We can talk about this later, but now we really need to move."

Fenna studied Burwardsley's face for a moment, searching for signs of evasion, or lies, she found only guilt and something far worse – a worried expression that she had never seen before.

"What is it?" she said.

Burwardsley whistled for Bahadur to bring the girl. He clapped his hand on Fenna's shoulder, encouraging her forward along the path they had struck across the ice.

"Tell me."

Burwardsley peeled the sling over his head and shifted his grip on the carbine. He checked the magazine, slapping it home with a soft metallic thud.

"The team in the woods was good. Well trained," he said, as Fenna increased speed to match the pace he set with his long legs. She glanced over her shoulder to see Bahadur at the rear of their tiny column. Alice was a few steps ahead. Fenna looked at her hair as the setting sun highlighted Alice's natural blonde colour, pushing up from the roots. She made a mental note that they should dye it, and soon. Burwardsley sighed and said, "The grenades shook them up a bit. They weren't expecting that. But they rallied quickly. Thomas caught one in the arm and another in the leg – shattered his tibia. He's going to slow us down."

Fenna thought about that for a second, and then she said, "But you got them? All of them?"

"Yep, all five. Dead."

"But you're worried."

"Yes, love. I am. These guys were better coordinated than the majority of goons we meet – even in this line of work." Burwardsley slipped suddenly, skidded for a second and regained his balance. Fenna saw a spot of blood on the ice. She grabbed his arm. "It's alright," he said, "just another scratch. I'll fix it later."

"You're sure?"

"Yep." He nodded, but Fenna caught the grimace

of pain he bit back. She started to speak, but he interrupted her. "You remember the guys Vestergaard had in Nuuk? His protection detail. The ones in the chopper."

"Yes."

"They reminded me of them. Meaning, they're not some home-grown local types. He put these guys into play."

"I'm not following, Mike."

Burwardsley stopped, glancing around Fenna to gauge the distance between them and Alice. "If I'm right, then Vestergaard is putting his best men into the field, which means he is trying to cover this up as fast and as efficiently as possible."

"We knew that," Fenna said and frowned.

"I know, but at this stage in the game, well, I think he is scared."

"Good." Fenna turned at the sound of Alice and Bahadur catching up. Burwardsley gripped her arm.

"No, Fenna. Not good. It means he's dangerous, unpredictable."

Burwardsley stopped talking as Alice stopped beside Fenna. He nodded at her before moving past the two women to talk to Bahadur. Fenna watched him for a moment, thinking about what he said, before slipping her arm around Alice's and continuing down the icy path in the direction of the rocky trail below them. She could see Thomas resting beside their packs and she waved.

"Who's that?" said Alice.

"An Australian. He's with us."

Alice laughed. "We couldn't be any more international if we tried."

"You're right. You know I'm from Denmark? I

can't remember if I ever told you."

"I don't remember either." Alice paused and Fenna wondered if she was thinking back to the canteen on the desert base where they met. "I never thought you'd come to get me."

"I promised myself that I would."

"Thank you," Alice said and slipped her fingers into Fenna's hand. "He was nice."

"Who? Nicklas?"

"It was him who said you would come. It's like he was waiting for you. How well did you know him?"

"Well enough, I suppose." Fenna felt a tremor pass through Alice's body. "You've never seen a man killed, have you?"

"No."

Fenna slowed as they neared the trail. She lowered her voice, and said, "Not even the President?"

"Not even him. I just…" Alice's voice faltered and Fenna pulled her close.

"It's okay. You can tell me some other time."

"Yeah, but…" she said and stopped.

Fenna took Alice's free hand and smiled. "What is it?"

"I didn't kill him. Not really. They just wanted me to dance for him. To show him a good time. They said the President chose me. They said if I was going to be close to him I had to have special training."

"He chose you?"

"Yeah, from some catalogue or other. I danced a bit at High School. I was on TV. But I never danced like that woman showed me." Alice's lips twitched and she whispered, "I think she was a stripper."

"I think you're right."

"Anyway. They said the President was real tired, that he never had a chance to relax, and that he really needed to, that the job was getting to him. I like the President, I mean liked. I even voted for him – I was just old enough."

Burwardsley passed them. He tapped Fenna on the shoulder and held up his hand, fingers splayed. *Five minutes*, she thought, and nodded that she understood. Bahadur remained on the ice, a few metres away, scanning the tree line.

"Sorry," Fenna said. "Tell me more. If you want to."

"Sure," Alice said. She let go of Fenna's hand and ran her fingers through her hair. She gripped her hair just above her ears, as Fenna might have done. "They said I should dye my hair, that he liked girls with black hair."

Fenna nodded and thought about how they really were meant to look like one another. *It was all in the details*, she thought. She looked up as Alice took a long breath.

"They told me I should put it in his drink," she said, clenching her hair in her fists. "They said it was a relaxant."

"But it wasn't?"

"I don't know. He was pretty relaxed." Alice shook her head. She let go of her hair and crossed her hands across her chest. Fenna noticed her right foot as it began to tap on the ice. "I danced. I even took my shirt off. They told me he might ask me to."

"Where were you?"

"Some hotel in New York. It was pretty fancy. They snuck me in through the kitchen."

"They?"

"The same men from the desert. Oh, and this other guy."

"Nicklas?"

"No. This one had a funny accent." Alice's brow wrinkled as she looked at Fenna. "Come to think of it, he said some words the same way you do."

"He spoke to you?"

"Just a little. Then they took me up in a service lift. I was already in the room before the President arrived. Just waiting on the couch. I was real nervous."

"Fenna," Burwardsley called. He waved his hand when she looked at him.

"One second," she said and looked at Alice. "What happened next?"

"The President walked in, and I was so nervous. I think I shook his hand. I think I apologised for being so sweaty. He said something sweet like *not to worry*, and I *couldn't guess how many sweaty hands he had shaken,* and how mine were the softest. He was really, really sweet. And I thought about all the things he had to do, and how difficult it must be, how stressful and…" Alice took a breath. "It sounds crazy, but, I just felt right there, that if I could give him a break, make him happy, just for an hour, then I would, and that I would maybe, in my own way, make a difference. You know? Do something for my country. Does that sound crazy?" She didn't wait for Fenna to respond. Alice continued, "and the stuff they said I should put in his drink. They said his doctor prescribed it. I mean… Why shouldn't I believe them?"

"You had no reason not to."

"For sure. And anyway, he was so sweet, and he

just kinda started to doze off right after I took off my shirt. He said something about how pretty my bra was and I remember giggling like I hadn't done for a while. And all that time I'd spent in the desert, it kind of made sense. I had a job to do, for the President. For my country."

Alice tapped her foot and Fenna saw the tears on her cheeks. She hugged her, stepped back, wiped the tears from her cheeks with her thumb, and said, "What happened next?"

Alice bit her bottom lip and Fenna reached up to curl a lock of Alice's hair behind her ear.

"They told me I should wait until they came to get me. That the President would leave first. They said he would probably sleep after I put the powder in his drink. That it was normal. Well, it didn't look normal, and I got scared. I put my shirt on and I just wanted to leave, but there was a guard on the door. We had music on – real low – but enough so they couldn't hear us. I opened the door to the balcony." Alice surprised herself with a smile. She laughed at the memory, and Fenna saw a spark in her eyes. "I told you my dad was a climber, right?"

"Yes. You did."

"He taught me good. I climbed up onto the balcony on the floor above, and I promised my dad that if I got away I would come here. This is where he wanted to be at the end. I figured if this was the end of my life, then at least we would be together. You know, our spirits. Is that crazy?"

"No, it's not."

"You're sure? I think it's crazy. Anyway, climbing up one floor, and then another. That *was* crazy. That's how I got away. Once I got to the street I ran so fast.

I got to a bus station – that's where they must have taken the photo of me, 'cos I was more careful after that. I started wearing a beanie. And I got some climbing gear, food – I had some money. They had paid me up front. Then I just came here. As fast as possible. I was here about a week before Nicklas showed up. I saw no-one else. The weather has been crappy. Until today." Alice smiled. "It must be because you came. You brought it with you."

"I'd like to think so," Fenna said. She pulled Alice into a tight hug as Burwardsley called out one more time. Fenna whispered in her ear, "I'm going to take you somewhere safe."

"Okay."

"You're going to have to trust me."

"I do."

"And do whatever I say."

"I will."

Fenna felt Alice's body shake as she began to cry.

"These men, they are my friends. They are going to help us."

Fenna turned her head as Bahadur coughed softly beside her.

"We go now. Mike say so."

Bahadur walked past them and Fenna let go of Alice. She held her hand as they followed the Gurkha to the beginning of the trail. The sun started to sink behind the peaks and Burwardsley looked at his watch. He picked up a spare German Heckler & Koch G36 assault rifle. The stock was folded and he snapped it into place before handing it to Fenna.

"You alright with this one, Konstabel?" he said, as he handed her two spare magazines.

"Yes."

"Konstabel?" Alice said. She stared at the rifle as Fenna did a quick physical check of the weapon.

"That's right," she said, "although I think rogue agent is what they prefer to call me now."

"Who?"

"The same men who put you in that hotel room."

"You know them?" Alice said. The look on her face suggested she found that hard to believe.

"You could say that," Fenna said and laughed. Her lips flattened into a tight smile. She picked up her pack from the pile at Thomas' feet, nodded at the Australian and slipped her arms through the shoulder straps. Fenna tightened the straps and fastened the waist belt before tucking the rifle against her chest. She nodded that she was ready.

"Okay," Burwardsley said. "Thomas, you've got the rear."

"For as long as I can, mate."

"Understood. Bad?"

"Yes, *Saheb*?"

"I want you on point. Keep a good pace, with a break every twenty minutes. Don't let us fall more than two hundred yards behind. Fenna, I want you and Alice in front of me."

"Where are we going?" Alice asked, as Burwardsley directed her onto the trail.

"Canada," he said.

"And then? What happens after we cross the border?"

"One step at a time," Fenna said. She would have said more, but the flick of Thomas' head in the direction of the meadows caught her attention.

"What is it?" Burwardsley whispered.

"Movement on the trail." Thomas paused. He

cocked his head to one side and closed his eyes. "Four men, heavily armed."

"Okay." Burwardsley pressed his hand on Thomas' shoulder. "You know what to do."

"Yeah, mate. I know." Thomas reached into his pocket. He pulled out part of a map, folded in half, and pressed it into Burwardsley's hand. "I had some time while you were playing on the mountain."

"Alright," Burwardsley said. He glanced at Thomas' handwriting on the map and slipped it into his pocket. "I'll make sure your family gets it."

"Thanks, mate," Thomas said. "Now fuck off before I change my mind."

Bahadur and Thomas exchanged a brief look before the Gurkha turned and began to jog along the trail. Fenna followed with Alice right behind her. Burwardsley waited for a moment, and Fenna thought she heard him say a few more words to Thomas before the heavy tread of his boots on the trail confirmed that he was following them. She swallowed and surprised herself at how the thought of Burwardsley behind her, and Bahadur in front reassured her. *We met on the ice as enemies*, she mused, *and now we're heading back there. But as what? Friends? Allies?* The thought occupied her for the first few hundred metres, until the familiar bark of Thomas' M4 carbine ricocheted around the mountain walls, and along the trail behind them.

Chapter 12

The trail widened just before they reached the tree line, descending into the valley several kilometres from the border. Bahadur had increased the pace twice, and they had barely stopped since the first exchange of bullets behind them. Burwardsley had halted once, when Fenna paused to speak with him, only to be pushed on.

"Stay with the girl. Keep up with Bad."

"And Thomas? What about him?"

It was too dark to see Burwardsley's expression, but Fenna could *feel* his response, hear the way he breathed, the soft click of the fire selector switch as he flicked it to full automatic.

"Stay with Bad," Burwardsley said. He jogged down the trail in the direction they had come. Fenna watched him for a moment. She turned and caught up with Alice, pushing her on with short, soft words of encouragement.

They were well inside the tree line when the first burst of Burwardsley's M4 caught Fenna's attention. She slowed, unslung her assault rifle and took a step in the Royal Marine's direction.

"No," Bahadur said, his voice a whisper. Fenna flinched, amazed he had arrived so quickly, so quietly. "Mike say we go for border. I take you there now. Mike come later."

"You don't know that," Fenna said.

"Yes. I do. Mike say." Bahadur gripped Fenna's arm and pulled her down the trail. He let go when they found Alice leaning against a tree. "The border is close. Come."

Fenna's hair flicked across her cheeks as she

nodded. She looked up when Alice took her hand. "It's okay," she said.

"You said you wouldn't leave me."

"And I won't. I just…"

"You want to go back for your friend?"

Friend. The word tumbled inside Fenna's head. In the darkness beneath the thick pine needle canopy, she shut out the dark images of Burwardsley, picturing instead the more recent memories in Greenland's capital, exchanging banter and bullets as they did their best to escape and evade her countrymen. "Yes," she said as she recalled the moment of their capture. "I suppose he is."

"What?"

"A friend."

Alice tugged at Fenna's hand. "I understand if you want to go back. But I'm scared, Fenna. I want to get out of here."

"I know." Fenna slung the assault rifle over her shoulder and squeezed Alice's hand. "Run," she said. "I'll be right behind you." Another short burst of automatic weapons fire gave her pause, but Fenna shut it out, released Alice and followed her down the path through the trees. *If Burwardsley makes it,* she thought, *when he makes it, I'll tell him…* Fenna stubbed the toe of her boot on a tree root. She stumbled, her feet thudding on the trail, arms flailing, until she found her balance, righted herself, and kept going. Another burst of weapons fire – an exchange this time – ricocheted around her mind as she processed her priorities. *The girl, it had to be the girl. That's what we agreed.* Fenna ran, bringing up the rear, surprised at Bahadur's speed, pleased that Alice could keep up.

Bahadur pushed them on, stopping after two

hours at the rotten door of a small moss-clad cabin. He rested, his carbine held loosely in the crook of his arm. He grinned when Fenna slowed to a stop beside him, her chest heaving. She considered removing her pack, but thought better of it. Alice, she noticed, seemed to be in better shape that she was. It started to rain once more, and Fenna looked up at the canopy in anticipation of a few drops of relief splashing onto her face.

"Mike is okay," Bahadur said.

"You can't possibly know that," Fenna said.

"Yes. He tell me he will be okay."

"I'm sure he did, but…"

"No." Bahadur said. He shook his head and she caught the shadow of movement between the trees. "He is okay. We keep going. Meet him at the road, and cross the border."

We are never going to get across the border, Fenna thought. *It will be guarded, from the highway and into the hills.* She looked at Alice. *And I will have failed her. Failed another young woman. For what? Some twisted sense of…*

"What are you thinking?" Alice said.

Fenna bit her lip, said nothing. She flicked her gaze from Bahadur and back to Alice.

"You're thinking about something."

"Yes," she said.

"It's the border, isn't it?"

"Yes."

"You don't know how we will cross it?"

"That's right."

Alice smiled. She lifted a finger and pointed in a north-westerly direction. "We'll go that way. Once the trail widens into a road, we'll cut through the trees to the west, then north and over the border." She lowered her hand and searched in her pockets for a pair of thin gloves. She pulled them on and said, "Dad had a thing for Smarties."

"What?"

"The chocolate? They're like M&Ms."

"I know," said Fenna, "we have them in Denmark."

"Well, they don't in the US, so dad used to sneak across the border after a climbing trip, just to stock up. There's a gas station a few miles after the fire road. He would buy Smarties to last a month." Alice laughed. "Of course, they lasted about a week. He ate most of them walking back into the Cascades."

"And you can find the fire road?"

"Sure."

"At night?"

"Is there a better time to cross the border?"

"No," Fenna said. She laughed and looked at Bahadur. "What do you think?"

"Good plan."

"What about your friend?" Alice asked. "He won't know where to find us."

"He find us," Bahadur said. "Thomas not the only tracker I know. And, I leave sign. Show him way."

"Okay. Alice, we'll follow you." Fenna slipped the assault rifle from her shoulder, readjusted her pack and carried the weapon in her hands. She followed Alice, just a few steps behind her, as Bahadur moved to the rear. She could hardly hear his footsteps. Nor could she hear Alice's. *Just my own*, she mused. Fenna smiled in the darkness, amusing herself with thoughts of being *the only elephant in a herd of gazelle*. She shook the thought from her mind and concentrated on following Alice, and staying alert to any threats on the trail ahead of them. When Alice paused to find her bearings, Bahadur caught up. Fenna watched as he plucked three stones of equal size from the path and positioned them in a line indicating the direction Alice was about to lead them.

"What if it's not Burwardsley who finds them?" she whispered.

"If not, Mike, then it not matter. We all dead."

"Right," she said. Fenna took one last look at the stones and then followed Alice off the path and into the trees.

The lower branches of the pines caught in Fenna's hair, scratched her cheeks, and slapped at her body and pack. There are no trees in Greenland. The climate ensures that shrubs don't extend their reach beyond what is required for mere survival. *A bit like me*, Fenna thought. She remembered missing trees during the first few months with the Sirius Sledge Patrol, but then she grew accustomed to the wide-open surroundings of the stark Arctic landscape, the long fetch of wind across the sea ice, hurling snow needles into her face, the scale of the mountains on the land, the bergs in the sea. Everything was bigger, open, an agoraphobic's nightmare. Even in the desert, where she had first met Alice, the trees were just arrogant shrubs, too stubborn to remain close to the surface like their Arctic cousins, yet too parched to do more than twist in the desert wind a few metres higher than the dirt. Fenna had seen decades-old saplings clenched between rocks in Arizona and the Arctic, both deserts of a sort, with extremes that tested every living thing. Only the dead would outlive the living, as the extreme conditions parched skin, desiccated bones, and preserved the last rigors of the body for all to see, once the ravens and foxes had picked the bones clean of nourishment. Yet here, in the valley below the high peaks of the Cascade Mountain Range, in the lush, wet forest, Fenna felt claustrophobic all of a sudden, and wished for a break in the trees, no matter how exposed they would be, she just wanted to breathe.

"Hey," Alice said, and Fenna felt her hand on her cheek.

"Huh?" There was something tugging at Fenna's head. She reached up and brushed at a thin spiny branch twisted into her hair and slipped.

"Let me." Alice pinched Fenna's wet hair and pulled the branch out of it, showering Fenna's face with a thin storm of old, brown needles. "There," she said and knelt in front of Fenna. "You keeled over. You alright?"

"Yes," Fenna said. She brushed at a pine needle on her lip. "I must be tired. We haven't stopped since we boarded the plane." Fenna adjusted her grip on the assault rifle in her lap, the sling had caught in the belt of her pack. "Where's Bahadur?"

"Over there," Alice said, and pointed in the direction they had come. "Although, I can't see him."

"Okay." Fenna used the rifle butt to get off the floor. It sank a few centimetres into the loam before pressing against something firm. *Tree roots*, Fenna imagined, as she stood. Alice reached out to support her as she swayed.

"I can take your pack," she said. "I left mine in the cabin. She unclipped the clasp at Fenna's waist. Fenna shrugged the pack from her shoulders and Alice put it on the ground.

"Wait." Fenna opened the lid of the pack and dug around inside for a bottle of water and a bundle of energy bars taped together. She passed the bars to Alice and drank from the bottle. Bahadur joined them and Alice split the energy bars between them.

"It's quiet," he whispered, between mouthfuls. He took the bottle from Fenna's hand and drank.

Fenna scanned the area as they ate. She noted a line of boulders, *a good firing position*, to the right of the path they were forging, and a shallow ditch to the left. Given the darkness, the dense configuration of the trees, it was the best ambush position they might find all night, and the best place to wait. She took the bottle from Bahadur and offered it to Alice. "Finish it," she said, "so it doesn't slosh when you move."

Alice emptied the bottle, screwed the lid on tight, and stuffed it inside the pack. She collected the wrappers from each of them and zipped them inside the top pocket, smiling as she did so. "Reminds me of dad," she said, "always thinking of the environment." She closed the lid and lifted the pack onto one shoulder.

"We're going to wait," Fenna said, and put a hand on Alice's arm. "See those boulders? I want you to tuck in behind them. I'll be there in a second."

"You're sure? The road is real close. Maybe just forty minutes away."

"I'm sure. We're going to wait for Mike."

"No," Bahadur said. "Mike say keep going. He say…"

"He said some things about you, too," Fenna said, and Bahadur stopped speaking. "He told me about when you carried him away from the Taliban."

"Okay, maybe I do that."

"You did. And now we're going to wait."

"But Mike my boss."

"And he's not here. So, you do what I say. We wait."

"Lady," Bahadur said, "you not my boss."

"No, I'm not, but you killed *my* boss. Remember?"

Bahadur fiddled with the carbine in his hands. He looked away before staring straight at Fenna. "It was my job," he said. Alice took a step backward, toward the rocks.

"And this is mine," Fenna said and pointed at Alice, "to get her out of the US and somewhere safe. It's your job too, ever since Mike called you, and put you on the mountain. Now you do what I say, you little shit, because when you said yes to Mike, you said yes to me. My job. My orders. You understand?"

Bahadur let the carbine rest in the sling, and folded his arms across his chest. He spat to one side and glared at Fenna. "Mike say you one tough bitch. He also say you save him from freezer."

What freezer? Oh. Fenna almost smiled when she remembered the *freezer* – a refrigerated container converted into a torture chamber, hidden in plain sight on a building site in Nuuk.

"So, he owes both of us," she said.

"Yeah. Maybe."

"Well, he can't repay us if he's dead." Fenna wiped the dirt and wet needles from the butt of her assault rifle. "You take the ditch over there." Bahadur looked in the direction she pointed.

"It not very big."

"Neither are you."

"Okay, fuck it. I take little ditch. We wait. Mike

sort all this out later." Bahadur took a step backward, turned, and melted into the darkness.

Fenna thought she heard him wriggle into position, but it could have been the wind as it teased the upper branches and the very tops of the pines. She followed the route Alice had taken to the rocks and knelt down beside her. Fenna leaned the rifle against the rock, took out the spare magazines and placed them on the ground, side by side. She unzipped her pocket and pulled out the Glock.

"Did they teach you to shoot at Yuma?"

"No," Alice said, "and neither did my dad."

"But you're American?"

"Right, and every true American girl knows guns?"

Fenna laughed. "Just like every Dane is a Viking."

Alice didn't laugh. She lowered her voice and said, "You are."

The wind caught the trees in another gust, fresh air spiralling down the trunks to flick and tease at their hair. Fenna pressed the Glock into Alice's hand and nodded. "Maybe I am a Viking, and now it's your turn to learn about guns."

"I don't know." Alice let the weight of the pistol press her hand against her thigh.

"I just need you to look in that direction." Fenna waved her hand in an arc toward the trees behind them. "The Glock has a safety in the trigger, here," she said and guided Alice's finger to the trigger. "Can you feel it?"

"Yes."

"It's like a plastic switch in the middle. Be sure you've got it under your finger before you fire."

"You want me to shoot?"

"If someone comes. Yes."

"What if it's your friend?"

"It won't be. He'll come the way we came, or not at all. We'll wait until dawn."

"And if he doesn't come?"

If he doesn't come, Fenna thought, *he's dead*. She said nothing, as she picked up the assault rifle, smoothed one hand across the surface of the boulder, searching for the best firing position with a clear view of the path they had taken and the ditch where Bahadur lay in wait.

"Fenna? What if he doesn't come?"

"He will," she said, and, as she took a breath, the first crack of gunfire ripped through the trees, just a few hundred metres from their position.

Chapter 13

Aim, breathe, squeeze. It was a reflex now, muscle memory, trigger memory, Fenna had discovered a feel for it, a taste even. The rifle jerked in her grasp. She absorbed the kick, compensated with a change in posture, leaned into the butt, and fired. Short bursts of three, designed to keep Vestergaard's men in check, make them think twice.

When Burwardsley crashed into view and fell, Fenna prepared to move. She pointed at her last firing position, ordered Alice to stay put, to shoot at anything that moves within five metres of her, and to keep her head down. Then she was gone, twisting around the trees, a shadow pounding forward into battle. She caught a glimpse of a smaller shadow, Bahadur, as he pressed forward. She copied his stance – bent forward, the rifle an extension of his reach, head down, cheek tucked into the rifle, eyes forward. He was first, curling between the trees, his head never higher than the iron sights fixed before the muzzle of the carbine.

Fenna followed a parallel route, flicking her gaze to Bahadur, slowing when she was ahead of him, stopping when he stopped, stopping to fire. A stray round snapped through the air above her head before it thwacked into a tree, stripping the bark from the truck with a wet rip of woody fibres. She tucked behind the tree in front of her, scanned for movement, and loosed a burst of three rounds to the right of where Burwardsley had fallen. Then she moved, curling her body into shape of the Gurkha. Fenna ignored the scratch of the branches, didn't even feel them. She ripped her hair free of obstruction, tugging away the thin twigs of dead branches, ignoring the earthy resistance, and the silent plea to stop, take cover, hide. If that thought existed, she buried it. She moved on, watched as Bahadur reached Burwardsley. The Gurkha confirmed that his boss was alive, and then pushed forward, firing, blistering the trees with a mix of short bursts and full automatic when he located a target too close for finesse. Fenna heard the thud as one of Vestergaard's men collapsed beneath Bahadur's assault, and then a scream, "Ayo Gurkhali!" as Bahadur tossed his carbine at the dead man's feet and drew the kukri blade from his belt. It flashed once, and then he was gone, the wild sporadic bursts of enemy fire the only indication of the direction of his movement. Fenna pushed on and slid to a stop beside Burwardsley.

"How bad are you hit?" she asked as she ran her hand over Burwardsley's chest, pausing at each pulse of blood over her fingers. She tucked the assault rifle into her shoulder, her left hand trembling with the weight.

"I told you to go."

"Sure you did. Now shut the fuck up and tell me how bad you're hit."

"Konstabel," Burwardsley said, as he reached for her hand.

"What?"

"Go. I'm fucked. Just go."

"No," she said. Fenna grasped his hand, slippery with blood. "Not this time."

A scream from the woods and a sickening wet thud made both of them pause. Then the woods erupted with a fresh onslaught of bullets – new arrivals, more men from the meadow.

Fenna let go of Burwardsley, unclipped the sling from his carbine, and tied it around his chest. She tossed his empty weapon to one side, reached beneath his back and grabbed the sling. Fenna started to pull. Burwardsley groaned.

"Stop fucking moaning and help me," she said. The bursts of weapons fire intensified. Fenna could see the muzzle flashes, could see the arc of fire narrowing as the tracer rounds burned between the trees like green comets. The field of fire was narrow. They had found the Gurkha. Burwardsley pushed at the ground with bloody palms as Fenna pulled him behind her.

"How many?" she said.

"I killed three." Burwardsley paused between words. "There are two teams of four."

"Thomas?"

"Dead." Burwardsley stopped pushing as the roar of lead missiles diminished and the forest absorbed the sounds of battle. "Fenna," he whispered.

Fenna knelt down behind Burwardsley. She propped his body against her thigh and stomach, his head rested on her bended knee. The irony of Burwardsley's body being her only cover crossed her mind, before she switched her grip on the assault rifle and scanned the dark woods through the scope.

"It's quiet," she whispered.

"They'll be there."

"Seven?"

"Yep."

Burwardsley shifted to pull the Browning from his belt. Fenna heard him grimace as he raised it, the heavy pistol wobbling in his grasp.

"There," he said, and pointed. Fenna fired, the

bullet casings ejecting from the port in the rifle in high speed brass spins. The man dropped to the ground before he could fire. Burwardsley grunted, as Fenna shifted position.

"Keep looking," she said, and was still, as quiet once again descended on the woods.

Six, she thought. *No. That's four left. Bahadur dropped one, killed another with that sword of his.* She remembered the prick of the tip of the kukri when Burwardsley, the man bleeding at her feet, had stretched and stripped her in the house on Greenland's east coast.

"You're thinking," he whispered. "I can feel it."

"Shut up."

A scream, maybe fifty metres to their right, snapped Fenna's head in that direction, the rifle following her head as she synced her body to the fight. The second scream was duller, wetter, and Fenna remembered the kukri, the bent blade – Bahadur's sword.

"Three," Burwardsley said, his voice thick with blood. "Bad's having a good night."

Fenna spun slowly back to scan the shadows and trees in front of them. She could feel the soft bed of pine needles beneath her knee, they slipped as she repositioned the foot she was sitting on. The wet scent of damp humus tickled her nose, but did little to disguise the more sinister smell of blood. She wanted to look back to the rocks, to see Alice, but there were still three men in the woods. Three enemy combatants. Vestergaard's men. And Burwardsley was bleeding at her feet. "I have to get you to the rocks," she whispered.

"Forget it, Konstabel." Burwardsley paused for

breath. "I've my gun. Just go."

Fenna thought about responding, telling him what she promised herself she would, if they ever saw each other again, that he had, in fact, become a friend, and she wasn't about to leave him. Instead, the snap of brush twigs beneath the trees forced her to act. She flung Burwardsley to the ground and rolled to her left. Fenna's elbows slipped in the carpet of needles as she tucked the assault rifle into her shoulder and fired at the man running toward them. Her first burst forced him into cover, further left. He tripped, stumbled, and lost his grip on his weapon. Fenna's second burst caught him in the chest as he pitched head first into a tree. The air was still thick with gun smoke as Fenna kneeled and fired one more burst into the man's body. He was dead, but he wasn't alone.

A wild burst of fire ripped into the ground between Fenna and Burwardsley. Fenna swung the assault rifle up and aimed, only to pull the trigger on an empty magazine. She swore, dropped the rifle, and reached for her pocket with the Glock.

Empty.

"Fuck." She gripped the rifle and jumped to her feet.

The man sneered as she charged. He lifted his rifle and waited for her to close the distance from five to four, and then three metres. He waited too long. Fenna stumbled as the man's chest erupted in a spume of blood and he dropped his rifle. She turned to see Burwardsley shake his head. He pointed a bloody finger at Bahadur, as the Gurkha slammed a boot onto the man's back and shot him twice in the head with his pistol.

Fenna realised that the night was drawing to a close when she saw the blood dripping from Bahadur's wrist and onto the blade of the kukri in his hand. There was enough light to see his face too, and the Gurkha was smiling.

"I save you again, Konstabel Fenna," he said.

"Yes," she said.

"How many times shall I…"

The question died on the Gurkha's lips as a burst of bullets punctured his chest and dropped the short Nepalese man to his knees. His breath caught in his throat as he choked. He dropped the Glock, pressed the tip of the kukri into the earth and leaned on it. The last of Vestergaard's men stepped out of cover, ejected the empty magazine, and reached for a new one from his belt.

Fenna moved fast, as Bahadur drew his last breath, wrenching the kukri from his grip and flinging herself at the man as he jammed the fresh magazine into his weapon. He swung the rifle up to his shoulder, but Fenna slapped it to one side with the flat of the kukri blade. He reeled, took a step backward, as Fenna kicked him in the knee, raised the kukri, and swung the bent blade into the man's shoulder. It dug deep, stuck in the bone, and she let go to punch him in the face. The man slumped against a tree, fumbling for the pistol holstered below his belt around his thigh. Fenna grabbed his wrist, twisted it, and slammed her knee into his groin. As he slipped down the tree she pulled the kukri from his shoulder. He looked up, as she curved the blade in an arc into his neck. Fenna left the blade there, left the man to bleed as she crawled back to Bahadur, turned him onto his side, and cradled his head against her thighs. Bahadur blinked once, curled his lips into a half smile and died with the last rattle of air that spluttered from the ragged holes in his punctured lungs. Fenna closed his eyes with her palm and laid his body on the forest floor. She wiped her bloody hands on her trousers and stood up. The first face she saw was Alice's. The Glock, she noticed, twitched in the young woman's hand.

"It's okay, Alice. We got them all." Fenna followed Alice's gaze and nodded. "Yes," she said, "he's dead." She stepped around Bahadur's body and took the Glock from Alice. Fenna stuffed it into her pocket. She held Alice's hands, and said, "Are you hurt?"

"No."

"Are you okay?"

"No," Alice said, and shook her head. "The smell…"

"It's blood. Don't think about it."

"How can you say that? How can you…"

Fenna pulled Alice into her body, pressed her hand onto the back of her head, and held her tight.

"It's okay," she whispered. "I'm going to get you out of here. Keep you safe. Do you believe me?"

"Yes," Alice said, her voice muffled, her body trembling.

Fenna kissed the side of her head and said, "I need to go see Mike. Will you help me?" Alice nodded. "Okay then." Fenna took Alice's hand and guided her to where Burwardsley lay on the floor. He lifted his head as Fenna knelt beside him. "Bahadur's dead."

"I figured," Burwardsley said. He let his head fall onto his arm. His fingers were still gripped around the

Browning pistol, and Fenna tugged it gently from his grasp. He watched her.

"I have to see where you are hit," she said and turned him onto his back.

"Any excuse," he said and smiled. A trickle of blood ran from the corner of his mouth.

Fenna worked quickly, opening the Marine Lieutenant's jacket and shirt, lifting his arms, and rolling him, gently, from side to side with Alice's help. She found one of the bullet wounds beneath his left armpit. She sent Alice to grab the first aid kit from her pack. Fenna undid Burwardsley's belt, unzipped his trousers.

"I didn't see him die," Burwardsley said.

"He took a burst to his chest." Fenna struggled to lift Burwardsley's hips. "Help me," she said to Alice when she returned. She pressed a bandage into the entry wound, and bound it around his chest. Between them they lifted his hips, tugging his trousers and underpants to his knees. Fenna slipped her hands inside the cuffs of his trousers to the collars of his boots, found no more wounds, and decided to leave them on. There was another wound in his thigh, and the bullet was visible. "I have to get that out," she said.

Alice reached around her belt and pulled a multi-tool from a webbing pouch. "My dad's," she said and handed it to Fenna. "He had a climbing pack in a friend's garage. They climbed together. I snuck in and took it. I needed something of his."

"It was a risk," Fenna said and opened the tool. "You could have been caught." She fastened the pliers around the bullet and waited for Burwardsley to nod. She pulled, lost her grip, and pulled again, tugging the bullet out of Burwardsley's flesh as he groaned. "There's dental floss and a needle in the first aid kit," she said. "Alice?"

"I shouldn't have looked. I feel sick."

"Take a breath," Fenna said and smiled. "You're doing fine."

"Where did you learn that?" Alice asked, as she handed Fenna the first aid kit.

"Sirius," she said, and threaded a length of dental floss through the eye of a curved needle. "They didn't actually teach us to remove bullets, but we had to sew up the dogs after fights, clean our own wounds…" she paused to pinch Burwardsley's skin between her bloody fingers. "Pull teeth." The skin was slippery and she set the needle to one side to grip the skin in both hands. "Alice."

"Yes?"

"Your hands are dry. I need you to sew."

"No. No freaking way," Alice said, her face pale.

"It's alright, kid," Burwardsley said. He stared up at the grey light as it filtered through the branches above. "Just get it done." Fenna nodded, and Alice picked up the needle. Burwardsley gritted his teeth at the first prick of the needle in his skin, muttering a stream of soft curses.

Alice sewed under Fenna's direction. The tip of her tongue was visible between her lips, and Fenna stifled the urge to chuckle at the young woman's concentration. She explained how Alice should tie the knot at the end of the stitching.

"He'll never get it out," Alice said, as she looked at her needlework.

"Right now, it doesn't matter. But we do have to clean it."

"With what?"

Fenna pulled a small bottle of alcohol gel from the first aid kit. She squirted it onto Burwardsley's wound and he grunted. Fenna had expected a scream, and told him so.

"Konstabel," he said through gritted teeth.

"Not anymore," she said, as he scowled at her. "I decided something, with a little help from Alice."

"What's that?"

"You call me Fenna from now on, because that's what friends do."

"We're friends? That's cute, *Konstabel.*"

"Don't fucking spoil it, you ape," Fenna said and splashed more sterilising gel on Burwardsley's thigh. He cursed, and she waited until he was finished. "Besides, if we weren't friends, I would have left you to die." She looked at Alice. "You'd think he would be grateful."

"He should be," Alice said, as she rocked back on her heels.

"Listen, ladies, I *am* grateful, but I am also naked. And unless you fix the hole in my chest, I will probably die naked."

"Probably," said Alice.

"Well?" he said. "Fenna?"

But Fenna was silent, because the grey light of dawn was brightening, and she could see the outline of a fire road in the distance, between the trees. *We're close*, she thought. *One more country, and then Greenland.* Fenna sighed as she capped the bottle of gel and moved closer to the wound in Burwardsley's chest. *We're going to need a miracle to get out of Canada. A miracle, or magic.* "Fuck," she said as she knelt beside Burwardsley.

"What?" said Alice.

"I know what we have to do," she said and looked at Burwardsley. "You're not going to like it."

Chapter 14

"No," Burwardsley said. He tried to turn away from Fenna, but she pushed on his shoulder, forced him to lie still.

"I have to clean this, and sew it up."

"That's not what I mean."

"I know. It's the thing with Vestergaard."

"Too fucking right it is."

"But how the hell else are we going to get across the border? How are we going to get out of Canada?" Fenna said, and rocked back on her heels.

"I'm working on it."

"No. You're not. You're bleeding to death. Pretty soon this will be my problem, and mine alone."

"Well, love, it's a lousy fucking solution."

Alice helped Fenna lift Burwardsley. "I don't understand. What are you talking about?"

Fenna removed the dressing and cleaned the wound with water from a second bottle in her pack. They lay Burwardsley on the ground, turned him onto his side, and Fenna cleaned the exit wound. It was smaller than she'd anticipated, and better for it. She sterilised it, sewed it shut, and sterilised it again. Burwardsley said nothing beyond a few suppressed groans. Alice handed Fenna the items she asked for, but was otherwise quiet, waiting for Fenna to finish working on Burwardsley, waiting for an answer. The dawn sky lightened and lit the scene of battle on the forest floor. Alice kept her back to the dead bodies.

"Tell her," Burwardsley said.

Fenna removed her jacket and draped it over Burwardsley's shoulders. She picked up the Browning and pressed it into his hand. She held on as he took it.

"You know I'm right," she said, and let go of the pistol.

"Right about what?" Alice stood up, as Fenna dug in her backpack for a change of shirt. The one she was wearing was soaked in blood. Once she had changed she beckoned for Alice to step away from Burwardsley.

"He wasn't always my friend," she said. Alice frowned but said nothing. "We met in Greenland, on the ice, and he did his very best to get information out of me, and to clean up once he was done."

"To clean up?"

"Yes," Fenna said. She bent down to pick up their belongings littered on the forest floor. "He was ordered to kill me by a splinter faction of the Canadian intelligence service. I don't know what they are called, and it doesn't really matter. All you need to know is a young Greenlander killed herself because of what happened, and both he and I," she said and nodded at Burwardsley, "feel responsible. That's what brought us together. That and you."

"Me?"

"Yes." Fenna pointed at a few more things lying on the ground behind the rocks, items of gear that had fallen from the pack as Alice had dragged it over to where they were working on Burwardsley. "I couldn't save Dina, the Greenlander, and when I met you, when I saw how you were being treated, it struck a chord. I made a promise, to myself more than anyone, that I wouldn't let another girl die, not if I could help it."

"But why me?"

"Because, there's a man who is responsible for all this." Fenna gestured at the bodies sprawled between the trees. She paused at the sight of Bahadur, then moved on, grateful to look at Alice. "I know because he interrogated me, and, ultimately, recruited me. He sent me to the desert. He put me in the same place, at the same time, as you. There was even a time when they considered me for the role you played." Alice looked away and Fenna grasped her arm. "But here's where it gets difficult, and this is what Burwardsley, *Mike*, wanted me to say."

"Which is what?"

"That I used you, the knowledge of where you might be hiding, to bargain for my life."

"I don't understand."

"I told them I knew where you were, and that I would come and get you, – *we* would come and get you," she said and pointed at Burwardsley.

"You're going to give me to these people?" Alice said, recoiling from Fenna's touch.

"No. Never."

"How can I believe you?"

"You can't, but I won't. I won't ever give you up. I will make sure you are safe."

"But what Mike said…"

"Shit." Fenna twisted the gear in her hands as she spoke. "We can't keep running. Vestergaard – these are his men – will keep sending teams after us. He knew where you were. He put Nicklas in that cabin with you. He is always, and will always be, one step ahead of us. And I can't…" Fenna cleared her throat. "I can't protect you like this. I need to get us to a place where I am in control, a place I know and can use to protect you."

"Like Greenland?"

"Exactly. I know Greenland. I know the

environment, the people, I even have friends there, people who can help." She thought of David Maratse lying in a hospital bed, and wondered just how much help he could possibly be. And then another thought, the image of a hunter and his dogs, shivered into focus and she smiled. "And it's so far away from everything, so remote... I can protect you. I know I can. But I need to pretend to give you up, to get us there. All of us."

"You're going to give me up?"

"No. I'm going to pretend to. That's all." Fenna tried to smile, but Alice turned away.

The wind caught in the treetops, whistling down the trunks, showering them with soft needles, green and brown, new and dead. Alice spoke softly, her words barely louder than the whisper of needles, "It's not like I have much choice."

"No."

"How will it work?" She turned around. "What will you do?"

"As soon as we get to that gas station, I'll contact Vestergaard. We'll be in Canada. But you'll still be on the most-wanted list. We'll have to play it smart."

"But he'll just pick us up, and it will all be over."

Fenna shook her head. "Nicklas told me what is going on, that the countries using Vestergaard – his clients – are getting worried. They are starting to distance themselves from him. He needs leverage, and you're it."

Alice frowned. "I still don't get it. He'll want to pick us up. To bring me in."

"But he will want to wait until he gets you out of the country. He needs you somewhere safe and quiet just like I do. He even suggested a place."

"In Greenland?"

"Yes," Fenna said. She noticed movement to one side and watched as Burwardsley struggled into a sitting position and pulled on his shirt. He fiddled with the buttons and then, slowly, stood up.

"But I don't understand. Really, I don't. If he suggested this place, then he controls it. We're as good as trapped. And then, what's the difference? Dead here or dead there? He has control."

"We have to make him think that, yes," Fenna said. "We will agree to all his terms, so long as he gets us there."

"And what's to stop him killing or using us once we're there?"

"The Greenlanders," Burwardsley said. He leaned against a tree, the Browning still in his hand. "They are resourceful. They will help her," he said and nodded at Fenna. "Don't ask me why, but she has a way with them. She's earned their trust somehow."

"Fighting with you, mostly," Fenna said. "How are you feeling?"

"Stiff, sore. I need to pee."

"You need me to hold your hand?"

"Fuck off, Konstabel," Burwardsley said. He turned his grimace into a grin, and said, "Fuck off, *Fenna*. Is what I meant to say."

"So, we're friends now?"

"One step at a time, love."

Burwardsley pushed off the tree and took a few steps away from them. Fenna noticed the stiffness in his movement, wondered how far he would be able to walk, and then she heard him unzip his trousers. She took Alice's arm and walked her back to her pack, and the assault rifle. The ground was littered with bandages, shell casings, and patched with swathes of blood. Burwardsley grunted as he walked past them.

"Where are you going?"

"To see to Bad. You get our gear, and we'll put this crazy plan of yours into action." He staggered off. Fenna watched him as he paused to kneel beside Bahadur's body. She turned away to give him some privacy.

"I still don't understand," Alice whispered. "How are we going to get to Greenland, and how are we going to stop this man…"

"Vestergaard."

"Yeah, him. How do we stop him from using me, and killing both of you?"

"There's a charter flight from Iqaluit in Nunavut," she said, as she cleaned up the area and collected her gear into a pile. "It's an evangelist flight. They fly direct to Qaanaaq at the top of Greenland. I read about it in a magazine a while ago. Converting heathens, I guess, although the Lutheran church is dominant in Greenland, like it is in Denmark. There are close connections between the Inuit of Canada and the Greenlanders – in some cases, the Greenlanders in the north consider themselves more Inuit than Greenlander. Vestergaard can get us on that flight. It's private. It avoids the main hub, and it means we don't have to fly out of the States and into Europe. All other flights to Greenland are routed through Copenhagen, and we can't risk that. Neither can Vestergaard. He needs you in a country where extradition is difficult or time consuming. The more remote and challenging it is to get to you, the better. He'll want you there, and I will promise to deliver you."

"And once we're there, at this safe house of his, are you just going to leave me there? Job done."

"No. I won't do that. And neither will he," she said and gestured at Burwardsley. "Come on." Fenna shouldered her pack. "I'll tell you what I'm thinking later. Right now we need to bury a Gurkha warrior and cross the border."

Fenna led Alice to where Burwardsley knelt beside the body of his friend and fighting comrade. He nodded when Fenna suggested they bury him, pointing at the shallow ditch behind them, the same one that Fenna had ordered Bahadur to take as his fighting position. She dumped her pack, and encouraged Alice to help her carry Bahadur to the ditch. The young woman was willing, but Fenna could see she was struggling. The forest floor was littered with bodies, and Alice was finding it difficult to breathe.

"I'll need his kukri," Burwardsley said, as Fenna and Alice laid the body in the ditch.

"I'll get it," Fenna said. "I know where I left it."

She heard the scrape of soil, as Alice started to cover Bahadur's body. *He's dead*, Fenna thought, and realised that the sense of justice she might have felt that her partner's killer had been killed, was not there. She felt empty, not satisfied. *He was just following orders. He was good at that, and it killed him in the end – following my orders.* She stopped at the tree where the man was slumped, Bahadur's kukri buried in his neck, just where Fenna had left it. She gripped the handle and the man's eyes twitched open. Fenna caught the gasp in her throat, gritted her teeth and removed the blade. The man's head lolled forward onto his chest, and the last of his blood splashed from his neck. Fenna wiped the blade on his trousers.

"What have I become?" she whispered.

She didn't wait to think of a response, choosing instead to remind herself that she did what she needed to do, and if she hadn't, she would most likely be dead. Fenna picked up her pack and carried the knife to Bahadur's shallow grave. Alice had already covered his body with what little ground cover and top soil was available. Burwardsley asked Fenna to chop some of the lower branches with the kukri, and they arranged a blanket of pines over the grave. Fenna gave Burwardsley the kukri, and he buried the blade halfway into the ground just above Bahadur's head.

"I never thought the little runt would die. He didn't have it in him," Burwardsley said and laughed. His voice faltered, and he said, "Goodbye friend. Ayo Gurkhali." And then. "Give 'em hell." He tossed the Browning into a patch of young pine trees, and waited for Fenna to ditch her weapons. "We won't need them," he explained to Alice.

Fenna adjusted the straps on her backpack and nodded that she was ready. Alice led the way, picking a route between the trees to the fire road. Fenna wondered if she was going to run at the first chance, wondered if she had lost the young woman's trust. *And why not? Hell, I wouldn't trust me.* But each time Alice turned to check on their progress, to see if Burwardsley needed a break, she would smile, and Fenna allowed herself to be reassured, that there was still something that bonded them, that would allow them to trust one another.

They reached the fire road, and paused to remove or disguise the signs of battle. Burwardsley protested at the idea that he should remove his clothes, choosing instead to tie Fenna's jacket around his waist, and to hide the blood on his shirt with mud from the edge of the road. They walked on and heard the first car on the asphalt road just half an hour since walking out of the forest.

"There it is," Alice said and pointed at a small gas station less than a kilometre away. Fenna noted the single pump, and the wooden shop tacked onto a brick garage.

"And it's inside Canada?" she asked.

"Yes, and so are we." Alice took a breath and said, "I'm not a fugitive here. It feels good to be free."

"You're not free, kid," Burwardsley said.

"Not yet, she's not." Fenna took Alice's hand. "But I'm working on it." She lifted Alice's hand and pointed at the gas station. "You think your dad left any Smarties?"

"Yeah, I'm pretty sure," she said. Alice and Fenna walked a little faster, and Burwardsley let them go. Alice stopped to wait, but he waved her on.

"I know where you're going," he said.

A second car passed as they walked along the side of the asphalt road. Fenna tried not to laugh, but the absurdness of the situation, the gunfight in the woods, it took hold and she had to stop and let it out.

"What?" Alice said. "You going to tell me?"

"Give me a second."

"Fenna? Come on." Alice smiled, and then the smile broadened, dimpling her cheeks. She laughed beside Fenna, laughed until Burwardsley caught up with them.

"What did I miss?" he said.

"Well," Fenna said, as she curbed the last bout of

146

laughing. "It's just, when I saw the last car that passed us…"

"The Jeep?"

"Yes, whatever, it doesn't matter. I just imagined the driver picking us up and driving us into town. Chatting, you know, asking where we'd been, what we'd been doing."

"And that's funny?"

"In a way, yes. I mean, what would I say? What would I tell him? That we climbed a mountain to pick up the President's assassin, fought our way into the forest and buried a friend, and now, we're going to call the most evil guy we know to see if he can hook us up with a flight to Greenland. I mean, is that what I would tell him?" She laughed, and added, "Oh, and by the way, how was *your* weekend?"

Alice giggled as Fenna continued laughing. They looked at Burwardsley's face and spluttered at his dead-pan expression. He scowled at both of them, bit back a wave of pain, and said, "Alright, Konstabel. But remember, before you lose it completely, remember, it was your fucking plan." He brushed between them and continued on to the gas station. Alice followed, once she had contained her laughter. Fenna waited a few minutes more.

She looked back at the mountain, thought about the location of Bahadur's grave, tried to place it in the trees. The thought sobered her. She tugged the straps of the pack higher onto her shoulders, took a last look at the mountain, and said, "Okay, let's finish this."

Chapter 15

FRASER VALLEY, BRITISH COLUMBIA, CANADA

The helicopter must have arrived in the night. The dark blue Bell 206A JetRanger was tucked in behind the gas station. Burwardsley had seen it, and he waved at Fenna to slow down. Alice was visibly trembling, and Fenna could do little to reassure her when she caught up with them, one hundred metres before the gas pump. *This is it then*, she thought and reached for Alice's hand. Alice pulled back, her eyes darting from one side of the road to the other. Burwardsley caught Fenna's eye and looked at Alice. Fenna nodded. *I won't let her run.* The gas station door creaked open and a woman wearing a thin down jacket, plum-coloured, stepped out, followed by two men, the last of which gave Fenna pause; he looked Greenlandic. *Canadian Inuit*, Fenna thought, but she couldn't help thinking of Maratse.

The woman walked past the pump and stopped. The men flanked her, taking positions to either side, and opening their black waist-length jackets to reveal pistols in shoulder holsters. Fenna turned her attention to the woman, twice her own age with flame-red hair coiled in a tight bun at the back of her head. The woman's stance concerned Fenna more than the two men, she was indifferent somehow, casual, and yet there was no mistaking the woman's agenda as she stared at them.

"It's going to be a lovely day," the woman called out. Fenna relaxed for a second as she identified her as Canadian, not American. But only for a second. "We've been waiting for you. Why don't you come over?" The woman stuffed her hands inside the pockets of her jacket and waited.

"Fuck," Fenna whispered. She reached for Alice, but the young woman shied away again. "Alice, you have to stay with us." Alice tensed and flicked her head toward the trees on the side of the road.

"Fenna," Burwardsley said.

Fenna opened the buckle on the waist belt of her backpack, so that the moment Alice bolted, she was able to dump the pack and race after her. Alice was fast, but Fenna couldn't let her run, wouldn't give anyone the excuse to shoot her. Her heart pounded in her chest as her body began to compensate for Alice's flight, and the fight that Fenna knew was coming. Alice was just a few metres from the trees when Fenna tackled her. They slammed into the ground and the air whumphed out of Alice's body as Fenna landed on her. The girl might have been lighter on her feet than Fenna, mountain fit, but Fenna was all muscle, and she pinned Alice to the ground.

"Let me go," Alice cried. "Just let me go."

"I can't."

"You can. I don't want this. I never wanted this. Let me go."

Alice's body heaved between sobs. Fenna couldn't see her tears, but she could feel her own streaming down her cheeks, cleaning a path through the dirt, the blood, and the pine sap of the violent hours they had spent in the forest. *It wasn't meant to be like this*, she thought. *It was never meant to be like this.*

Fenna heard the swish of boots through the grass and felt rough hands on her arms. She let herself be pulled off Alice's body and onto her feet. The Inuit man whispered in her ear, something about stopping

Alice being the first smart move she had made since arriving in North America, but she ignored him, her focus was on Alice, as another man, a white Canadian, pulled her to her feet, and cuffed Alice's hands with thick plastic ties. Fenna recalled the feel of them, the bite of the edges, and then the memory was all too real, as the Inuit snicked ties around her own wrists, and marched her back to the road. He pushed her all the way to the gas station, shoving her back with a flat palm each time she tried to turn to see Alice. He grabbed the ties securing her wrists and pulled her to a stop in front of the woman with the flame-red hair. Fenna noticed that Burwardsley was sitting on the bench beside the door, flanked by two more men; one of them was working on his wounds. She heard Alice sniff as she was marched past her, all the way to the helicopter, and then the woman stepped in front of Fenna and blocked her view.

"Konstabel Fenna Brongaard," she said, "I have waited a long time to meet you."

It was the *you* that confirmed it, the *Canadian raising*, she wasn't American. Of course, that didn't mean she wasn't working for them, but Fenna had anticipated more drama, more flashing lights, more guns. This all seemed very low-key, making it even more menacing.

Fenna lifted her chin and said, "You're with Vestergaard?"

"Klaus Vestergaard?" The woman laughed. "Now what would make you say that?"

The Inuit shifted his stance, and Fenna heard the gravel crunch beneath his boots. She looked at the woman, caught the flicker of emotion in her eyes, and the tightening of the skin around her mouth. She was good, professional, but clearly very excited, and Fenna hoped that was in their favour.

"I would think he was a person of interest."

"Really?" The woman pointed in the direction of the helicopter. "You don't think she is more interesting?"

"Alice? No," Fenna said with a shake of her head. "She's just bait, or a bargaining chip, depending on how you want to play this."

"My, my, you have come a long way since running around with dogs, eh? Oh, yes," she said, as Fenna tensed, "I know all about you. Your history. Of course, the past several months is perhaps the most interesting."

"Then you'll know why I am here?"

"I certainly intend to find out." A weak gust of wind played with the gas station sign by the roadside. It creaked and the woman glanced at it. She looked beyond Fenna toward the mountains. "Do you know how much time it takes, how many resources, to clean up after you, Konstabel?"

"I can imagine."

"Then you'll appreciate that tolerance for your actions – in general, I might add – is growing thin among the community."

"What community is that?"

"Intelligence, of which you do seem to possess a fair share. That's why we're talking, just now. But I am not against using the full palette of options at my disposal."

"And I thought Canadians were supposed to be nice," Fenna said.

"We have a reputation for being polite. There's a difference. But let's not go there, Konstabel. I'm sure we can work things out."

"What is it you want?"

The woman smiled, and Fenna noticed a crooked tooth, one that she tried to conceal with a conscious dip of her top lip. Her lipstick caught on the edge of the tooth, and the woman licked it away with the tip of her tongue. It was a refined move, practised, and Fenna realised that a woman who was attuned to such small details, was likely to be equally tuned-in to the bigger picture. *She already knows my history*, she thought, *and quickly changed the subject from Vestergaard to Alice. Careful, Fenna.*

"What I want? What do I want, Yuka?"

The Inuit man let go of Fenna. He prodded her shoulder as he walked around her. Yuka, Fenna realised, was nothing like the Greenlanders she knew. While his skin was a similar tone, he was thinner in the face, his beard wispier, eyes narrower. He seemed sterner, and she had yet to see him laugh. She thought about Maratse and the hunter, remembered the way they laughed, remembered Maratse's boyish enthusiasm as they raced across the ice in the police Toyota. *And now he is recovering in hospital*, she thought. *Because of me.*

Yuka stared at Fenna, and said, "You want to finish this, Ma'am?"

"I do," the woman said, "that's right." She took a step closer to Fenna. Her perfume was subtle, but confirmed that if she had ever been in the field, it was a long time ago. Fenna thought of her own subtle fragrance, and almost smiled as the woman stepped back.

"Sorry," Fenna said, and smiled. "It's been a long time since I smelled sweet."

"Do you like this life, Konstabel?"

"I don't have much choice. And the longer we spend talking around the subject, the less choice I have."

"Choice?" The woman laughed. "It amuses me to think that you believe you have a choice."

"I believe I have a future, or, at least a purpose."

"And so do I, Konstabel."

"Then let's stop dicking around, and get right to it, shall we?" Fenna looked from the woman to Yuka and shrugged. "Whenever you're ready. Or do we have to wait for someone with more authority?" *Easy, Fenna. Don't piss them off.* From the look on Yuka's face, she knew it was too late.

"Dicking around, eh? Nice choice of words. Amusing, almost." The woman nodded, and said, "Leave us for a moment, Yuka."

"Ma'am," he said, and walked over to join the men guarding Burwardsley. Fenna watched him, studied his gait, looking for a weakness. She found none.

"You're smart, Fenna. I'll give you that. But you've made a series of mistakes, one after the other."

"I had no choice."

"Choice. That word again. Women always have a choice."

"Not in our line of work."

"You're wrong. But you're also young. And I have to remember that. I was, believe it or not, an agent in my younger days."

"RCMP?"

"Ah, no. I was not like your friend, Nicklas." She paused to study Fenna's face. "He was your friend, wasn't he?"

"Yes."

"And now?"

Fenna said nothing. She ignored the image of the lookout cabin, their last rendezvous.

The woman continued, "I'm not RCMP. I'm something else. You can call me Meredith. It's not my real name, of course, but it will do for now, until we get to know one another." She paused to pull her Smartphone from the pocket of her jeans. "Just give me a moment."

Meredith walked toward the pump and leaned on it as she made her call. Fenna smiled as she remembered the signs warning people not to use mobiles when filling their cars with petrol. She wondered if that wouldn't be the easiest solution, for them all to just blow up in an explosion. *But nothing about this is easy*, she remembered. And then she looked at Alice in the helicopter. Her head was against the glass, her beanie pulled low over her eyes.

"Let's get something to eat," Meredith said, as she walked back to Fenna. A large SUV appeared around the corner in the road, and Fenna realised there were probably more arranged in a road block, just out of sight.

"Okay," she said.

"This is going to take a while to clean up, and I could do with some pie."

"And my friends?"

"I'll make sure they get something to eat."

"That's not what I mean."

"I know. But then you don't have much choice."

She was right, of course, *but I don't have to like it*. Fenna tensed as Meredith opened a folding knife and cut the plastic ties from her wrists. There was a second when Fenna considered her options, but one look at Yuka suggested that she really didn't have any, and then the SUV pulled into the gas station, and Fenna was ushered inside by two female agents.

"Yuka is loyal," Meredith said, as she got into the back of the car beside Fenna, "but I like to have as many women on my team as possible." The agents climbed into the front of the SUV, and they pulled away from the gas station and onto the road, heading north. Fenna caught a glimpse of Burwardsley as he stared at the SUV. Her stomach cramped for a second, as she wondered if she would see him again.

"It wasn't supposed to end like this," she whispered.

"No?" said Meredith. "How did you imagine it would end?"

"I don't know. I don't tend to plan that far ahead."

Fenna was quiet until they pulled into a small diner. She smelled waffles as they entered, and coffee. Meredith showed her to a small table by the window. The mountains were visible in the near distance, but clouds threatened to obscure the view of the peaks. Meredith ordered coffee and pie, bantering with the waitress that it was never too early for pie. Fenna slumped into the seat, it had been a long time since she rested. The coffee, when it arrived, lifted her for a moment. It was black, and strong, it almost reminded her of home.

"What are you thinking about?"

"Denmark," said Fenna, as she turned the mug on the table.

"I went to Sweden once. Malmö."

"Sweden is nice. Denmark is..."

"*Hyggelig*? Did I say that right?"

"Yes," Fenna said. The waitress brought the pie and she started to eat.

"I read a book all about it," Meredith said. She picked up her spoon, and said, "But isn't it just a Danish way of being cosy? I mean it's not rocket science. Just light a few candles and eat cake." She waved her spoon at Fenna's pie. "How is it?"

"It's good."

"When I knew we were on our way down here, I wanted to find somewhere..."

"Listen, Meredith, can we just get on with it?" Fenna set her spoon down on the plate. "We don't really have time for small talk. We're not going to build a relationship. Honestly," Fenna picked at a crust of blood on her cheek, "I'll tell you whatever you want to know."

"Why would you do that?"

"Because you obviously need me."

"Based on what assumption?"

"I'm not dead."

Fenna sipped her coffee and cast a glance at the female agents smoking by the side of the SUV. They were about the same age as Fenna. She was sure they could shoot, *but can they kill?* Fenna thought about the man she had killed with Bahadur's kukri. She took another sip of coffee.

"Alright, Konstabel. I'll get to it." Meredith put down her spoon. Fenna noticed she had not touched her pie. "We have a mutual acquaintance."

"Living or dead?"

Meredith laughed. "Living. God, I didn't imagine you to be such a cynic. You've really been through some shit, haven't you?" Fenna shrugged, and

Meredith continued, "Vienna Marquez. Do you remember her?"

Alpaca wool, a beautiful apartment, and a shitty little dog, *yes*, Fenna thought, *I remember Vienna.* "We met on *The Ice Star.* How do you…" Fenna put down the mug of coffee. It occurred to her then that another name would connect Meredith and her, and it would be a stronger connection.

"Ah, I see that mind of yours is connecting the dots."

"You don't care about Vienna."

"No," said Meredith. She picked up her spoon and took a tiny piece of pie. She ate while Fenna talked.

"I know who you work with," she said.

"Worked. The past tense is more appropriate."

And then it all made sense, so much sense. It wasn't Vestergaard cleaning up on the mountain. They weren't his men blocking Nicklas, preventing him from leaving with Alice.

"They were your men," Fenna said. Meredith raised her eyebrows – refined, plucked, and with just the right amount of make-up – and spooned another small piece of pie into her mouth. "You wanted Nicklas dead."

"And yet, it was your little Gurkha who killed him."

"To protect me, and Alice. But you wanted vengeance."

"And I got it," Meredith said. Her spoon clattered on her plate as she curled her fingers around the coffee mug, the tips of her nails tapped on the glazed surface. "I don't condone what you did in Toronto, when you castrated my colleague with a bullet."

"You worked with Richard Humble," Fenna said. Her voice quavered.

"I did, and, despite his evil nature," she said, and shrugged, "he was effective, and devious. It was his deviant ways that got him into trouble, of course."

"So, this is personal?"

"Isn't everything?"

"And you wanted Nicklas dead, because he finished off Humble."

"That's right."

"But he was acting on orders. To protect me."

Meredith sipped her coffee. She wiped her lipstick from the rim of the mug with a napkin. She let Fenna think for a moment more, and then said, "Have you ever wondered, Konstabel, just how many times people have died to protect you and your identity?" She didn't wait for Fenna to respond. "Perhaps I should be thankful, because now I have you, and I can use you. You are *useful* to me."

"And that's why I am alive."

"Yes."

"And you want me to kill someone."

"Yes."

"You want me to kill Vestergaard," Fenna said, and smiled.

"Do you think you can do that for me? Konstabel?"

Fenna took another spoonful of pie. She almost choked on the cream, as it slipped the wrong way down her throat. Whether it was fatigue or euphoria, she couldn't tell, but suddenly, here in the Fraser Valley, she could see a way out. There was hope. "You'll get us to Greenland?" she said.

"You," said Meredith. "I'll get *you* to Greenland."

The Arctic

INUIT GOVERNED AREAS,
CANADA & GREENLAND

Chapter 16

IQALUIT AIRPORT, NUNAVUT, CANADA

The de Havilland Dash 7 was cramped. Fenna bumped against Alice's shoulder as Burwardsley sat down, squashing his huge frame into the seat. He grumbled something about his knees, huffed for a moment, and then settled. Fenna grinned at him as the evangelists chatted and sang around them, cramming the overhead lockers with sports bags and backpacks, shopping bags of groceries, fruit they could entice the Greenlanders with, and cheap plastic toys for the children. *They'd rather have a Smartphone*, Fenna thought, as a large woman bent over to pick up a collection of plastic cars that had fallen out of her shopping bag. Fenna nudged Alice with her elbow, but she ignored her. Burwardsley was, however, open to distraction, and Fenna decided she could work on Alice later, during the flight.

"Don't," Burwardsley said, as Fenna opened her mouth to speak.

"What?"

"It looks like you're going to take some kind of credit for getting us on this flight."

"And why shouldn't I?"

Burwardsley pointed at Yuka sitting two rows in front of them. "That's why."

"They weren't going to let you leave. I don't know about Alice, but you would be dead already. I had to make a deal. He is part of it. I had to agree that Yuka would come with us. My chaperone," she said and laughed.

"Listen, love, you made a deal with the devil."

"Hey," Fenna said, and shushed him. "Don't

mention him here."

"You are fucking kidding me," Burwardsley said. He turned in his seat, but Fenna clamped a hand on his mouth, giggling as she wagged her finger in front of him.

"And no swearing." She let go of him. Alice stirred beside her, and Fenna hoped she was smiling, at least for a moment. *That would be enough, for now.*

The steward announced that they would be taking off soon, and Fenna took a last look at the new terminal, a 300 million dollar project expected to put Iqaluit firmly on the map. She thought about similar projects in Greenland, and how the Greenlanders had been able to preserve their language to a far greater degree than the Canadian Inuit. The difference between using Latin letters and symbols, was, Fenna imagined, crucial in making the language accessible for later generations, especially in the digital age. And yet Greenland was split between those who could and those who couldn't speak Greenlandic. *Like the Inuit in Qaanaaq*, she remembered, *they speak a dialect that has more in common with the Canadian Inuit than the Greenlanders on the west coast.* It was a point of contention that ostracised the Inuit in the far north of Greenland. *As if life wasn't difficult enough.*

The roar of the Dash 7's four turboprop rotors forced the evangelists into their seats, and Fenna smiled at Yuka's obvious discomfort as the passenger next to him tried to engage him in conversation. It was going to be a long trip for the Inuit intelligence agent, and Fenna realised she didn't care. There were other things to worry about. She wished, for a moment, that Burwardsley could speak Danish, but whatever plans they needed to discuss would have to be talked about in the open. Discreetly. And, as he had often reminded her, *I don't do discreet*. Fenna leaned back in her seat as the Dash 7 taxied off the apron and roared down the runway, lifting off in under twenty seconds.

The journey to Iqaluit had been uneventful, almost anticlimactic. If Alice had opened up, and given Fenna the chance to explain, then it might even have been pleasant. Meredith, whoever she was, clearly had enough information on all of them, that no interrogation was necessary. She seemed to be on the clock, and they had been swept along in the urgency of her operation. Stopping Vestergaard seemed to be her sole motivation, and Fenna began to wonder why. *What was he planning?* Meredith's motive of revenge was a thinly-veiled cover for something greater, more sinister. And, while she had been reluctant to give up Alice, that same urgency seemed to drive her decision-making process. Fenna hadn't seen her make any calls, it appeared that Meredith's decision was final, there was no superior to check in with. *And that should worry me*, she thought.

"There's just one problem," Meredith said in the motel room, the night before the flight from mainland Canada to Iqaluit, Baffin Island.

"Thule Base," Fenna said.

"You have to fly over it get to the Uummannaq fjord area, and your final destination – the so-called safe house."

"Yes."

"The base is American."

"I know."

"And if there is bad weather…"

"We can be forced to land. I know."

Meredith shook her head. "That can't happen. These," she said and tapped her fingernail on the stack of three passports in front of her, "will only get you so far. If they question you… if they recognise Alice…"

"We"ll colour our hair."

"You and Alice?"

"We've been mistaken for one another before. I can mislead them long enough to stall them."

"Long enough for me to help you, you mean?"

"Maybe." Fenna shrugged. "At least this," she said, picking up a bottle of chestnut-coloured hair dye, "is my natural colour." *I get to be me again.* "Besides, they won't be looking for Alice in Greenland, and certainly not in Thule."

"You've considered everything. Haven't you?"

"Not everything." *I haven't even begun.*

As the pilot throttled back, and the engines settled into a rhythmical drone, Fenna looked at Alice, saw the wisps of chestnut hair sticking out from the hem of her beanie. She tried to catch her eye, but Alice ignored her.

"We need to talk at some point," she said.

"I know. But not now." Alice turned to look out of the window, tracing the outlines of icebergs, in the sea below, on the window with her finger.

The steward served coffee. A passenger at the front of the cabin plucked at his guitar, and Burwardsley swore.

They didn't speak for the rest of the flight. Each lost in their own thoughts. Burwardsley kept an eye on Yuka, and, when he wasn't sleeping, Yuka stared at Fenna.

"You'll want to watch him," Burwardsley said, as the pilot announced they would be landing soon in Qaanaaq.

"I know. But he's here for her," Fenna said.

"I'm not so sure."

The wheels of the Dash clunked into position as the pilot lowered the undercarriage, and then they were approaching, hurtling onto the gravel airstrip just four kilometres outside the village of Qaanaaq. Fenna caught a glimpse of Herbert Island in the fjord to the right as the pilot applied the airbrakes and wrestled the aircraft to a stop beside the airport building. Fenna enjoyed the sight of the familiar blue sidings, the red-striped yellow *Mittarfeqarfiit* pickups favoured by the airport authority. She spotted the standard dark blue police Toyota in the car park, and then she forgot all of it, and focused on the ice.

Qaanaaq is served by two supply ships each year, the first in July, and the last in August. The last ship even included Christmas trees, real ones, stored until December. To buy them, the locals had to order them in advance. The needles fell off the moment they brought them inside the house, but that hardly mattered. It was the thought that counted, and now Fenna's thoughts were focused on the ice, and the extent to which it covered the sea, greater than expected in these times of extreme climate change. The passengers had noticed too, even Yuka showed a passing interest before staring at Fenna once more.

The ice was a popular topic of conversation, and it continued as they disembarked and walked the short distance, beneath the wingtips, and into the airport building. The luggage carousel was a single track of rubber encased in metal. It was just a few metres long, and, from the looks of it, rarely switched on. The ground crew emptied the Dash's hold into shallow skips carried by a forklift truck. Fenna smiled as the passengers commented on how quaint it all seemed, before they entered the airport waiting lounge, and were given further instructions by the policeman and his assistant.

"Here we go," Burwardsley whispered as Yuka joined them. He stuffed his hands in his pockets and stood to one side.

Alice found a chair and sat down as they waited for their gear. Fenna joined her, only to pause as she pulled out a chair. There were two men sitting at the table in the corner, furthest from the carousel strip, but still no more than fifteen metres from the exit. They stared at Fenna and then started speaking quietly, the words barely escaping their beards. Fenna recognised their type immediately. Her stomach cramped again as she took in their tanned faces, the white stripes of skin where the sunglasses sat above their ears. They wore wool sweaters, worn and patched, and their trousers were military grade cotton with large cargo pockets – she looked down – much like her own. Burwardsley spotted them too, and he took Fenna's elbow.

"What the fuck are they doing here?" he said.

"You think I know?"

"It's not even September. Shouldn't they be fucking around with dogs in Daneborg?"

"Yes."

"But clearly, Konstabel, they are not."

"Don't call me that," she said. "Not now."

"What? You think they might recognise you?" Burwardsley let go of her elbow. "Bit late for that.

They're coming over." He stepped back and stood beside Yuka, flicking his gaze from Fenna to the two tall Danes of the Sirius Sledge Patrol.

The men smelled of dog, and Fenna took a step toward them, standing between them and Alice. But it was Burwardsley they were more interested in, him and Fenna. They spoke Danish as they approached, but they dispensed with any form of greeting, starting instead with a variety of accusations.

"Heard you were dead," said the taller of the two Danes. Fenna considered him to be the more experienced of the two. He was familiar, but she couldn't quite place him. The shorter man, by just a few centimetres, was the *fup*, the new guy, just starting his first year.

"That depends on who you think I am," Fenna said. She felt Alice stir behind her, heard the squeak of her chair on the floor.

"Who do we think you are? Hah," the man laughed. "You're a legend, Konstabel Brongaard." He turned to the first year man. "This is the one who killed her partner, Mikael Gregersen."

"Is that what they told you?" Fenna worked hard to keep her tone level, measured, as neutral as possible, but she could feel the adrenaline charging through her veins. *This isn't the place, it's not about Mikael anymore.* And yet, she knew it was, and that it always would be for the Sirius Patrol.

"They told us nothing. The first we heard of it was when Kjersing blew his own brains out. Then we heard that Mikael was dead, and you were lost at sea. Apparently, you and your team fell through the ice. That's what we heard. Then," he paused to point at Fenna, "we heard about some PET scuffle in the

167

mountains around Nuuk. A mine was set on fire, and some Chinese men were killed. Along with a couple of Danes. Oh, and there was a car chase, which…" he paused to laugh, "is pretty fucking funny considering how little road there is in Nuuk." He stopped talking and jabbed another finger at Fenna. "But I don't see you laughing, *Konstabel.*"

"Okay," she said. "It's me. I didn't fall through the ice. But before I tell you what happened, tell me, Noa Andersen – that's you, isn't it?"

"*Ja*," he said.

"Your beard was thinner when I met you."

"And I was fatter. Go on."

"What are you doing here?" Fenna glanced over her shoulder, as Burwardsley moved closer.

"We're looking for dogs. Daneborg needs new breeding stock."

"You usually don't go this far north."

"No, but hunters are shooting their dogs along the coast. Too many winters with poor or no ice," he said, pausing to nod in the direction of the fjord. "Ironic, really, as this winter looks like it's going to be a good one." He looked from Burwardsley to Fenna. "Your turn, Konstabel. What are you doing here? And, more to the point, why'd you come back?" Andersen waited, his eyes fixed on Fenna, but flicking occasionally in Burwardsley's direction as the Royal Marine moved closer.

"I can't tell you."

"*Ja*, of course," Andersen laughed. "How convenient."

"She means it," said Burwardsley. "Whatever it was she just said."

"Hey, man," Andersen said in English, as he took

a step towards Burwardsley. "Just who the fuck are you?"

"Me?"

"Don't," Fenna said. She glanced around at the evangelists as they collected their baggage. She could see their own gear on the luggage belt and tapped Alice on the shoulder. "Can you get our gear?"

"Sure," Alice said, happy to move away from the men crowding around the table.

"You didn't answer my question," Andersen said.

"You didn't ask nicely."

"Oh, for God's sake," Fenna said. She turned on the first year man. "Who are you?"

"Hansen," he said. "Konstabel."

"Great. Hansen meet Burwardsley," she said and grabbed the *fup* by the arm, dragging him between the two men. "I don't have time for this testosterone Navy bullshit."

"Navy?" said Andersen, as he shoved his partner to one side. "British?"

"Royal Marines," Burwardsley said. "Heard of them?"

It was Fenna who threw the first punch. A brawl seemed inevitable, and, with Alice safe collecting their gear, she decided it was best to get it over with. *Besides,* she mused, as she curled her fingers into a fist, *there's no better way to break the ice. And,* she added as an afterthought, *we might need them.* Fenna extended her middle knuckle and slammed her fist into Burwardsley's ribs, just below his bullet wound, just enough to slow him down. She whispered in his ear as he grunted, "Let me handle this. Stand down."

Burwardsley staggered backward into Yuka, creating a gap large enough for Fenna to stand between them. As Yuka shoved Burwardsley onto a chair, she whirled toward Andersen, knees bent, adopting her preferred fighting stance, projecting just enough attitude for a large opponent to take her small frame seriously. She glared at him as he opened his mouth.

"Not one fucking word," she said in Danish, "or I will drop you like a sack of shit."

He lifted his hands and took a step backward. Hansen leaned against a table near the window. The ground crew had stopped working on the Dash, and were gathered at the glass, on the outside of the building.

"Mike?" Fenna said, switching to English. She kept her gaze fixed and focused on the two Sirius men. "Are you alright?"

"I am bleeding. Again. Thanks to you."

"Sorry about that..."

"He's bleeding?" said Andersen. He switched to English. "Why is he bleeding?"

"Because we pulled at least two bullets out of him," said Alice, and she dumped their gear onto the table. "And before you ask *how* or *why*, or some other dumbshit question, then let me tell you..." She paused to look at the two men. "It was to protect me. Now," she said, "if you've got nothing better to do, you can help us with our gear. It's been a long flight. I'm tired, and I can't remember when I last had something to eat." Alice sighed. She looked at Fenna. "What?"

"Just you," Fenna said, and smiled. She lowered her fists, relaxed her stance, and laughed.

"You're laughing?" Alice said.

"And you will too, if you know…"

"What?"

"If you want to."

"Yeah, I want to," she said, and smiled.

Fenna bit her lip to stop laughing as the policeman walked over to their table. He tucked his hands into the broad belt around his waist and looked at each of them. He paused to nod at Yuka, and then stopped to focus on Fenna. She decided she liked him.

"*Allu*," he said. "*Ajunngilaq?*"

"*Aap*," said Fenna. "*Ajunngi.*"

"You speak Greenlandic?"

"A little," she said.

"And everything is alright here?" he said, and again in English.

"We're fine," Fenna said.

"*Torrak*. Good then." The policeman nodded in the direction of the exit. "My name is Akisooq Jessen. Welcome to Qaanaaq."

Chapter 17

QAANAAQ, GREENLAND

The ground crew drifted away from the window and Akisooq stood to one side, making room for the airport leader. The Danish man glanced at Fenna as he talked to Andersen.

"Air Greenland called. Your flight's been cancelled," he said.

"Shit."

"Technical problems."

"Should've gone with *Flugfélag*."

"They call them Air Iceland today, boss," said Hansen, his smile barely hidden beneath his beard.

"Thanks, whelp," Andersen said and slapped him in the stomach. "But they've still got *Flugfélag* written on the side of the plane. Until they change that... Well," he shrugged. Andersen scratched at his beard as the airport leader returned to the office. "I guess we're stuck in Qaanaaq one more night." He looked at Fenna.

The policeman checked their passports, passing quickly over Fenna's to concentrate on her companions. He spent a long time with Yuka's, flipping the pages back and forth, before handing it back. He looked at Burwardsley, and nodded at the blood seeping through his fleece. "Do you need assistance?"

Burwardsley lifted his arm and prodded at the area. He winced, and said, "Might be a good idea."

"Then I'll give you a ride to the hospital. Where are you staying?" he asked, and looked at Fenna.

"We don't know yet," Fenna said. "We also need a ride south. Noa?"

"*Ja?*"

"How many dogs have you got on your flight?"

Andersen shook his head. "Not gonna happen," he said, and switched to Danish, "You can't just come back from the dead, Konstabel, and expect to roll back into your previous life."

"No?" Fenna lifted her chin. "But you're curious, aren't you?"

"About what?"

"The truth," she said. "Give us a ride south, and I'll give you all the details."

"Like I said, Konstabel. The last I heard, you were dead, and then you were working for PET, maybe. Now you turn up on a flight from Baffin Island with a Royal Marine, a pretty girl, and a Greenlander lookalike." He paused to lean close to Fenna. "Do the words *untrustworthy bitch* mean anything to you? Or are you so far gone, so damaged, that this all seems perfectly normal?"

Fenna almost smiled. "Normal doesn't quite cut it anymore, Oversergent."

"Apparently."

Andersen pulled Hansen to one side. He stared at Fenna as they talked, soft words through long matted whiskers. She pictured them both with ice clinging to their beards, sparkling in the sun, their breath misting into clouds before freezing into another layer of ice. She smoothed a hand over her chin, remembering how the wind, the snow, the freezing temperatures had hardened her skin, rubbed it raw. She had envied her partner's beard during each day on patrol, and teased him about it each night as he plucked food from his whiskers. *I miss it*, she realised, as she watched the two Sirius men talk. The thought of flying south, stuffed in the cabin – seats removed to make space for dogs and gear, thrilled her. *It was what I was meant to do.* She looked at Burwardsley. *Before him.* And then at Yuka. *Before them.*

"I can give you a lift into Qaanaaq," Akisooq said. "They…" he pointed at the bearded Danes, "have their own vehicle. From the hotel."

"There's a hotel?" Alice asked.

"Yes," Akisooq said. "Very small. And full," he said, "of evangelists. We will have to find somewhere else for you to stay."

The small airport emptied. Akisooq showed them to the Toyota, and they loaded their gear into the back. Burwardsley pulled Fenna to one side, nodding at the Inuit intelligence officer as he walked beside Alice.

"We're going to have to deal with him, and soon," he said, his voice low, hidden beneath the crunch and scuffle of gravel at their feet.

"I know."

"And you know it has to be you, right?"

"Me?"

"Fenna," Burwardsley said, "look at me." He lifted his arm to show her the blood seeping through his clothes. The stain was bigger than when he was sat in the chair. "I need to get fixed up before I can do any of the fun stuff. You're on your own, love."

Again, she thought. Fenna stopped at the car and helped Burwardsley with his gear. Yuka was the last to shove his pack into the car, and, when the policeman tried to make conversation, he ignored him and climbed into the back seat. Fenna opened the passenger door and got in. With a quick glance at the two Sirius men as they got into the hotel pickup, she shut the door. Akisooq backed up and drove away from the airport, the grit of the gravel road peppered the Toyota as he accelerated. They passed small groups of Greenlanders, families, children, young couples out for a walk. Akisooq slowed as they passed each group.

"I usually have a car full," he said.

"You still do," Fenna said.

"Right."

The ice sheet was just visible on the plateau of the mountains running parallel to the road. The hard granite sides seemed closer with the dusting of snow, it reached all the way to the lower slopes, close to the road and the village. Fenna pointed, and said, "Winter is coming early this year."

"Maybe."

Fenna looked out at the sea, at the ice just beyond the shore. She thought about global warming, and the anomalies that can't be explained, the ones that buck the trend. *Perhaps this year will be one of those years?* She forgot all about the ice when she saw Yuka staring at her in the wing mirror. She stared back.

"Your passports are all in order," Akisooq said, breaking the contact between Yuka and Fenna. "But I still don't know what you were doing on the charter flight. You're not evangelists."

"No, we're not," Fenna said.

"We're students," Alice said and leaned forward in the gap between the seats.

"You don't look like students."

"Yeah," she said, with a flash of a smile at Fenna. "We're not *all* students. I guess it is just me, really, and my sister is along for the ride. Together with her guy." Alice said and punched Burwardsley on his

175

thigh.

"And you?" Akisooq said, as he turned the rear view mirror to look at Yuka. "You look familiar. Have you been to Greenland before?"

Yuka leaned back in his seat and raised his eyebrows.

"When?"

"2016," Yuka said, and turned away.

Akisooq looked at Yuka for a moment longer, and then repositioned the mirror.

They entered the village, driving past wooden houses – brightly painted, sorely loved. The climate blistered the walls, and a lack of money shifted priorities from furnishings and fittings to food. *Nothing was cheap in Greenland*, Fenna remembered. Akisooq stopped outside a yellow house on a curve in the gravel road. The neighbour had dogs chained to the rocks between the two houses. The policeman's house was exposed on the eastern side to the gradual granite slope leading to the mountains, with a line of three newly-built wooden houses above it. The first house, painted dark blue, sank each summer to the permafrost, only to rise again each winter. Akisooq said as much when he turned off the engine.

"Those houses are fit for Danish summers."

"Then why did they build them here?" said Fenna.

He shrugged, and said, "Somebody did somebody else a favour. They should never have been built." He turned in his seat. "You can stay here. It's the police house, but I am just the summer replacement. My family is in Maniitsoq. There's plenty of room. If you get out, I will take your friend to the hospital." He got out of the car and walked over to the house, opening the door as Alice and Yuka emptied the boot and carried their gear inside. Fenna pretended to have lost something inside the car.

"He's not stupid," Burwardsley said. "He knows you want to talk."

"You're right," she said and looked at Yuka waiting by the door. She started to speak but stopped when Andersen pulled up alongside them in the hotel pickup. He wound the window down and Fenna did the same.

"Hansen and I have had a chat, and, seeing as we're all trapped in this wonderful town for the night, how about we start again? We're staying in a house just up from the hotel. We'll cook. We even have beer. What do you say, Konstabel?"

"You have beer?"

"Brought it with us. No one can afford what they have in the store."

"Right," Fenna said. She looked at Burwardsley. He nodded, and she said, "What time?"

"About sundown?" Andersen said, and laughed.

"Fucking hell, he's a comedian," Burwardsley said. "I liked him better when he was an arrogant Dane."

"Shut up, Mike," Fenna said. "Alright, we'll be there for dinner."

"Good. We can talk about your flight, tomorrow," he said. Gravel and grit spewed out from beneath the wheels as he accelerated up the slight rise in the road.

Fenna watched him drive away. Two of the neighbour's sledge dogs lifted their heads for a moment, only to rest on their paws as the pickup disappeared between the row of houses leading to the hotel. Fenna heard the pickup stop, and wound up her window.

"Tonight then," Burwardsley said.

"Yuka?"

"Yep."

Fenna nodded. She opened the door and got out. Akisooq was waiting by the door to the house. He stopped Fenna as she approached.

"You're not students," he said.

"No." Fenna waited for him to say more. She noted the way he wore the USP Compact on his belt. There was fluff between the snap of the holster and the grip. *He doesn't clean it very often. Doesn't need to.*

"I can't place your strange Canadian friend," he said. "But I have seen him before. As for the rest of your friends – you are a strange mix."

"Yes, we are." She wondered where their conversation was taking them, wondered if their strangeness was what encouraged him to offer them a bed in the police house. *Why not the police station?* She mused, and remembered the single cell in Ittoqqortoormiit. *Not enough room.*

"Greenland is a small country," he said.

"Yes."

"And did you think you could come back, without people recognising you?" he said with a nod in the direction of the hotel.

"I came back to finish things."

"What things?"

"I can't say."

Akisooq sighed, and said, "I could lock you up."

"For what?"

"I could think of something."

"But you're alone."

"Was that a threat?"

"An observation."

A group of children clambered across the rough ground beside the house. They were full of energy, buoyed by the thought of the evening's evangelical entertainment. Fenna heard them chattering, and imagined the stories they might tell their younger brothers and sisters. They stopped talking when they saw Fenna, clustering around her and the policeman.

"I'm not alone, Konstabel," he said.

"Hey," Fenna said, as one of the girls tickled her leg. The girl giggled, as Fenna tickled her back. Soon, she was surrounded, and it was all she could do to keep them at arm's length. Akisooq retreated to the car, waving as he sat behind the wheel. "You're just going to leave me?" she said, as she picked up the smallest of the boys, and tucked him under her arm. The children giggled, regrouped, and attacked, as Fenna whirled the boy around her body. He whooped and she set him down on the ground. A girl immediately filled the vacant spot, lifting her arms for Fenna to swing her too.

"They should keep you occupied until I return," Akisooq said. He drove away, as Alice stepped out of the house.

"What's going on?" she said, only to back away as the children split up to engage both targets at once. "Fenna?"

"We're outnumbered, Alice," she said and made the mistake of sitting on a large boulder by the side of the road. Three children crawled onto her lap and they toppled into a heap on the ground.

Alice staggered over to Fenna, with one boy wrapped around each leg and a girl pushing her from behind, her tiny hands hooked into the belt loops on Alice's trouser. Yuka watched from the door, before retreating inside the house. Fenna saw him go, before the two boys on Alice's legs let go of her and leaped onto Fenna. Alice giggled as Fenna groaned beneath a pile of children.

The girl pushing Alice from behind slipped her hand inside Alice's and beamed at her. She pointed at the boys, and said, "Ungaaq, Kaaleeraq, Luka."

"Okay," said Alice.

"Birgithe, Frederikke," she said, and pointed at the girls.

"And you?" Alice tugged at the girl's hand.

"Pipaluk."

"Hi, Pipaluk. I'm Alice."

Pipaluk smiled and tugged on Alice's hand, pulling her forward until they were close to the squirm of children crawling over Fenna. She pulled her down until Alice sat on the boulder. Fenna said something in Danish, something else in Greenlandic, and then, finally, she said stop, in English. The children crawled off and giggled as Fenna stood up.

"I guess," Alice said, as Fenna dusted herself off, "stop is the same in any language."

"Right," Fenna said, licking at the dirt on her lips. The children started talking. They scrabbled about on the rocks and Pipaluk let go of Alice's hand. She chased one of the boys until they were all involved in a seemingly random and altogether confusing game of tag.

"Do you ever think about children?" Alice said, as they watched the game develop.

"Like having kids, you mean?"

"Sure," she said and moved to make space for

Fenna on the boulder.

"Maybe. I don't know. It's seems trivial somehow."

"But nice." Alice brushed a patch of dirt from her knee. "Dad said I should have kids. He said it the day before he died. Something about seeing life in a different light once you have a child. I don't know about that. It's difficult to imagine life – a different life to this one. And there's no light. I mean," she paused to shrug. "Sure, here, there's lots of light."

"It won't start to get dark before sometime in September."

"Really?"

"That's right. And then the sun disappears late October, and the light gradually diminishes until it is pitch black."

"I can't imagine it."

"It takes some getting used to," Fenna said. She looked at the house, saw Yuka at the window, frowned as he lowered the blinds. "But," she said, "so long as you keep busy, try to maintain a routine, try to adapt…" Fenna stood up.

"Fenna?"

"Stay outside, with the children."

"What are you going to do?"

"Don't let them come into the house."

"Fenna?" Alice moved to stand up, but Fenna pressed her hand, gently, on her shoulder.

"Stay here. I am going inside. Don't come in, no matter what you hear."

"You're scaring me," Alice said, as Fenna walked toward the house. "Fenna?"

The interior of the house was not dark, the light streamed in from around the blinds, through the gap beneath the door. Fenna saw the strip of light on the toes of her boots as she stepped inside the house, shut and locked the door. She heard the children playing, calling Alice's name. She pictured them crawling over the rocks, scuffing the palms of their small hands on the rough clusters of black lichen. She knew the touch, could almost hear the dry crunch of the thicker patches of lichen as one stepped on them. *Black*, she thought. *And stubborn*, surviving each winter despite the desiccating cold, the evaporating wind, and the long dark night. *A survivor then*. Fenna turned at the sound of soft footsteps on the linoleum floor. Yuka stepped into view, blocking the door to the kitchen. Fenna recognised the fighting posture, looked for an edge, saw the kitchen knife.

Chapter 18

Yuka was the first to move. The kitchen knife blurred in his hand as he attacked. Fenna dodged to the right and tripped over the shoes and boots littering the floor. Yuka spun on his heel and stabbed at Fenna's thigh. The tip of the blade caught in her trousers, peeling a triangle of material from the pocket and nicking her skin. Fenna rolled onto her back, hooked her foot around Yuka's ankle, and slammed her boot onto his shin. He swore as he kicked free of her grip, giving Fenna time to find her feet. She lunged after Yuka's knife hand, gripped his wrist, and bent his hand backward until he dropped the knife. It clunked onto the floor and Fenna kicked it to one side. She moved, searching for a better position and grip, but Yuka grabbed her hair with his free hand and yanked her head backward. She released his wrist and he jerked his knee into her stomach.

There was nothing pretty to the fight, but it was bloodless, until Fenna slammed an elbow into Yuka's nose. He let go of her hair, and she twisted to grab his bloody nose between her fingers. His head followed his nose, his body followed his head, and Fenna pulled him across the short floor of the hall into the living room.

She hadn't thought about the door frame, or how he might grip both sides with his hands and yank his nose free of her bloody fingers. Fenna toppled into the living room, and Yuka followed, lunging at her body, slamming into her back. They crashed through the glass surface of the coffee table, the shards cutting their faces and hands, and slicing through their clothes. Fenna scrabbled across the floor, grabbed a

183

shard of glass, and thrust it into Yuka's face as he found his feet. The shard tore a flap of skin from his cheek. He ignored it, powering inside Fenna's defence. He wrapped his arm around Fenna's and punched her in the face. She spluttered blood, gasping for breath as he punched her again.

Yuka held her arm above her head, pausing for a second at the sound of a knock at the door. Fenna reached for another shard, but Yuka slammed his boot on her hand, pressing jagged pieces of glass into her palm. She wanted to scream. The thought of a handful of glass, embedded in her hands like nails, made her sick. She bit back on the first convulsion, tensed the muscles in her legs.

The knocking changed to a steady pounding, vibrating through the house. Yuka glanced again at the door, then focused on Fenna.

"You really thought we were going to let you go?" he said through gritted teeth.

Fenna said nothing. Her blood was raging in her temples. She rasped each breath into her lungs through bloody teeth, yanked her hand out from beneath Yuka's boot, heaved down on his grip and lurched to her feet. She slashed at his face with the palm of her hand. He let go of her arm, swatting at her hands, as she gripped the back of his head and pushed his face into her palm of glass. Yuka cursed her as the glass ripped through his flesh. He staggered back and Fenna kicked his legs out from under him, following him down onto the floor, never letting go. She could feel the blood streaming from his face, down her wrist. She could taste it in her mouth, or perhaps it was her own, she didn't know, didn't care, until she felt strong hands grip her arms and pull her up and off Yuka.

"Easy, Fenna, easy," Burwardsley said. She squirmed in his grasp until he let her go, shoving her into the corner of the room as Akisooq wrestled Yuka onto his back, and slipped a pair of handcuffs around his wrists. He sat on the floor beside the Canadian, as Yuka spat blood and shifted his head from side to side until he found Fenna. He snorted blood as it bubbled beneath his nostrils as he glared at her.

"It looks like this man attacked you, Fenna, is that right?" Burwardsley said.

"I…" Fenna started to speak, but Burwardsley cut her off with a look.

"This man joined our group in Iqaluit. We don't know who he is beyond his name. I think it best if you arrest him," he said, and looked at Akisooq.

Yuka spat and laughed, as he rolled onto his side. He sneered at Burwardsley, and said, "You should be an actor. What a perf…"

Burwardsley slammed the toe of his boot into Yuka's chin, snapping his head back and silencing him. He bent over him to check Yuka was still breathing and then apologised to Akisooq. "I am sorry. I thought he was going to attack again."

Akisooq raised his eyebrow and glanced from Burwardsley to Fenna. He stood up, brushed shards of bloody glass from his knees and cast a glance at the door. "First time I've ever had to break into my own house," he said.

"Clearly, he had it all planned," Burwardsley said.

"Mike," Fenna whispered. "Cut it out."

Akisooq gripped his belt and looked around the room. Fenna followed his gaze from the bloody remains of the coffee table, to the spots of blood leading past the kitchen knife to the front door. A picture frame had smashed on the floor, she didn't remember that. The door frame was splintered, and, framed in the light that streamed in from outside, was Alice, and a clutch of children staring around her legs.

"Go home," Akisooq said. "Now." The children let go of Alice. Fenna heard them chatter down the road as they ran away from the policeman's house. He nodded at Burwardsley. "Help me get him into the car."

"I can help," Fenna said, as the men started to lift Yuka's body.

"It would be best," Akisooq said, "if you worked on your part as the defenceless victim. Don't you think?"

"Okay," she said, watching them as they carried Yuka toward the door. She sat down as Alice stepped out of the way and joined her.

"It was you who locked the door," Alice said, "wasn't it?"

"Yeah, that was me."

"Why?"

"I thought I could take him. I was wrong."

"Sure, maybe, but he's the one they are carrying into the police car."

They sat quietly as Akisooq started the engine and drove away. Fenna waited for the sound of Burwardsley's boots, but heard nothing more than the muted rattle of a chain as the dogs settled again after all the excitement.

"Let me see your hand," Alice said. She rested Fenna's hand on her lap and peered at the glass sticking out of it. "I need more light," she said and stirred.

"No," Fenna said, "don't open the blinds. Not yet."

"Okay, but I can only see the big stuff."

"Then start with that."

Fenna sucked a sharp breath through her teeth as Alice teased the largest shard out of Fenna's palm. When it was free she looked around for somewhere to put it, and then tossed it onto the floor of the living room.

"He'll be missed, won't he?" she said.

"Yes."

Alice pulled another shard from Fenna's palm, and said, "Why did you do it?"

"What? Attack Yuka?"

"No. Not that. Why did you talk them into letting me come to Greenland?"

"I wasn't going to leave you behind."

"But why here?"

Fenna winced as Alice worked at a stubborn shard, the jagged edge ripped at her skin until Alice tore it loose.

"Well, we're not there yet. We have to fly south."

"With the Danes?"

"Hopefully, yes."

"Where to?"

"There's a house in a small settlement – maybe seventy people live on the island."

"Whose house?"

"It belongs to a shaman."

"A shaman?" Alice laughed. "As in Native American? A medicine man?"

"Sort of," Fenna said, and smiled. "I don't know for sure, but that's what I was told."

"By who?"

"Vestergaard. He chose the house."

Alice pulled Fenna's hand onto her own lap. "I really need more light," she said, and stood up. Fenna squinted as Alice opened the blind and disappeared into the kitchen. She returned with a wet cloth and a towel. "Neither of them are clean," she said, and sat down. She took Fenna's hand and inspected it. She talked as she turned Fenna's palm in the light. "This man, Vestergaard, he's the same one you talked about before, right?"

"Yes."

"The one who wants to use me and kill you?"

"That's right."

Alice wiped the blood from Fenna's palm. The tip of her tongue was visible as she worked and Fenna tried not to smile. "What I don't get," Alice said, "is why we are going to a house that Vestergaard suggested. Why not go somewhere else?"

"There is nowhere else, Alice."

"Nowhere?" she said, and wrapped the towel tightly around Fenna's hand.

"No," Fenna said. She sighed and said, "I'm sorry."

"It's okay, I guess." She bent Fenna's hand at the elbow and pressed it to her chest. "Keep it elevated." Alice stood up and paced the length of the living room, stopping at the far window to stare at Herbert Island in the distance. The snow dusted the spine of the island, making it look like the back of some great sea beast, breaching the surface and breaking through the ice. Fenna joined Alice at the window, taking her hand and squeezing it.

"I'm sorry," she said.

"I know."

"But, if we can just get to the house, we can make things right."

"How?" she whispered. "Yuka almost killed you."

"I wasn't ready. He had the advantage."

"And Vestergaard doesn't? He knows we are coming, and where we are going?"

"Yes, but I'll be ready. More prepared."

"I don't know, Fenna."

They turned at the sound of the police car pulling to a stop outside the house. They listened as Burwardsley kicked the grit from his boots and stepped inside. He joined them in the living room, the keys to the car hooked around his little finger.

"How's your hand?" he said.

"Alice fixed it. Where's Akisooq?"

"Processing our friend at the police station." Burwardsley laughed, "more of a house, really. We took him to the hospital, then Akisooq called his assistant, and they took him to the station. I've got the spare car."

"One policeman, and two police cars?"

"This is an old one. Apparently, it would cost more to ship it out than to keep it running."

Fenna nodded. *Typical Greenland*, she thought. "Did Akisooq say anything?"

"We agreed you were lucky, but it's Yuka who is going to be scarred for life. He's not going to forget you, love."

"But what about us? Akisooq could probably arrest us for disturbing the peace."

"I've been wondering about that." Burwardsley sat down on the sofa. "Greenland is a small place, small community. Everyone knows everyone else, despite the distance. What are the odds that he knows your friend from Ittoqqortoormiit?"

"Maratse?" Fenna said, and shrugged. "He probably does."

"That's it then."

"And you think he'll let us get on that plane tomorrow?"

"With the Sirius boys? Fenna, I think he'll drive us to the airport just to make sure we do get on it. He's got enough paperwork to sort out with Yuka. He can't keep an eye on the village and deal with us." He drummed his fingers on his knee. "Which reminds me, I bumped into the boys on the way back from the hospital."

Fenna cringed, and said, "Just bumped into them?"

"Christ Fenna, what do you take me for? I'm hardly going to mix it up with them in the street. Can you imagine it? Oh, by the way, I'm the guy who offed your pal on the ice…" Burwardsley paused. "Sorry, love."

"It's okay." She frowned and said, "But you are pretty upbeat for someone with a couple of bullet holes in them." Then she laughed. "Ah, they gave you something at the hospital, didn't they?"

Burwardsley reached into his pocket. "They gave me a whole bottle," he said, and shook it between his fingers. "I have to say, Konstabel, I probably feel better than you do right now." He looked at Alice. "What about you? Ready to party?"

"Party?"

"It's Friday night. Did you know that? Eh?" He stood up. "I saw the beer they bought, and I don't mind admitting that Carlsberg is equal to the best of

190

British lager, so long as it's cold. Oh, and we're eating whale steaks tonight."

"Mike?"

"Yes, Konstabel?"

"How many pills did you take?"

"Shit, I don't know," he said and stood up. "They said I should take some for the pain. They didn't say how many." He stuffed the bottle in his pocket. "You going like that?" he said and nodded at Fenna's hand. Blood was seeping through the towel.

"It's either that or the hospital."

"Fine. Grab another towel, there's beer to be drunk." Burwardsley walked out of the living room and waited for them at the front door.

"He's going to be impossible, isn't he?" said Alice.

"I think he is." She tugged Alice across the floor, doing her best to ignore the crunch of glass beneath her feet as they walked out of the house. "Are you going to be alright with this?"

"A party?"

"Parties in Greenland can get a little rough," Fenna said. Burwardsley got in behind the wheel and waved at them to hurry up.

"Rough? Did you just say that?"

"I guess I did."

"Amazing," Alice said, "with all we've been through." She let go of Fenna's hand and jogged to the car.

"Hey," Fenna called out. "Remind me? What's the drinking age in America?"

"Who are you? My mother?" Alice said as she opened the passenger door. She called out, "Shotgun," and climbed in beside Burwardsley.

Once Fenna was in the car, they drove less than half a kilometre, before Burwardsley stopped and announced they had arrived. Fenna smiled as she stepped out of the car and saw nine sledge dogs secured to a travelling chain stretched along the road, secured at both ends to rusted fuel drums full of rocks. Each dog had a short length of chain clipped to a collar and attached to the long chain between the drums. One chain was missing a dog.

"If they work together they can pull those barrels down the street and escape," Andersen said, as he stepped onto the porch outside the wooden house. He had an open beer in one hand, and three cans stacked in the other. He gave Alice and Burwardsley a beer each as they stepped around the dogs and walked inside the house. Fenna dawdled by the dogs, fussing each of them with her good hand, appraising them for size and weight, the condition of their fur, how hydrated they were. "If you keep pinching their skin like that, they'll bite, Konstabel."

"Maybe," she said and fussed another dog as she worked her way along the line.

"Do you miss it?"

"You can tell?"

"*Ja*, I can tell," Andersen said and gave Fenna the last can of Carlsberg. "*Skål*," he said and took a slug of beer.

"*Skål*." Fenna popped the can and drank.

Andersen smiled as a neighbour cranked up a radio, and the revellers inside raised their voices over the distorted sounds of Johnny Cash. The dogs twitched at the ends of their chains, and Andersen knelt to make a fuss of the one between him and Fenna.

"Friday night in Qaanaaq," he said and crushed the empty can in his hand.

Fenna nodded and looked at the house. She heard Alice giggle, and smiled at the thought of winding down, for one night at least. She gestured at the chain.

"Just nine dogs?" she said.

"Nah," Andersen said and grinned. "There's one more inside."

"A bitch?"

"*Ja.*"

"And she's in heat?"

"She is."

"Well," Fenna said, and laughed, "us girls can be a handful."

"I've heard that," Andersen said. He nodded at the towel around Fenna's hand. "You weren't wearing that before."

"No," she said. "No, I wasn't."

"Want to talk about it?"

"Inside, maybe."

"Come on, then." Andersen tossed the empty beer can in the direction of the bin, muttering something about cleaning up in the morning.

He led Fenna up the stairs to the house, and she heard Alice giggle again, before a twenty-kilo bundle of energy, fur and claws, skittered across the floor and leaped into Fenna's arms.

Andersen laughed, and said, "What were you saying? Something about girls being a handful."

Fenna pulled the bitch into her chest and held it tight, as it licked at her face. *It feels good*, she thought, *to be with friends, for as long as it lasts.* She slipped the bitch onto the floor and gave it a soft kick on the rump to

193

send it back inside, and away from the dogs straining at the chain behind her. Fenna waved at the dogs and closed the door. She took a breath, let go of the handle, and joined the party.

Chapter 19

The bitch finally settled at Fenna's feet as the neighbour's music beat through the thin wooden walls, and the Sirius men found another crate of beer to wash down the rich, dark whale meat. Fenna rubbed the fur between the bitch's ears, teasing one ear between her fingers. She listened to Hansen tell Alice about his first year in Sirius. Fenna guessed that he was only a year or two older than the American, about the same age as Fenna had been when she tried out for the sledge patrol. Andersen, she noticed, was far more interested in Burwardsley, although he cast a furtive look in her direction more than once during his conversation with the Marine Lieutenant. He was pumping Burwardsley for information, she knew, but trusted that the Englishman would be guarded. Despite the pills he had taken, Burwardsley had hardly drunk any beer, unlike Andersen. *But then what's a Dane to do on a Friday night in Qaanaaq?* she thought, as the corners of her mouth curled into a smile.

Fenna leaned back against the wall, her legs stretched flat on the floor. She curled her hand around the base of the bottle of beer, pushing it back and forth along the floor as the bitch turned on her side and slumped against her legs. Fenna laid her arm along the bitch's flank and smoothed her fingers between the dog's matted fur. She couldn't remember the last time she had felt so safe, so relaxed. *It feels good. How long will it last?*

The scrape of a chair leg vibrated through the floor and Fenna looked up as Alice walked to the bathroom. She smiled at Fenna as she passed, blushing as Andersen said something about not leaving, because Hansen was going to be inconsolable if she left without a kiss. It was all so very far removed from the bullets, the blood, and the bursts of adrenaline that typically defined Fenna's more recent experiences. She heard the bathroom door click as Alice turned the key in the lock. Hansen went outside to smoke, and Burwardsley joined him.

"He's a close one," said Andersen, as he opened another can of beer and joined Fenna on the floor. "He knows Greenland, and he's been around, but he won't say where, or when... I can't get anything interesting out of him."

"And what do you want to know?" Fenna said and took a sip of beer. It was warm. She didn't care.

"About you. How he knows you."

"Why?"

"Because nothing adds up, Konstabel. Gregersen, a car chase in Nuuk – nothing makes any sense."

"That's PET for you."

"No." Andersen shook his head. "I don't buy that."

"But you'll have to. I can't tell you anything."

"That's your problem then," he said.

"What do you mean?"

"Well, unless you open up, I've got no incentive to put you on my flight, tomorrow." He took a slug of beer, wiped the froth from his beard, and said, "None."

The bitch twitched, and Fenna stroked it as she thought about what to tell Andersen. *How do I tell him that the man responsible for Mikael's death is sharing a smoke with his* fup? She bit at her lip, wondering what had changed. *Because I need him*, she realised, and almost laughed at the irony.

"What's so funny?" Andersen asked. He stretched his legs and rested his arms on his knees. Fenna saw the holes he had patched in his trousers, recognised the ragged hems for what they were – wear and tear on patrol, and wondered at the route he had chosen, and which cabins he had visited.

"Are they going to rebuild *Loch Fyne*?"

"They've talked about it. There's not much left. It'll have to be rebuilt from scratch."

"It's a good location."

"Which is why they're talking about it."

If she closed her eyes, Fenna knew she would see Bahadur pressing her Glock to the back of Mikael's head, hear Burwardsley give the order, and then turn away as her partner's body slumped to the floor. If she closed her eyes. She chose to look at Andersen instead, and, as the bass from the neighbour's stereo diminished in favour of a raucous chorus of English songs from the seventies, Fenna decided to tell the Sirius man what had happened that day on the ice, with just one omission, Burwardsley.

Alice returned as Fenna finished her account of the shootout at Loch Fyne, her capture, how the helicopter crew had doused the cabin with aviation fuel, right before they drugged her.

"And that's when my interrogation began," she said. "When they woke me up."

"Jesus," Andersen said. He glanced at Alice, and then said, "No wonder Kjersing killed himself. If he was privy to what was going on…"

"It was a test. He was being used."

"That's no fucking excuse. He was a traitor."

Fenna took another sip of beer, studying Andersen's reaction as she lowered the bottle from her lips.

"What happened next?" he said, and, with another glance at Alice, he switched to English. "You were interrogated?"

"By a Dane, or so I thought."

"Vestergaard? You mentioned him before."

"That's what he called himself. He's also called *the Magician*."

Andersen bit at the longer whiskers of his beard, the ones curling into his mouth. "And you got away?"

"I had help."

"Who?" he asked and nodded at Burwardsley. "Him?"

"No. Mike helped me later," Fenna said. "It was a Greenlander, two in fact. A policeman called Maratse, and Kula, a hunter."

"We heard about an anti-terror exercise…"

"That was the cover story, yes."

"And a car chase across the ice," he said and raised an eyebrow. "Really?"

"The truth is stranger than fiction."

"No shit."

Alice excused herself, and joined the men talking outside. It was past midnight, but, with no visible difference in the light, the night seemed like it would never end. *If only that could be true*, Fenna thought. *But the winter dark will come, and I need to be prepared for what it might bring. If we live that long*, she added. She watched Alice as she walked across the floor and stepped out onto the deck. Fenna turned back to Andersen.

"You want to know why I'm here?" she said.

"*Ja.* I do."

"The girl."

"Girl? She's not much younger than Hansen." He

snorted and lifted the can to his lips. Andersen licked beer from his lips and said, "What about her?"

"I need to her to get to Vestergaard."

"Her?"

"Yes," Fenna said. She took a moment to explain what Vestergaard wanted with Alice, finishing with a plea for help. "We need to go south, as far as Uummannaq, and then into the fjord."

"I can get you as far as Qaarsut. We can land there before going on to Ilulissat."

"That works. We can get a boat to the settlement."

"Which one?"

"Nuugaatsiaq, I think. I'll know when we get there, when I call the Magician."

"You're actually going to call him?"

"He has a safe house arranged for us. The girl is important to him."

"Why?"

"It's complicated."

"See," Andersen said and crossed his legs. He lifted the can of beer, one finger extended, pointing at Fenna as he spoke. "This is what I don't understand. After all you've told me, you are going to call the man that ultimately got Mikael killed, and tell him... tell him what, exactly?"

"That he can come and pick up Alice."

"You're going to give him the girl?"

"No. I'm going to kill him." Fenna leaned forward, a frown on her brow, as she looked at Andersen. "You don't think I can?"

"Fenna..." he started. "Have you heard yourself, lately? I mean, this is not normal talk, even for the first female Sirius *fup*. It's like you're deluded, or something. Have you considered getting help?"

Fenna waited for Andersen to laugh. Only to realise, when he didn't, that her own reality had shifted tectonically from what even the elite Sirius Sledge Patrol considered normal. *It's a whole other world*, she thought, and looked at Burwardsley as he bummed another cigarette from Hansen. Alice was by his side, swapping glances with the young Sirius man. Burwardsley turned and caught Fenna's eye, and that connection, however brief, grounded her in that other world, the one so far removed from Andersen's.

"I don't expect you to understand," she said, her focus still on Burwardsley. "But I do need your help."

"To kill a man?"

"Oh, I don't think he will send just one."

"Jesus," Andersen said. He ran a hand through his long, greasy hair, so matted and twisted from the trail that the division between his hair and his beard was indistinguishable. Fenna looked at him as he tried to process what she had told him. He laughed, suddenly, just as the neighbours stopped singing and found another CD for the stereo. Andersen coughed, nodded once, and said, "Of course, it's all a joke, right? A story?"

"Sure," Fenna said, and smiled as she recognised one of Alice's words slipping into her vocabulary. "It's all a joke."

"And the stuff about Mikael? What really happened on the ice? That's a joke too?"

"No, that's real enough, but you'll never see it written, or hear it said in public." She held the bottle of beer at the mouth and tapped the base on the floor. "Only a few people know. And most of them are dead," she added, in a whisper.

"Well," Andersen said, as he stood up, "true or not, the story is worth a lift to Qaarsut. I'll have to put your names on the manifest, but the pilot owes me a favour. We just have to have things in order, especially as we're flying over Thule Base."

"But not stopping? Right?" Fenna said and looked up. Andersen towered above her. He and Burwardsley were the same height, she realised.

"We'll fly to Upernavik. Touch down, and then on to Qaarsut. We'll only stop in Thule if there's…"

"Bad weather. I know." Fenna looked out of the window, scanned the clouds and then looked at Alice. *She looks happy*, she thought, laughing at something Hansen said. Burwardsley came in and closed the door behind him.

"Three's a crowd, and all that," he said and smiled at Fenna.

"*Ja*," said Andersen. "They'll be talking all night, but I need my bed," he said and yawned. "You'll see yourselves out?"

"Yes," Fenna said, as the bitch stirred beside her. "Thanks, Noa."

"My pleasure. Of course," he said and looked at Burwardsley, "we'll be sharing the plane with the dogs."

"I figured that," he said. "Just glad for the lift."

"*Ja*," Andersen said. He walked to the bedroom door, paused, and turned around. "What about the Inuit guy? Where is he? Has he got family in Qaanaaq?"

"Something like that," Fenna said. "He'll be staying here."

"Fair enough. Goodnight."

Andersen walked into the bedroom and closed

the door. Burwardsley pulled out a chair and sat at the table. Fenna got up off the floor and joined him.

"Everything alright, love?" he said.

"Everything is fine."

"You got us on the plane."

"Yes."

Burwardsley lowered his voice. "Tell him anything interesting?"

"A little," Fenna said, and then shook her head. "Not about you though," she breathed.

He nodded and rooted through the open cans and bottles of beer for one last mouthful. He gave up and plucked Fenna's bottle from her hand. "Thanks, Konstabel," he said, and finished her beer.

"You're quieter than earlier," she said. "Pills worn off?"

"Yep, that and jetlag. I'm tired," he said.

"We haven't stopped since, Nuuk."

"Nope."

Fenna's chair creaked as she leaned back. She looked around the walls. They were bare, stained with cigarette smoke, faded by the long low sun of summer. Alice giggled, and Fenna turned to look, just as the young Sirius man made his move. She watched as they kissed, as Alice curled her hand around Hansen's neck and pulled him close. *What would he think*, she wondered, *if he knew he was kissing the woman who killed the President of the United States of America?* Fenna smiled. She looked at Burwardsley and laughed.

"What?"

"It's all so surreal."

"Yep," he said.

Fenna rapped her knuckle on the table. "Let's go

for a walk," she said. "See the sights."

"Sights? This town is an armpit, Konstabel."

"Surrounded by glaciers, with the ice sheet just up there." Fenna pointed toward the front door.

"I'm not walking up the bloody mountain, just to see the ice sheet. I've seen enough ice for a lifetime."

"Fine. We'll walk down to the beach," she said, and stood up.

Burwardsley put the bottle down on the table and nodded at Alice. "We're just going to leave her here?"

"Let her have some fun," Fenna said.

Burwardsley grunted and followed Fenna to the front door. The dogs tugged at the chain as they shut the door behind them, fidgeting and wagging their tails as Fenna made a point of fussing over each of them. Burwardsley shook his head, "I haven't got all night, Konstabel."

"Yes, you have," she said, and nodded at the sun low in the sky.

"Smart arse," he said and started walking along the length of chain link fence that separated the front yard of each house in the row. Children tramped along the bitumen roofs of the wooden siding insulating the water pipes above the ground. They chattered and waved at Fenna, before chasing each other down the street.

"It's almost two o'clock in the morning," Burwardsley said. "What are they doing up?"

"They're playing."

"They should be in bed."

"Why?"

"Because…" He stopped and shrugged. "What do I know, eh? Not my culture. Not my kids."

"Exactly," Fenna said.

They walked down the main street, past the store, painted red, and the bar, spilling drunks onto the dirt. The tide was out and the fishing dinghies and small skiffs were stranded on the sand between sharp boulders of ice. Fenna explored the *qajaq*s on the wooden rack, as Burwardsley picked his way between the boats, leaning against one closest to the sea. Fenna watched as he pressed a hand to his side and checked for blood.

"Does it hurt?"

"It's sore."

"What about your thigh?"

"That's just stiff. You did a good job sewing it up."

"It was Alice."

"That's right, now I remember."

A raven cawed above them, settling on the beach to pick at a rotten seal carcass. Fenna watched as the raven tore at the flesh, tugging at it with its beak. Now she had seen the carcass, the smell reached her nose, the smell of death.

"We're still going through with this?" Burwardsley asked.

"Yes."

"Good," he said.

Fenna thought about the evangelists, wondered where they were, what they were doing, or planning. *Bringing God to the godless*, she mused, *in this godforsaken land*. But in truth, despite the harshness of it, the extremes of winter and summer, Greenland was as close to God as she imagined any country to be. There was little to distract the people from their belief, their faith, no interference, just a very thin and fragile boundary between life and death. *Death*.

"You're thinking, Konstabel. I can hear you."

"Yes."

"Well? What about?"

"Death," she said.

"We all have to die sometime," Burwardsley said. "Hell, I feel pretty lucky to have gotten this far, all things considered. This past week…"

"Yes," Fenna said. "This past week…"

Burwardsley pushed off the boat and stood up. The raven cawed and flapped a couple of metres along the beach, before stalking back to the carcass.

"Are you ready to die, Konstabel?"

"Yes."

"Then let's get on with it."

Burwardsley rapped the hull of the boat with his knuckle, and starting walking back up the hill. Fenna waited a moment longer, staring at *Politiken's Glacier* on the other side of the fjord. She stifled a yawn, turned her back on the sea, and followed Burwardsley up the hill.

"It's time," she said.

Chapter 20

All but six seats had been removed from the interior of Nordlandair's de Havilland Canada DHC-6 Twin Otter. Fenna recognised the cramped interior as an older airframe with a new livery. *Lucifer bit me in this old bird*, she remembered as she grabbed the collars of each dog in turn and lifted them into the aircraft. Andersen and Hansen secured the dogs, relying on a passive temperament and a warm cabin temperature to pacify the sledge dogs from Qaanaaq. Burwardsley made a point of teasing Alice as they watched Hansen bumble around the Twin Otter's interior, only to spur into action each time Andersen barked an order in his direction. Alice blushed, tugging the collar of the young *fup*'s jacket up to her cheeks and peering over the greasy stitching.

They loaded the aircraft within an hour of it landing. As Andersen closed the door on the dogs and Hansen, the pilot did a visual check of the aircraft while Fenna waved at the policeman. He nodded for her to step to one side so they could talk.

"Your Inuit friend has been asking about you," he said. "I can't hold him much longer, unless you press charges."

"Okay."

"Do you want to press charges?"

"That depends. Can you give us time to get airborne?"

"*Aap.*"

"And when's the next regular flight out of Qaanaaq?"

"Wednesday."

"Then I don't need to press charges."

"Good," Akisooq said. The first of the Twin Otter's engines fired, and he looked around Fenna's shoulder, as Andersen helped Alice climb onboard. "Your passports are in order," he said, "but I could keep you here for all kinds of reasons." Fenna waited for him to continue. "Do you understand?"

"Yes."

"The thing is," he said, as he rested his hands on his belt, "we have a mutual friend."

"Maratse," Fenna said.

"*Aap.* We studied together at the police academy in Nuuk, several years ago."

Fenna saw a spark light up the policeman's eyes, and she wondered just how much hell they had raised in class, and on the weekends. Akisooq disclosed nothing, and Fenna was left with the hope that one day she might be able to ask Maratse, to tease him about his days as a cadet.

"He told me about what happened in Uummannaq, about Dina," Akisooq said. "Are you sure you want to go back there?"

"I don't have much choice. We need to finish this," she said, "for Dina, for Alice…" Fenna glanced at the Twin Otter as the pilot started the second engine. Andersen waved for her to hurry.

"But what about you? Will *finishing this* bring you peace?"

Fenna shrugged, "One way or the other."

"Then go," Akisooq said. He looked up at the sky. It was a brilliant blue, with just a few cirrus clouds and mare's tails, above the Twin Otter's preferred flying altitude. "If you leave now, you should pass Thule without any problems."

"Thank you," Fenna said, and shook the

policeman's hand. She whispered in his ear before letting go, "Sorry about your living room."

"I didn't like the table anyway," he said. "Good luck, Konstabel."

"Thank you." Fenna turned toward the aircraft, but Akisooq caught her arm.

"I can probably have your Inuit friend deported."

"Thank you."

"You're welcome, but remember, whatever part he has to play in this – and, really, I don't want to know – it is personal now. You made it so when you cut up his face."

Fenna bit her lip. Andersen shouted from the aircraft. She looked at Akisooq one last time, turned, and jogged to the Twin Otter, grabbing Andersen's outstretched arm as she reached the cabin door. He pulled her inside, secured the door, and pointed at an empty seat next to the window. Fenna sat down and closed her eyes, picturing the ragged mess of skin Yuka now wore as a permanent reminder of her. *Great. Just one more man determined to get even.* The word *driven*, came to mind, and she regretted the fact everything always became personal. She almost laughed, for what was more personal than her own need for vengeance?

The pilot turned the Twin Otter in a tight circle, taxied on huge tundra wheels a short distance from the airport building, before accelerating down the gravel runway, pulling back on the stick, and guiding the small aircraft into the blue sky above Greenland's most northerly village. There was a smaller settlement fifty kilometres or so to the north and west, but Fenna had never been there. She took a last look at Herbert Island before closing her eyes once more, making herself comfortable, and succumbing to the stuffy, doggy interior of the cabin. Andersen said it would take a couple of hours to reach Upernavik, she would sleep until then.

Fenna didn't wake up until the pilot bumped the Twin Otter onto the asphalt runway on the island of Upernavik. She opened her eyes just as Andersen stirred in the seat opposite her. Fenna looked over her seat to see Alice curled onto Hansen's shoulder, and Burwardsley, doing his best to ignore them. He looked like he was the only one who hadn't slept. The pilot shut down the engines and clambered out of the cockpit. He shoved a dog to one side with his boot and stepped inside the cabin.

"We have an hour," he said, his Danish laced with Icelandic roots. He pointed at the aircraft building. It was quiet, with only a few ground personnel waiting to receive them. "There's coffee inside." He stepped over the dogs and opened the cabin door. "Make sure they piss," he said, and hopped out onto the apron.

"Pee break," Andersen said. "Everyone grab a dog."

The dog at Fenna's feet growled and she cuffed it on the nose. There was not enough space for a dogfight. *Finish it before it gets started*, she thought, smiling at the idea that it was a pretty good mantra, one she might consider adopting. Burwardsley grunted something about hating dogs, as he stumbled over a large male fidgeting in the tiny aisle between the seats. The cool air from outside had woken them up, and the cabin began to fill with whines and growls. Alice stirred as Andersen leaned over her to

209

thump his partner awake.

"Wake up, Romeo," he said. Hansen stirred and Andersen squashed Alice as he tugged at the *fup*'s beard. "There's work to be done." He grinned at Alice as he backed into the aisle and arranged with Fenna which dogs should pee first.

Fenna walked two dogs on short leads to the flat area overlooking the sea. The top of the mountain on Upernavik island had been blasted flat to build the runway. The Danes living on Upernavik had dubbed the island the aircraft carrier. Seen from the air, it was easy to understand why. Fenna was less interested in the island, and far more occupied by the sight of pancake ice clustering around the island's rocky coastline. It did feel colder, and she had once seen snow in September. But she was still surprised. *Already?* Even if the ice began to form, the wind would determine its reach, and how quickly it would settle. Experienced hunters were known to sledge across newly formed ice barely a few centimetres thick, only to have to wait another week or month after a period of autumn winds broke up the ice, and grounded the dogs. The autumn and winter storms also tended to wreak havoc on the sea ice, but deeper in the fjords, even in this period of global warming, it was not unheard of for ice to form in more sheltered areas earlier than expected. *I wonder*, she thought.

"You're thinking of ice," Andersen said, as he approached. "I can tell."

"It's colder, isn't it? You can feel it."

"*Ja*, but it's probably just a freak cold spell. I wouldn't get your hopes up."

"Wasn't the winter of 2008 a good one? I thought they told us that in training."

"I remember it pissed a lot of journalists off," he said. "Something about wanting to record climate change in progress, but all the locals wanted to do was get out and hunt."

"Maybe this winter will be a good one."

"Planning to get out on the ice, Konstabel?"

Fenna didn't answer. She took a last look at ice crusting the rocks below her, and walked back to the aircraft. The pilot was already there, sipping coffee as he watched Alice help Hansen with the dogs. Fenna waited for Andersen to catch up, and they loaded the last dogs before climbing into the cabin. Burwardsley was already seated, slumped as he was with his chin on his chest. *His turn to sleep*, Fenna thought, as she buckled into her seat. Andersen closed the door as the pilot talked to the tower. They took off just five minutes later.

Fenna swapped places with Andersen so she could look at the snow-clad cirque glaciers of the Svartenhuk Peninsula to the north of Uummannaq fjord. The dark bands of exposed granite in stark contrast to the snow and ice leaped out at her, and Fenna pressed her nose to the glass. She heard Andersen laugh over the drone of the propellers. She turned and said, "What?"

"You," he said, "you're like a kid in a toy shop."

Fenna flicked him the finger and turned back to the window. There were muskoxen down there, one of the nine areas in Greenland where they could be hunted and harvested. She lifted her nose from the glass and warmed it with her hand. Then the Twin Otter began to descend and Fenna's stomach began to churn. Her fascination with the glaciers and the wildlife surviving in the harsh arctic environment below would have to wait; it was her own survival that was at stake now. She thought about the phone call she was about to make, and the actors and elements that call would set in motion, all the way into their approach to Qaarsut airport. Fenna barely felt the wheels bump down on the gravel runway. She almost didn't react when the pilot parked the aircraft and shut down the engines. It was Burwardsley's hand on her shoulder that startled her into action. She looked up and realised they were alone in the aircraft, the Sirius men and Alice were walking the dogs.

"You alright, love?" Burwardsley said.

"I think so."

"Okay," he said, but the frown on his brow suggested he wasn't sure. This was the fjord they had sailed into on *The Ice Star*, and just thirty kilometres from here was the cabin where Dina had killed herself. Burwardsley sat on the edge of the seat opposite Fenna and waited for her to speak.

Fenna began to nod, slowly, rhythmically, as she processed the next steps. "We'll need a boat to get into the fjord. I'm not waiting for a helicopter."

"I'll find us a boat."

"Maybe call in at Uummannaq first, get some supplies."

"I'll make a list."

"Right," Fenna said. She unbuckled her belt and clenched her fists on top of her knees. She looked at Burwardsley and said, "I'll find a phone. I'll make the call."

Fenna stood up and climbed out of the cabin. She ignored Andersen's shouts, and the concerned look on Alice's face. Fenna walked to the airport building, past the patches of early snow on the

212

ground, opened the door, and looked for a phone. There was an old payphone on the wall, and she searched in her pockets for change. She looked at the five, ten, and twenty kroner coins in her palm, and figured she had enough for a few minutes. *Plenty of time to arrange my death*. Fenna picked up the phone, pressed the coins into the slot, and dialled the number she had written on a slip of paper tucked into her passport.

The line buzzed with static and the long rumble of cycling digits before a ringtone sounded in her ear. The voice that answered was distant, but no less destructive. Fenna's stomach cramped when he said, "Hello."

"It's me," she said, and waited.

"I see." Fenna heard movement in the background, as if the man she was talking to was moving to a more private location, or just making himself comfortable. "I've been expecting your call."

"Yes."

"Any problems?"

"No."

"And everyone is with you?"

"Yes," she said, and pressed more coins into the slot. The grip the man's voice had on her stomach tightened as each coin fell.

"You are in Greenland? I assume that is why you are calling."

"Yes."

"And you want to know who to contact?" he said and paused. "Do you have a pen, Konstabel?"

"No. Just tell me."

"Very well." More muffled noises, and a beep on the line, as if he muted her for a moment. When he spoke again, the man's voice was clearer, but there was another sound on the line. Fenna didn't think they were alone. "You need to get to the settlement of Nuugaatsiaq. It's the most northerly settlement in the fjord."

"I know that."

"Ask for the shaman. I honestly can't pronounce his name, so I won't try."

Fenna said nothing, aware only that someone was standing next to her, but too intent on the man at the other end of the line to look. *It's Burwardsley*, she told herself. *And he's probably found a boat already*. But there was one more pressing detail to have in place, and she wasn't going to hang up before she heard the man say it.

"Vestergaard?" she said, at last.

"Yes, Konstabel?"

"You'll be there, won't you?"

She waited for his answer. The cramps in her stomach were gone, just as Burwardsley, standing right behind her, was as good as gone. It was as if nobody else could exist in that moment, everything hinged on the answer, whether he was telling the truth, or just stringing her along, Vestergaard's answer would define her next move, perhaps even her last. She could taste it, the end, the moment when one or the other of them – perhaps even both at the same time – pulled the trigger, plunged the knife, wrapped bloody fingers around one another's throats. It didn't matter how, it just had to end, and she had to know that the end was coming. She had to hear it, taste it, believe it, and so, she waited.

The phone began to beep as the credit for the call expired. Fenna pressed the receiver closer to her ear, clapped her hand on her other ear, took a step closer to the payphone, and stared – she stared through the wall, picturing Vestergaard – standing, sitting, it didn't matter – she saw him take a breath, open his mouth, move his lips, and then she heard the words.

"Yes, Konstabel. I'll be there. You can count on it."

The line went dead, and Fenna started to tremble. Burwardsley put his hand on her shoulder. He tugged the phone gently from her hand, turned her body toward him, and gripped her shoulders in his hands.

"Fenna?"

She looked up. "He's coming," she said.

The Icefjord

UUMMANNAQ FJORD, GREENLAND

Chapter 21

NUUGAATSIAQ, UUMMANNAQ FJORD, GREENLAND

The fisherman driving the boat smoked a cigarette as they sailed toward the settlement of Nuugaatsiaq. They hugged the coastline, close enough to reach it in an emergency, but not so close they might be swamped with waves reflecting off the rocks from a calving iceberg. Burwardsley chatted with Alice, the driver stared straight ahead, and Fenna zipped her jacket all the way to the top of the stiff collar. She always seemed to be caught out by the cold at sea, as if her knowledge of cold weather clothing was limited to the land. *And yet the sea is an extension of the land when it freezes*, she thought. Further thoughts of sledging, the dogs that Noa and his partner had bought for Sirius, and the training runs along the east coast beaches, occupied her for another few minutes until the hull of the boat clunked against ice debris. Fenna peered over the side as the fisherman eased back on the throttle. It wasn't debris from an iceberg, she realised, but softer pancakes of ice clumping in sheets across the flat surface of the sea. Each pancake was clear in the centre, and white at the edges, as if the sugar frosting had been spread to the sides. Fenna caught the fisherman's eye and nodded at the ice.

"What do you think?" she asked in Danish. "Is winter coming early this year?"

"*Imaqa*," he said. "Maybe." He flicked the butt of his cigarette into the water and increased the throttle with a turn of his wrist. The bow of the boat lifted gently like a mini-icebreaker, pressing the hull down on the ice and ploughing a path to the settlement.

"What's up?" Burwardsley said.

"Nothing," Fenna said. "Just the ice. It's forming early."

"It's also colder than I remember this time of year."

"An anomaly."

"No, just cold." Burwardsley shifted on the bench seat stretched across the centre of the small vessel. He made room for Fenna to one side, Alice sat on the other. "Best I sit in the middle I think, love."

A glance at Alice revealed the young woman's delight at sailing between icebergs. She remembered the time she saw icebergs for the first time, and felt a pang of longing, wishing that this was her first time too, and that the circumstances were different.

"You said he was coming?" Burwardsley said.

"What? Oh, yes I did."

"And what do you intend to do when he arrives?"

"That all depends on when," Fenna said and studied the coastline. She could see the brightly-painted houses and buildings of Nuugaatsiaq in the distance, and the deep tongue of the fjord stretching toward the glaciers calving into the sea to the right of the settlement.

"When?"

"If the ice does form early, even just a thin layer, I'll lead him away from the settlement."

"Just like that?"

"Yes."

Burwardsley scoffed and shook his head. "And what happens if that doesn't work?"

"That's where you come in."

"Me?"

"I need you to plan our last stand."

"There?" Burwardsley said and pointed at the settlement as they approached it. "Christ, Fenna, we've got no weapons to speak of, and we can't exactly make a stand inside any of the buildings – they're all made of wood."

"We'll find weapons."

"Really? Where?"

Fenna looked around the boat, slapping Burwardsley's knee when she spotted a hunting rifle nestled between ropes and fishing lines in the bow of the boat. "That's a .30-06," she said. "I bet there's at least one rifle in every boat and another in every house on the island. There'll be ammunition in the store, maybe even a shotgun or two to buy."

"Vestergaard and his men will have automatic weapons. You want us to make a stand with a bunch of rusted saloon rifles and the odd high calibre rifle?"

"Yes," Fenna said and pointed toward the mountains on the island as the fisherman throttled down in anticipation of beaching the boat on the narrow strip of sand in front of the schoolhouse. The ice was thicker near the shore, slowing the boat, and forcing the fisherman to pick his route carefully, following the channel ploughed by the locals. Fenna pointed again and said, "There's plenty of high ground, and good cover if it comes to that. We can draw Vestergaard away from the village and pick him and his men off as they climb after us."

"And if they have a helicopter, Fenna? What then?"

She shrugged. "We'll think of something." Any further discussion was cut short as the boat bumped onto the beach and two Greenlanders walked down

219

to the water to steady the boat as they climbed over the side and unloaded their gear. Fenna spotted an older Greenlander wearing a cornflower-blue smock and thick cotton trousers. He watched them from where he waited beside the schoolhouse. She risked a wave and was rewarded with a smile.

"Do you know him?" asked Alice as she took her holdall from the fisherman. She thanked the Greenlanders as they took it from her and carried it up the beach.

"No, but I have an idea that he has been waiting for us."

"He has been waiting a long time," said the taller of the two Greenlanders. He smiled at Alice as he introduced himself to her and Burwardsley. "My name is Inuuteq, and that man is my father, Tulugaq."

"Tulu...?" said Alice. The name caught upon her tongue and Inuuteq laughed.

"It means raven," he said. "My father is a shaman, if you believe in such things."

Fenna looked at Tulugaq, as his son continued chatting with Alice. She might have been impressed by his English language skills, had it not been for the fact that Inuuteq's father was the shaman, and suddenly everything was coming full-circle. "Right before the end," she whispered.

"...and this is Fenna," Burwardsley said, punching her on the arm, as he introduced her to Inuuteq. "Come on, love, be polite."

"What?" Fenna frowned as Inuuteq clasped her hand. He let go just as quickly, waving at his father and beckoning him onto the beach. Burwardsley paid the fisherman and helped him push the boat back into the water. Fenna did nothing, said nothing, just watched the shaman approach and waited for him to speak. When he did, it was in Greenlandic. She shook her head, and he switched to English.

"I am not so good as my son. Only enough to sell things to tourists," he said.

"What about Danish?"

"Better."

"Good," Fenna said, "because my Greenlandic is terrible."

Tulugaq smiled, and Fenna caught the twinkle in his eye as the late summer sun reflected on the ice crowding the bay. For a brief moment Fenna thought she saw something else reflected in the old man's eyes, *a sadness*, she thought, only for it to disappear as he led them up the beach, past the schoolhouse, and onto the path leading to the store. The shaman's house was opposite the store, looking out onto another beach on the north-western side of the island. A bony finger of rock stretching from the island into the sea provided a natural but low wall protecting the beach in front of the schoolhouse.

The shaman led them between fishing boats and broad sledges, and it wasn't long before they were surrounded by sledge dog puppies of all sizes. The smaller ones tumbled between the legs of those just a few weeks from being put on a chain. Alice bent down to tickle the pups and was bumped to the ground by three of the larger dogs. She laughed as she fell, protesting that she was okay as Inuuteq scared the pups away and helped her to her feet.

"We can't take her anywhere," Burwardsley whispered to Fenna.

"No," she said, as she caught the look in Inuuteq's eyes as he brushed the worst of the dirt from Alice's jacket. *We really can't*, she thought as the young man suddenly realised he was touching parts of the young American that he probably shouldn't. He pulled his hand away, hiding the colour in his cheeks with a few quick commands in Greenlandic aimed at the dogs. Alice forced more colour into the Greenlander's face with a smile, and he was lost. Fenna saved him with a few questions about the dogs. "They look well fed," she said.

"Yes," he said. "You won't find any skinny dogs on the island." He nodded at the ice lapping the beach in crusts of varying thickness. "We might get the first ice a few weeks from now, if the temperature continues to fall."

"What about the wind?"

"We're a bit more sheltered here," Inuuteq said, as he picked up Alice's holdall. "The ice forms deeper in the fjord, and it can stretch all the way here if the conditions are right."

"This early in the year?"

"It is September," he said. "If we are lucky, we might have ice in the fjord by October, and a thin layer surrounding the island."

"October," Fenna said. She looked at Burwardsley, and hoped that Vestergaard would take his time to get here. *Maybe the shaman knows?* she thought, as they walked to the house.

Fenna was the last to enter. Tulugaq ushered them past the tupilaq on the shelves in the kitchen. Alice lingered beside one carved figure in particular, hiding an embarrassed laugh behind her hand as Inuuteq commented that the figure was a self-portrait. Fenna waited in the kitchen as the others sat down in the living room. She was alone with the shaman in the kitchen, as he poured water from the plastic container into a pan and put it on the stove to boil.

"We collect our water from the tank," he said, "but the house has electricity from the generator."

"One generator powers all the houses?"

"Easily, but," he said and shrugged, "sometimes it breaks down."

Fenna watched as he wiped the lips of dirty mugs with a tea towel. She heard Inuuteq and Burwardsley swapping stories about travelling in Greenland, together with a laugh or two from Alice, as the Greenlander said something funny or mispronounced a word. She corrected him, gently, and they laughed again.

"He studied in America," Tulugaq said. "An exchange."

"That must have been expensive," Fenna said.

The shaman wiped the last mug and nodded at the tupilaq on the shelves. "How many do you see?"

"Nine," Fenna said, after a quick count.

"There were forty more before the last cruise ship came."

"You nearly sold out?"

"*Aap*," he said. "And this year was the worst of the last three years."

"So, you paid for Inuuteq's exchange by selling carved figures?"

"With help from a government grant. What I have left, I send to my wife in Nuuk."

Tulugaq stopped talking as the water boiled. He made tea in one big pot, and pointed at the bowl of sugar cubes on the counter beside the mugs. Fenna carried them into the living room, and smiled as Inuuteq taught Alice how to take her sugar in tea in

Greenland, pinching the cubes between finger and thumb, before dipping them in the tea and popping them in the mouth.

Fenna waited until they were all quiet before speaking in English. "You were expecting us, weren't you?"

"*Aap*," Tulugaq said. He looked at Inuuteq and the young man nodded.

"My father asked me to explain," he said. Inuuteq put down his tea and folded his hands in his lap. "First, he wants you to know that you are welcome in this house. All of you," he said, looking at each of them in turn. "But especially you, Konstabel Fenna Brongaard. My father was told you would be coming, and he has been looking forward to your arrival."

"The sea told me when you would arrive," Tulugaq said. "It tells me many things, so long as I keep her happy."

"*Sassuma Arnaanut*," said Inuuteq. "The mother of the sea."

"Sedna," said Alice, as she sipped her tea.

Inuuteq nodded, and continued. "My father also wants you to know that you are in grave danger, and that you are not safe here." He paused as Tulugaq stood up and walked to his desk by the window. Fenna watched as he pulled a figure from the drawer. He sat down, the figure half hidden between his fingers. Fenna stared at it, almost drawn to it, as Inuuteq spoke again. "There is a Danish man who wishes for you to be killed – all of you – and he has arranged for that to happen."

"It's alright," said Burwardsley. "We know. In fact, that's why we're here."

"Yes," Inuuteq said, "we know you know, but

you cannot possibly beat this man. You cannot possibly survive. He has many resources, and once he knows you are here, he will come."

"We're counting on it," said Fenna.

"Yes, I know," Inuuteq said. Fenna caught the urgency in his voice and pulled away from the figure to look at him. "But you cannot win."

"The plan is not to win," she said, "but not everyone has to die." She shrugged. "Just him. Just Vestergaard."

"But how will you do this?" Inuuteq frowned. "I have seen this man. He has bodyguards with automatic weapons, and probably a whole army."

"Probably," said Burwardsley. "Is there more tea?"

"More tea?"

Fenna laughed, and said, "Don't mind him, he's British." She felt the pull of the figure in the shaman's hands and focused on it, as Inuuteq sighed and said something in Greenlandic.

"My son does not understand," said Tulugaq. He spoke in English, the words slow, cumbersome, but clear. "He thinks you have come here looking for somewhere to hide."

"You know different," said Fenna.

"*Aap*," he said. "You came here to wait."

"Yes."

"You are waiting for him."

"And whoever he brings with him," said Burwardsley.

The shaman smiled. He looked at Alice and said, "My son knows where it is safe on the island. When the time comes he will take you there."

"Thank you," she said and looked at Fenna, "but

I will stay with my friends."

"*Imaqa*," said Tulugaq. "Maybe. But I think it would be best to hide." He looked at Fenna, uncurling the fingers of his hands as he spoke. "And what about you? Will you hide?"

"No, I will fight."

"Then you will need this."

Tulugaq revealed the crude bone figure in his hands. Roughly ten centimetres tall, it was bound in the shape of a woman. The legs and arms were made of bone, held in place by lengths of grass stems and a single strand of orange plastic fishing line. The figure had small shells for breasts, a crude bone-carved face, and a brush of black hair tacked into its skull with two slim slivers of metal bent at right angles. Fenna didn't need the shaman to tell her – she knew the figure was carved in her likeness. There was only one thing that she couldn't explain.

"You are wondering if it is your hair," Tulugaq said.

"Yes."

"It is yours. The man you call Vestergaard gave it to me."

"What do you call him?"

"*The Magician*," Tulugaq said, and laughed. "But his magic is not as powerful as mine. It has no soul." He reached out to give Fenna the tupilaq.

"But yours does?"

"Yes," he said, pulling the figure back as Fenna reached for it, "if you believe in such things."

"I might," she said. Fenna wrinkled her nose at the smell of the figure. It was rank like rotten seaweed, with something deeper, an odour that was dark like the earth, like powdered brimstone mixed with old leaves. It smelled of ancient magic, unrefined, wild like the sea. *Wild like me*, she thought.

"This is a tupilaq. A real one. The Magician asked me to make one to use against you. I was to throw it in the sea, to turn *Sassuma Arnaanut* against you, but I could not. This man is evil, and I could not turn such a thing loose without meeting you. Without knowing you. This then is my gift to you. Part of you is bound to it, as is my magic, and if you take it, it will make you strong. Do you believe me?"

"Yes," Fenna said, amazed that she did.

"Then take it. You will need it."

Fenna took the figure from the shaman's hand, cursing under her breath as she tried to explain the tingling in her fingers. *Adrenaline*, she thought, *that's all it is*. But there was something deeper, something buried beneath the smell, and the touch of the tupilaq. It was as if some earthly magic from the roots of Greenland was twisted within the fibres and bones of the figure and was now seeping into her fingers. She looked up as Burwardsley clamped his hand on her shoulder.

"That's enough magic for one day, love." Burwardsley let go as Fenna stood up. She slipped the tupilaq into her pocket, and whispered thank you to the shaman.

"Okay," she said. "I'm ready."

"Good," said Burwardsley, "because now we've got to turn this village into a death trap."

227

Chapter 22

Fenna closed her hand around the tupilaq in her pocket. The grass, hair, and fishing line tickled her palm, as she stood on the beach and breathed in the scent of the ice-choked sea. Chunks of ice from calving icebergs bobbed in a broad swathe of white, arced like the path of a scimitar's swing, and grinding against the curve of rock breaching the water's surface. Fenna wondered what would happen if she was to toss the tupilaq into the sea. Would Sedna rise against her? Would the ice weaken beneath the runners of her sledge? She let go of the tupilaq and pushed the thought from her mind. *Sedna can wait*, she decided. *There are other things to take care of.* She took her hands out of her pockets, felt the tiny hairs on her skin begin to prickle in the cool wind, and nodded to Burwardsley that she was ready. He was waiting further along the beach, chatting with a hunter, admiring the rifle in the man's hands.

"Fenna," he said, as she approached, "this is Svend. I am going to buy his rifle."

"Hi," Fenna said, and smiled. The hunter raised his eyebrows. "How much?"

"We were just getting to that, but I don't speak Danish." Burwardsley leaned in close and whispered, "We can't buy all the rifles in the settlement, and I've already spent what cash we had left on the 12 gauges from the store. See if we can do a deal — we borrow the rifle, and he keeps the shotguns once we're done."

"Once we're done?"

Burwardsley shrugged and said, "Yeah, done. I didn't want to say dead."

"But you were thinking it…"

"Come on, love, just make the deal." Burwardsley took a step back and let Fenna finish negotiating. He leaned against an upturned boat and surveyed the row of houses along the shoreline. The wooden houses were barely two deep, with the majority clustered around the store near the shaman's house built on the thick finger of land pushing out into the fjord. Fenna completed the deal with the hunter, thanking him as he pressed the rifle into her hands together with a box of 7.62 ammunition.

"We're borrowing it," she said, and laid the rifle on the boat's hull. She gave Burwardsley the box of ammunition and pointed at the dogs chained just above the beach. "He has a team I can borrow too."

"And how much did that cost us?"

"The other shotgun."

"Fair enough," Burwardsley said and looked out at the fjord. "You really think the ice will come early?"

"I don't know, but the signs are here. There's a nip in the air, little wind. We might be lucky."

"Maybe."

Fenna waited for a moment before pulling Burwardsley away from the boat. "Come on. Let's go have a look at the dogs."

Burwardsley picked up the rifle and followed Fenna along the beach. They climbed up the embankment, picked their way around the lumps of shit between stumps of grass and approached the team of sledge dogs.

"I'll wait here," Burwardsley said, and sat on a weathered crate. The side of the crate had been removed and two fat puppies were snoring inside. They fidgeted as the crate creaked under

Burwardsley's weight, rolled over, and ignored him. Fenna stepped inside the circle of the first pair of dogs, their chains running long and free from a metal swivel wedged into a hole bored in the rock.

"Down," Fenna said, cuffing them on the nose and pushing them down onto the ground as they jumped up to greet her. She grabbed one by the collar, lifted her leg over its back and clamped the dog's body between her knees. She inspected the dog's paws, teeth, pinched the skin on its flank to see how well hydrated it was, nodding as the skin flashed back into position. *This hunter looks after his dogs*, she thought. Fenna looked up and saw the hunter drinking coffee on the deck outside his house. He waved and she waved back before releasing the dog and checking its partner.

"Well?" Burwardsley said, after Fenna had checked the ten dogs chained outside the hunter's house. She ignored the puppies, brushing them away with soft sweeps of her foot.

"They're in good condition. A little thin, but that's to be expected after the summer."

"And the sledge?" Burwardsley said and nodded at three sledges stacked one on top of the other, the largest at the bottom.

"The one in the middle looks lightest," Fenna said, as she walked over to them. "Metal runners, tight bindings," she said and plucked at the cord securing the thwarts. "It'll be fine." She straightened her back at the sound of footsteps on the packed earth that served as a footpath. The shaman smiled as he walked toward her, a clutch of children bobbing around his legs. The children descended on Fenna like a wave crashing onto a beach, and she was reminded of the kids in Qaanaaq, when she and Alice had tumbled with them outside the policeman's house, just before she had fought with Yuka. She paused as the image of his face, the stitches holding the flaps of skin together on his cheeks, flashed before her, only to be erased as the children tugged at her clothes and tried to drag her away from the sledges.

The shaman said a few quiet words in Greenlandic and the children let go of Fenna. They drifted away to play with the puppies, pointing and laughing at Burwardsley, as they stood on tiptoes and spread their arms to mimic his height and reach. Fenna laughed with them and the shaman took a step closer.

"You don't have children?" he said.

"No. Not yet."

"But maybe one day?"

Fenna bit her bottom lip as Burwardsley rose up from his seat on top of the crate, spread his arms and growled, chasing the children around the dog yard. They shrieked and giggled as he stumbled around the rocks, stepping over the chains, as the dogs joined in. She realised she had never seen him around children.

"I don't know," Fenna said. "I haven't had time to think about a family."

"One day, then," the shaman said. He gestured for Fenna to join him, and they walked along the path away from the chaos of kids, puppies, and one Royal Marine Lieutenant clearly out of his depth. "He will be alright," he said. "I have something to show you."

The children's cries and giggles carried on the cool wind from the fjord, pressing at Fenna's back as she followed the shaman out of the settlement. They moved on beyond the makeshift landing pad and the digger used to carry luggage and mail from the helicopter to the store. Then they climbed up a narrow path on the side of the mountain. The path wound its way up and onto a plateau beneath the steep sides of the mountain. The shaman stopped beside a cairn overlooking the settlement behind them, and the icebergs crowding the glacier just beyond the very tip of the island. Fenna held her breath at the sight of so much debris and the blue-white walls of the glacier, but it wasn't the ice the shaman wanted her to see. He took her arm and led her around the cairn to a slab of rock, Fenna could see there was a cavity beneath it.

"Take a look," the shaman said, gesturing for Fenna to crouch on the rock and peer through the crack in the surface.

Fenna kneeled on the slab and pressed her face to the crack. She saw bones resting on the earth inside, and at least one skull, maybe two. She shifted to one side to confirm that this was the resting place for more than one person.

"Our ancestors chose this place for the hunting."

"Not the view?" Fenna said and stood up.

"*Imaqa*," the shaman said and shrugged. "I don't know, but can you think of a better place to be buried?"

"No." Fenna looked at the glacier, breathed the chill of the ice deep into her lungs.

"I will die here," he said. "That is my choice. But, Konstabel, I think you should choose a different place to die."

Fenna looked at the shaman and said, "I will draw Vestergaard away from here. I won't let anything happen to the people of Nuugaatsiaq."

"That is not what I mean. The people are my responsibility," he said and pointed back to the settlement. "Do you see the red house, standing by itself, away from the village?"

"Yes."

"That is also my house. It is old, but strong. When the time comes, we will gather there."

"Okay."

"And your friend, the young woman…"

"Alice."

"*Aap*. She will come with us." The shaman laughed. "I think my son is falling in love with your friend."

Fenna smiled as she remembered the way Inuuteq had looked at Alice when they first arrived, when he had carried her bag. "Yes," she said.

"Then she will be safe. He will make sure of that."

"Thank you."

"But your other friend, the big soldier.

"Yes?"

"I think he should come here, to this place. It has a good view of the village, and it is protected from behind by the mountain. It is a good place from which to fight."

"Yes, it is," said Fenna, and she turned a slow circle to fully appreciate the shaman's eye for a good, defendable position.

"It is also a good place to die," he said. The shaman turned and walked along the path in the direction of the glacier.

"What?" Fenna said and followed him. "Do you think he will die?"

"It is not his death you should worry about, but your own." He stopped at another rise in the path, and drew an arc with his arm from one side of the glacier to the other. "You can see that the ice is forming here. The glacier has slowed for the winter, and soon it will stop. Winter has come early this year, and it will be to your advantage."

Fenna followed the shaman's direction and noticed the thicker ice trapping the smaller icebergs in front of the glacier. The larger bergs were still in motion, moving in and out of the bay on the tide. But even they were slowing as the sea thickened around them. *The early winter might be an anomaly*, she thought, *but I'll take every advantage I can get.* Fenna traced an imaginary route to the glacier wall, picturing the journey she would make with Svend's dog team. The shaman nodded, as if reading her thoughts.

"Svend's dogs are good," he said. "They are used to pulling on thin ice. Svend is the first on the ice every winter, and the last to leave."

"But the fjord is not frozen yet," Fenna said.

"You have time. I have consulted with the mother of the sea. I have read the signs. You have time."

"How much?"

"Enough," he said. The shaman began walking back to the village. Fenna took one last look at the glacier and turned to follow him.

Burwardsley was sitting beside the cairn when they reached it. The rifle was in his lap. He wiped the scope with the corner of his shirt and nodded as they approached.

"It's a good spot," he said. "Good visibility."

"*Aap*," the shaman said. He waved at Fenna as he

passed the cairn, and she let him go on to the settlement alone, choosing instead to sit beside Burwardsley.

"It's a nice view too," she said. "You've seen the glacier?"

"Hard to miss it."

"There's bones beneath the cairn," Fenna said.

"Human?"

"Yes."

Burwardsley nodded. "Yep," he said, and looked around. "There are worse places to make a last stand."

"You really think this is it?"

"Don't you? I thought that was the plan?"

"Sure, I mean…" Fenna paused. "Yes, it is the plan. Draw him here. Finish this."

"But now?"

"Now…"

Burwardsley lifted the rifle from his lap and rested it against the cairn. He took a breath. "We've been through a lot in a short space of time, Konstabel. If this is the end, then let's accept it and just get on with it. God knows, the journey here wasn't pretty. But this…" he said and looked out at the fjord, "…this is as beautiful as it gets. It's peaceful, and maybe we'll find peace here."

"You think so?"

"Why not?" he said and smirked, "Alice certainly has."

"What do you mean?"

"She's out in the bay with the shaman's son. He's showing her the sights."

"She is?"

"Yep," he said. "Although, I'm confused. I

thought she had the hots for that young Sirius fella, but what do I know…"

What do *we know?"* Fenna wondered. She remembered the shaman's words, *she will be safe*, and she sank onto the rock, letting her body sag against Burwardsley's. *We've done it*, she thought. *She's safe.*

"Mike," she said. "Does this even things out?"

"What do you mean?"

"Alice. If we save her, does that make up for Dina? Is it enough?"

Fenna trembled as Burwardsley took a deep breath and sighed. He was quiet for a long time, and Fenna didn't prompt him, focusing instead on the wind that tugged at the strands of her hair. Finally, he spoke, and Fenna closed her eyes, listening to his words as the deep bass of the syllables flooded through his body and into hers.

"It will never be enough, love, but it's a step in the right direction."

"But we tried, didn't we?"

"To save Dina?"

"Yes."

"You did," Burwardsley said. His voice drifted on the wind and he was silent for another moment. Then he said, "Bad would have liked it here. The little runt would have been up and down the mountain already."

Fenna felt her muscles tighten at the sound of the Gurkha's name, but she resisted, and willed herself to relax, enjoying instead the sight of the glacier, and the cool wind that filtered her thoughts.

"I am sorry he died," she said.

"You don't have to be," Burwardsley said. "He killed your partner after all."

"I know."

"Just as long as you don't blame him," I think he will be alright with that."

"And what about you?" Fenna said. She moved her body, turning to look at Burwardsley. She reached out for his hand, slipped her fingers within his, felt his rough skin brush against her own. "What about us?"

"I don't know, love. If I had done my job right, you'd be dead."

"Yes. I know that. But what about now?"

Burwardsley took a breath and smirked. "Let's take it one step at a time, eh? If we get off this rock – alive – then I'll be happy to say I've done my bit, and if you want to say that we're quits, I won't argue. But that's another day, Konstabel," he said and stood up, tugging his hand free of Fenna's fingers. "I want to walk to the end of the island. If you really intend to sledge to the glacier to finish this, well, maybe I can cover you, at least before you get too far from the shore."

"That all depends on the ice, but yes, let's do that."

"Of course," Burwardsley said, as he picked up the rifle. "Vestergaard might never come, and we'll be stuck on this island, just waiting."

"There are worse places to wait," Fenna said. "You said as much."

"I did. But that was before I realised the Internet was lousy, there's only one channel on the TV, and all the women are taken."

"The women?"

"No offence, Konstabel, but no matter how good you clean up…" Burwardsley grinned as Fenna clenched a fist to throw a punch, "and even if you were the last woman on the island…"

"Yes?" Fenna said, a smile playing across her lips as she positioned her feet and bent her knees, slightly – a fighting stance.

"You still smell of dog."

Fenna relaxed, smoothed her hands along the sides of her trousers and laughed. She followed Burwardsley, as they walked along the path parallel to the shoreline, identifying good defensible positions and rally points. They joked, but it was all business, *the killing business*, Fenna thought, as they passed one more boulder on a rise in the path. She glanced down at the ice brushing against the rocks below them, stopping to study a figure in a small boat. Burwardsley walked on, increasing the distance between them as Fenna studied the man in the boat, recognised the familiar cornflower-blue smock, and wondered at the shaman's actions as he beat a slow rhythm on a sealskin drum. She was surprised that she could hear the beat, and then realised that she couldn't just hear it – she could feel it. Fenna slipped her hand inside her pocket and curled her fingers around the tupilaq. She felt a surge of energy through her body and shook her head to clear her mind.

"Get it together, Fenna," she whispered.

The drum continued to beat through the hull of the boat, through the water, into the earth and up the sides of the mountain. She could feel it in her toes, thudding through her soul. She glanced at Burwardsley as he called out her name, hurrying her along the path. Fenna waved that she was coming, let go of the tupilaq, and jogged along the path to join him. The beat continued until it was lost beneath the pounding of her boots on the packed earth. Lost, but not forgotten.

Chapter 23

It was the children who saw the ship first, five weeks and one centimetre of sea ice later. The autumn storms had been mild, and the warm winds skirted the island with what Fenna imagined to be a supernatural reverence, almost as if the island was marked and somewhere to be avoided.

Life on the small Arctic island, so Fenna had come to appreciate, was a healthy mix of claustrophobia and cosiness. There were birthdays to attend, celebrated in the traditional Greenlandic *kaffemik,* where a steady stream of guests visits the house of the birthday girl or boy, man or woman, giving small presents and sitting at the savoury table of traditional Greenlandic food. Then it is time for the cake table, drinking strong black coffee before slumping on the couch with chocolates and spirits. Reluctant to let them leave, the children were quick to drag Alice and Fenna from the sofa and back to the cakes. Burwardsley was too heavy and too big to pull off the sofa, but they tried anyway, and it was during one last concerted and combined effort that the ship was spotted by one small girl, Nuka, as she skipped along the path to the *kaffemik.* Fenna caught the change of mood among the guests as she announced the arrival of the ship in Greenlandic, and one of the men left to fetch Tulugaq. Fenna pulled Alice to one side, away from the cake table.

"This is it then," she said, "you remember what we talked about."

"Yeah, but I don't agree. This is as much my fight as yours."

"Alice, stop," Fenna said. "You'll go with

239

Tulugaq and Inuuteq. You will stay in the house with the children, keep them safe, just as we agreed."

"But it's me he wants. I'm the reason he's coming here." Alice began to tremble. She looked at Burwardsley as he joined them.

"Listen to Fenna," he said. "We'll take care of the rest."

"No..." Alice started, but Burwardsley silenced her with a look.

"Christ, she thinks this is a democracy," he said and looked at Fenna. "Deal with this. I'm going to have a look outside." He brushed past the children, stepping to one side as Inuuteq clomped up the weather-beaten stairs and onto the deck before entering the house. The young Greenlander kicked the snow from his shoes and walked inside, nodding at Burwardsley as he searched for Alice.

"We have to go," he said, as he skirted around the table to take Alice's hand. She pulled back, resisting, squirming her stockinged feet onto the floor into a firmer stance, only to succumb to Fenna's hug as she wrapped her arms around her and whispered in her ear.

"Go," she said. "Do this for me. Live a long, beautiful life, raise six kids, love them so hard they melt. Do that for me. Go."

"I can't."

"Yes," Fenna said, as she smoothed her hands down Alice's arms and stepped back, "you can." She nodded at Inuuteq. "She's ready. Look after her."

"Yes," he said, and took Alice's hand.

Fenna waited until the room was empty, and the *kaffemik* was officially over. She picked her way around the chairs, grabbed her jacket, stuffed her feet inside her boots, and left the house. She found Burwardsley on the rocks above the surface of the sea ice at the far end of the settlement, past the store, beside the oil tanks. The snow crunched beneath her feet as she stepped off the worn path that led to the store entrance, and followed Burwardsley's tracks to the ice. The hunter's rifle was slung across his chest, and he was looking through a cheap pair of binoculars he had bought in the store.

Fenna took a breath of crisp air, used it to slow the adrenaline racing through her body, and looked toward the horizon. There was the ship. Red-hulled, a prominent bow, curved for the ice. The stack was white, and it could have been just another ship of the Royal Arctic Line servicing the towns, villages and settlements of Greenland. It could even have been a Canadian or American Coast Guard vessel, but Fenna knew it wasn't. She knew it was him.

She watched as the ship sailed closer. She could almost hear the soft crumpling of thin ice as it nosed its way forward, effortlessly. The ship could easily sail all the way to the island, she realised, even as far as the glacier if it wanted to. *But it won't, it's too dangerous.* Fenna looked over her shoulder at the glacier in the distance, beyond the island. She turned back to the ship at a grunt from Burwardsley.

"What is it?" she asked.

"They are stopping."

"Let me see," she said. Burwardsley handed her the binoculars and she looked through them, adjusting the focus with her fingers, aware of the cold pinching her skin.

The binoculars revealed the detail of the ship, the helicopter landing pad at the stern, but no hangar, and no sign or sound of the aircraft itself. There was activity at the rails, and, as the ship turned to starboard, the port side was exposed, and Fenna saw the crew lower a staircase and organise a small floating dock that they pushed onto the surface of the ice.

"Talk to me," said Burwardsley. Fenna heard the scratch of cotton as he stuffed his hands inside the white smock he wore on top of his thermal and fleece layers.

"The ship has stopped. The crew are getting ready to put something on the ice," she said. "Either they are concerned about getting too close to the glacier or…"

"It's a blocking action. They are sealing off the fjord."

"But then how are they going to get…" Fenna paused. She adjusted the binoculars, tried to hold her breath to stop the mist obscuring her view. "Dogs," she said. "They are putting teams onto the ice."

"Teams? How many?"

"Three sledges so far. Sleds, actually, the toboggan kind." She handed the binoculars to Burwardsley. "They are running Nome traces behind narrow sleds."

"That's great, love. Now what does it mean?" Burwardsley looked through the binoculars.

"Nome traces means they are running the dogs side by side, Alaskan style. They also have Alaskan Huskies, by the looks of it."

"Which means?"

"Mixed breed, bred for speed."

"So, fast dogs?"

"Yes, and banned in Greenland. The Greenlandic

Sledge Dog is pure bred, the closest thing to a wolf. No other dogs are allowed above the Arctic Circle or on the East Coast. This is against the law…"

"Fenna."

"Yes?"

"Focus," said Burwardsley. "Tell me what it means."

"It means they will run fast and smooth all the way to the island."

"And the good news?"

"If the ice breaks they are screwed." Fenna remembered the time Mikael had plucked her from the sea when their team, running Nome traces, had broken through a patch of thin ice. "Sirius runs with Nome traces on land, switching to fan traces on the sea ice, mostly, unless the ice is really good."

"But this ice is new and thin."

"Which means they are sacrificing safety for speed."

"I like that," Burwardsley said and lowered the binoculars. "Get your dogs ready, Konstabel. I am going to grab my gear and find a position to start picking off the leaders. Give them something to think about." He offered Fenna the binoculars. "One last look?"

"No," she said.

"Take them anyway. I have the rifle scope."

"Alright." Fenna slipped the strap around her neck and stuffed the binoculars inside her jacket. She pulled the zip to the top of the collar and looked at Burwardsley. She could feel her eyelashes crisping in the cold and chose to focus on that rather than her emotions. *Is this the last time we will see each other*, she wondered.

"Stop thinking so hard, love," Burwardsley said. He smirked and reached out to touch her hair, pinching the rime ice frosting the very ends of the strands framing her cheeks. "There was a time," he said as he let his hand fall, "when all I could think of was putting a bullet in your brain, Konstabel."

"Thanks," she said, choking on a laugh.

"It was completely professional, you understand? I was given one job, by that man." Burwardsley hiked his thumb over his shoulder in the direction of the ship. "Perhaps the instruction was from someone else, but he was the one who spelled it out. We know that. But you were so fucking stubborn. You just wouldn't die."

"You say that like it was a bad thing." Fenna smiled, but her lips flattened as she saw the look on Burwardsley's face.

"Be stubborn, Konstabel," he said. Burwardsley nodded once, tugged at the rifle sling across his chest and walked past Fenna toward the shaman's house.

"Mike," she called out, but he didn't stop. She watched him all the way to the steps of the house opposite the store, and then she turned to look at the ship. There were three black stripes on the ice, three teams, all of them moving, and moving fast.

Fenna turned and ran to the hunter's house, his dogs were howling, fidgeting, biting, raring to go, as he gripped each one between his knees and slipped a harness over its head. He bent the dogs' front legs at the elbow and slipped them through the harness. Once they were in harness he attached them to their traces, and made them ready for Fenna to attach the fan of dogs to the sledge. Fenna thanked him as she raced past the dogs and stopped at the sledge bag hanging between the uprights at the rear. She opened the envelope flap and pulled out her sledging gear, stripping on the snow behind the sledge as the hunter continued preparing the team. The dogs whined with enthusiasm, yipped and half-barked. Fenna could have been alone for all the attention anyone gave her as she peeled off her layers down to her bra, building the layers up again with a thermal top, leggings, fleece, and military trousers. She checked the contents of the cargo pockets, tightened the belt around her waist, tested the snap securing the knife in its sheath, pulled on her socks, and tightened the laces of her boots. Fenna left her jacket on the ground, favouring instead the waist-length padded canvas jacket she had seen a young mother wearing in town. She had bartered for it, and now enjoyed the snug fit around her waist and the thick ruff of dog fur the woman had sewn onto the hood. She hung the sealskins mitts – a gift from the same woman – on a length of cord around her neck, checking the rifle in its canvas holster with bare fingers. She pulled the rifle out, worked the bolt, checked the magazine, and slid it home again. The holster was secured to the right-hand upright, reminding Fenna, as it always did, of a cowboy's rifle wedged beneath the straps of his saddle. *Or hers*, she thought. *Women can fight too, and this one has too*. She fished a fleece neckie from her cargo pocket, pulled it over her head, and tugged a thin beanie over her hair. Fenna took a long breath and then brushed her fringe beneath the rim of the beanie. *I'm ready*.

Inuuteq appeared on the path, sliding along the packed snow in sealskin *kammiks*. He said something fast in Greenlandic to the hunter, and then turned to Fenna. "Burwardsley said to hurry. They are almost within range of the rifle."

"Right," Fenna said and nodded to the hunter. She was just about to release the rope anchoring the sledge to a thick hawser wrapped around a boulder, when she remembered the tupilaq. She reached down and pulled it out of the jacket laying on top of her discarded clothes. Fenna studied the tupilaq for a moment before zipping it inside one of the cavernous pockets on the front of her jacket.

"Fenna, you must go," Inuuteq said, as he helped the hunter attach the dogs to the sledge.

They all paused at the sound of the first gunshot, rallying on the second, and tugging the dogs and sledge down to the ice on the third. Fenna hoped Burwardsley was thinning the field, as the hunter dragged the lead sledge dog up and over the ice foot where the land met the sea. Inuuteq helped Fenna bump the sledge over the same icy obstacle as the dogs gathered on the ice.

"Go back to the house," Fenna said to Inuuteq. "Svend will help me with the dogs. You must look after Alice."

"What about you?"

"It's me he wants. Burwardsley and me. When the men come, they will ignore everyone else. But just make sure you keep Alice hidden. If she can't be seen, she will be safe."

"There is a space beneath the floorboards."

"Good. Use it. I will draw them away from the settlement."

Another gunshot rattled the dogs into a frenzy of excitement. Fenna pushed Inuuteq in the direction of the house, insisting that she would be fine. Then she turned her attention to the hunter as he explained for what seemed to Fenna like the hundredth time, that the ice was still too thin to stand still just beyond the island, thickening only once they got close to the glacier. Fenna knew he had tested it each day since the ice had begun to settle. She had watched him go out to set his longline from a hole dug in the ice, checking each day to brush the newly formed ice up and over the wood he had placed on each of the four sides.

"Follow my tracks," he said. "Once you are past the longline, the ice will be thicker. But beware of the icebergs, they are not settled yet."

Not settled. Fenna thought about it, remembering the bergs that were locked in the ice on the east coast, new bergs and new positions each winter. Until the temperature really dropped, there was still plenty of movement to cause an iceberg to roll, presenting Fenna with a hazardous opportunity. *If all else fails, I'll draw them close to the bergs and...*

The thought vanished at the sight of the first of the three dog teams as it slid around the corner of the island. The team had been thinned, and Fenna could see where dead dogs had been cut from their traces. Burwardsley had been busy, but he had not stopped them. She risked a glance toward the mountain, and saw the big Marine Lieutenant pounding up the path, a rifle in each hand. He would be running for the cairn, where they had cached supplies and ammunition in anticipation of Vestergaard's arrival. *And now he is here*, she thought, as she took one last look at Burwardsley.

"*Tuavi*," Svend shouted. "Hurry." He tugged at the dogs, leading them out onto the thin ice. Fenna followed, slipping the soles of her boots along the icy surface, avoiding pressing her toes downwards, keeping her feet flat, balanced, spreading her weight.

The first crack of automatic weapons fire spurred her and the team into action. She heard a cry, felt the slap of the hunter's hand on her back as she shushed past him, and then she was on the ice, leaping onto the sledge and reaching for the whip, as the dogs dug their claws into the pitted surface and followed the familiar lines left by the runners of the hunter's sledge.

The shushing sound changed to a harder, more brittle grating, as the metal runners slid along ice, clean of snow, black, almost transparent. Fenna kept her head down at the crack of gunfire. She checked that Vestergaard's sled teams were following her, and felt the familiar extra thump of her heart at the sight of her quarry. He was there, in the lead sled, riding in the bucket as two of his men skied by the side, one hand on the curved handle attached to the uprights, the other curled around the grip of a Heckler Koch MP5 submachine gun. The echo of each burst of 9mm urged Fenna's dogs to claw at the ice, fantailing the sledge and forcing Fenna to make corrections with the heels of her boots and the wooden butt of the whip. She whooped and encouraged the dogs with clicks and whistles, as the hunter did, ducking every so often at another burst of lead above her head.

"Come on, boys," Fenna yelled. "Let's go."

Fenna's team was fresh, they were following a familiar route, and the sledge was broad and light. She felt the cold pinch her cheeks and allowed herself a smile. The plan was working.

Chapter 24

Burwardsley could see Fenna from his position in front of the cairn. He watched her bump and steer the sledge onto the track leading to the hunter's fishing hole in the ice. There was one team following Fenna, and he was sure he had glimpsed Vestergaard sitting in the basket seat of the sled. That left two teams for him, the first of which he could see through the rifle scope as they left their dogs at the beach and spread out between the houses. Two teams of dogs, six men, all of whom carried MP5 submachine guns. Burwardsley recognised the sound and calibre of the weapon, the same he had trained with so many years earlier.

It's a good weapon for short range, he thought, as he wormed his body into the snow and tracked the first of the men. The trick to taking on six men armed with submachine guns with only a hunting rifle, Burwardsley realised, was to lull them into a group, to bring them closer before taking out the man at the rear. Burwardsley waited, letting the lead man climb the slope, and focusing on the third and fourth man in the group. He lifted his hand from the grip of the rifle to check the position of the shotgun. He would take the first man out with a scatter of pellets, then pick off the last of the group with the rifle. He spared another second to picture the location of the second shotgun further along the track in what he had dubbed his *last stand position*.

"If I make it that far," he whispered.

He heard the lead man slip on the slope just below him, switched the rifle for the shotgun, kneeled and fired as soon as the man's torso was in plain view.

The blast of the 12-gauge shotgun caught the man squarely in the chest, pitching him backwards over the lip of the rise. Burwardsley lunged forward to grab the sling of the man's MP5, only to miss. He was rewarded with a burst of fire over his shoulder, a single bullet of which singed his neck as it sped past him. He swore as he squirmed back into his firing position, tugged the butt of the rifle into his shoulder and searched for a target further down the slope. He saw the last of the group exposed on the open ground between the houses and the start of the incline. He tracked the man through the scope, as he dashed for cover behind the digger that was gathering snow by the side of the landing pad. Burwardsley's first bullet caught the man in the back of the thigh, his blood spraying the side of the digger, then Burwardsley jacked another round into the rifle and shot the man through the spine.

"Two," Burwardsley said, as he chambered another round in the rifle.

He sensed movement to his left, pictured the terrain he had explored to that side of the slope, and remembered how steep it was. Burwardsley crouched in the snow, slung the rifle around his chest and grabbed the shotgun. He pumped a shell into the chamber and moved closer to the slope, firing when he saw the top of the man's head. The man ducked and Burwardsley fired again. He missed, but the man lost his footing and started to slide down the slope. Burwardsley fired a third time and helped the man on his way, the impact of the shotgun blast propelling the man down the side of the mountain. Burwardsley pumped another shell into the chamber and moved backward in a crouch toward the path.

He knew the path well, having studied the terrain over the previous month, in all kinds of weather. He knew where to run, where to slide, where to jump, and made good progress. But the men following him were younger, faster, and likely had fewer wounds than he did. Burwardsley could feel the recent gunshot wounds protesting as he moved, he grunted and tried to ignore them. It was his shoulder that bothered him the most, and each time he pulled the butt of the rifle or the shotgun into his body, the recoil reminded him of when he had last been in combat, when he had last been hit. Even if his memory had failed him, he didn't have to wait long for the familiar burning pain that tore through his upper body as a three-bullet burst bit into the ground and a single bullet ricocheted off a lichen-crusted boulder and into his ribs.

"Fuck." Burwardsley stumbled, and a second burst of lead tore through the snow behind him into his right leg. He stumbled, rolled onto his back and fired the shotgun back up the path, catching the first man to run into his line of fire. The man cartwheeled into the snow in front of Burwardsley, bleeding profusely but alive. His MP5 was within Burwardsley's reach, and the Royal Marine Lieutenant considered grabbing it, only to hear an inner voice chide him that cover was better, and that he should get going. He rolled onto his knees, used the shotgun to lever himself up onto his feet, ignored the pain, and ran.

Burwardsley focused on the trail to quash the pain in his ribs and leg. He picked out his visual markers, and realised he was just a few hundred metres from a more defendable position. He was close to the end of the island, and had even chosen a spot that meant he could cover Fenna from the land if she needed help. But a few hundred metres was a long way for a wounded man. He pushed on, aware of the scrape of the men's boots over the lichen and rocks behind him, and the softer tread of their soles through the deeper patches of snow.

The wind blew spindrift into Burwardsley's face, and he spared a kind thought for the sudden cloud of snow and stars of ice masking his descent toward the tip of the island.

The only thing I don't understand, he thought as he ran, *is why they pushed so hard so fast. Why didn't they take their time? Why didn't they try to flank me?* The question occupied him for another hundred metres, and he even picked up the pace, only to slow as he realised the answer. *They don't have the time. This has to be done fast.*

The opposite side of the island and position of Vestergaard's ship in the fjord was obscured from view by the mountain. Burwardsley didn't have the vantage point he needed to second-guess why his pursuers had abandoned caution in favour of speed. But, he had to admit, speed was something they did have, and they were gaining on him. Two three-round bursts convinced him to stop thinking and start running. He pounded down the path only to stumble over a boulder. For the first time since they had sledded into the settlement, the men slowed, choosing two firing positions from which to torment the Royal Marine with a bullet from each position into his thighs.

"You bastards," he yelled. Burwardsley bit back a cry of pain and looked ahead. The position he had chosen for his last stand was only fifteen metres further on, through the snow, down the slope. "But I won't make it," he said, his words jarring through gritted teeth. The path was still high enough that there was a steep slope to his right, running all the way to the ice below. Burwardsley heard the soft click of metal as the men changed magazines, and that's when he pressed the barrel of the shotgun flat against his chest and pushed off over the edge of the path.

Burwardsley laughed as he heard the men swear, but the first boulder he hit with his ribs forced him to concentrate on rolling, or falling as it appeared to the men above him. They tried a few single shots, anticipating where he might be before he rolled into their line of fire, but the slope was uneven, and two sudden drops saved Burwardsley from more bullets in his body, only to knock the wind from his lungs as he slammed onto the rocks below. Snow plumed and geysered around his body as he fell, until the slope smoothed and he rolled and slid the last twenty metres to the ice foot that braked his fall.

The snow settled around him. Burwardsley took a moment, and then spat snow from his mouth. He rolled onto his back, ignoring the pain from the bullets and the fall. He watched as the two men picked their way down the slope, slipping around the larger boulders and stumbling over the smaller ones. When one of the men slipped and pitched forward, Burwardsley pushed himself up, levelled the shotgun and fired.

The hammer clicked but the weapon did not fire. He tossed it away and groaned onto his feet as the man regained his footing and ran down the last few metres of the slope. He crashed into Burwardsley and they fell backward over the ice foot and onto the slippery surface of the sea ice. Burwardsley's opponent was first onto his feet. He moved backward a step, reaching for his weapon, only to tug at an empty sling.

"That's just too bad," Burwardsley said as he pressed one foot down onto the ice, and kneeled. The man kicked at him, and Burwardsley caught his foot and pulled him off balance. The combined weight of the two men and the sudden impact splintered the ice. The current streaming through the water was strongest at low tide, it degraded the ice from beneath, thinning it. The man was masked, like his teammates, but his eyes were visible. They no longer focused on Burwardsley, but on the black water beneath them. Burwardsley looked at the man, lifted his elbow, and slammed it into the ice.

"No," the man shouted, as he struggled to pull free of Burwardsley's grasp. Burwardsley slammed his elbow again, and again, until it splashed through the ice and the frigid water of the fjord swelled onto the thin frozen surface. "What are you doing?" the man cried.

"Killing you," Burwardsley said, and rolled the man onto his back, pushing down on his chest until the water was rising around the man's neck. Burwardsley ignored the man's kicks and cries. He ignored the cold water turning his fingers and hands to wooden implements, unable to bend or feel, only push. "What's the rush? Who's coming?"

The man said nothing. He tried to kick, but Burwardsley's weight was too great. The water rose to the man's cheeks and he yelled at Burwardsley to let him go, but he kept pushing, until the man's forehead was below the surface. Burwardsley could feel his knees beginning to cool as the ice bowed beneath the weight of the two men. He pushed once more and the man's head disappeared beneath the water. Burwardsley held him there as the last of his breath bubbled through the fibres of his ski mask.

"I asked you a question. Answer me." Burwardsley started to pull the man out of the water, to lift his head, but he had forgotten the man's partner, at least until he felt the butt of the MP5 crack on his head. He slumped down onto the man beneath him, trying to focus on the icebergs in the distance, where he imagined he might see Fenna, just one more time, as she sledged toward the glacier wall. He forgot all about the man beneath him, thinking only of how much his head hurt, and how much more it hurt as he received another blow. Burwardsley's head slumped into the sea, he tasted the salt on his lips, felt its cool kiss on his cheeks, and in the blackness beneath him, he saw a young Greenlandic woman, her hair so black, so long, it twisted around her naked body, beckoning him to join her.

"Dina," Burwardsley said, the seawater bubbling from his mouth and onto the man's chest. "It's you."

"*Iji*," she said, in her native Greenlandic tongue.

"You can speak."

"Yes." Dina smiled, beckoning once more. "Come."

"I will," he said. "I'll be right there, only, just give me a minute." Burwardsley spluttered as the last of the team sent to kill him pressed his foot onto his back. "I just need a minute." He coughed. "I just need to see Fenna. Just one more time. To say I'm sorry."

"She knows," Dina said. "Come."

"Yes. I'll be right there, love. I will. I promise. Just one minute." He coughed another mouthful of sea water, and the man pressed him down, harder, kicking him again and again. But Burwardsley resisted, spreading his hands flat against the surface of the ice, a cold crucifixion as he tried again, one last time, to scour the ice for a sign, a trace, a glimpse of the young Sirius woman, Fenna, as she sledged to the glacier.

"Come," Dina called again, beckoning him to the depths. "It will be alright," she said, as she curled her slim hand around his neck and pulled him down beneath the ice, until his body was immersed to his boots. The man on the ice kicked at Burwardsley's hands, propelling him down into the water where Dina took care of him, rolling him onto his back so that he might have one last look at the sky.

Vestergaard's man, the last of the team of six, stepped back from the hole in the ice, slid the soles of his boots on the surface until he felt confident he could turn his back on the ice and walk to the safety of the land. He frowned at the sound of tapping on the air, checked the swivel mount securing his weapon to the sling, pressed his hands over both attachment points and paused on the ice to search for the source of the noise. He found it when he looked up and saw a man in a cornflower-blue smock tapping a thin bone instrument against a sealskin drum. The man cocked his head to look, exposing the side of his neck, and giving the shaman a perfect point at which to strike. The tapping noise stopped when the shaman plunged the length of bone into the man's neck and kicked his body back toward the hole in the ice. It was just one more thing that Fenna did not see, but then, as the shaman knew, she was fighting for her life.

Chapter 25

Fenna's dogs slowed as they passed the fishing hole and entered the ice fjord. The light was failing and the shadows from the icebergs created pockets of darkness, as long as the icebergs were tall. The team pursuing Fenna loitered at the fishing hole, as the men checked their gear before entering the maze of icebergs. Fenna let her team rest as she watched her pursuers through the binoculars. She saw their breath steam through their ski masks and imagined it freezing on the swathe of ice clinging to the fibres of the masks. Only Vestergaard's face was unmasked, and she studied him, the raw colour of his cheeks struggling to cope with the cold. He looked like a Russian, with the arms of his glasses tucked behind his ears, beneath a large fur hat. She wondered for a moment if there was a connection, another group in the shadows, pulling on strings, before deciding it really didn't matter anymore.

From her position, she could just see Vestergaard's ship beyond the island. It had turned, the gantry and floating deck had been retrieved and stowed, and it seemed to be moving slowly toward Nuugaatsiaq. Fenna thought she could hear the sound of a helicopter approaching, and a quick glance at Vestergaard through the binoculars suggested he had too. She watched as he hurried the two men with sharp gestures and trails of mist from his nose and mouth. *He looks like a dragon*, Fenna thought. *Let's see if we can put that fire out.*

She stuffed the binoculars inside the sledge bag and got off the sledge. The dogs were uncertain among the icebergs, and the air was colder, as the dense behemoths of ice pushed the temperature several more degrees below zero. Fenna imagined it to be close to minus twenty degrees Celsius. She walked to the front of the team, tracing slow circles with the tip of the whip on the ice. The dogs fidgeted as she bent down to fuss over the lead dog.

"Hey boy," she said, and smiled at the lead dog. Its face was scarred with the challenge of being an alpha dog and keeping the job. Ice beaded the fur around its eyes, and hung from its muzzle in the same way it hung from a man's beard. Fenna could feel the same tiny beads of ice clinging to the fine hairs on her face, could feel the crust of ice on her neckie each time she moved her chin, and she knew the tips of her hair were frosted white like icing. She pressed her forehead to the dog's and whispered, "I need you to follow me, keep the team in check, and we'll be alright." She lifted her head and looked at the dog. "Deal?" The dog licked at the ice on its muzzle and Fenna took that as a *yes*.

She stood up, and in the lull between the supernatural creaks and groans of the icebergs settling, she could hear the shush of the approaching dog team.

"Trust me," she said to the lead dog.

Fenna scanned the ice between two large icebergs. It was convoluted, a mess of jagged shards like toffee broken from a pan. Between the shards she saw patches of free plates of ice, bobbing in a white mass. The route she was considering was not frozen solid, far from it. There were larger plates of ice that were frozen in place, but the gaps between them were not be trusted. It was unlikely they could bear the weight of a sledge.

"Perfect," she said, even though the tumult in her stomach and the jag of adrenaline that peaked at the thought of venturing between the icebergs suggested otherwise. Fenna lifted her chin, ignored the sound of the runners grating across the ice behind her, and led her team between the bergs.

She took a step and heard her team follow, the creak of the hunter's wooden sledge magnified by the amphitheatre of ice. She took another step, picking her route toward a large floe that was flat, big enough for her team. She hoped the jagged shards and smaller bergs littering the route would provide ample cover from Vestergaard's men and their submachine guns, and counted on the fact they would be forced to follow. She pushed on, avoiding a smooth chunk of ice the size of a washing machine as it rolled within a chilly soup of small clumps and grains of brash ice. One of the dogs was not so observant. Fenna heard the splash as it slipped. She turned, lunged for the gangline and pulled it out of the water. There was more ice than water, and the dog had been lucky. *I'll check his paws later*, Fenna thought, and continued."If there is a later."

Fenna reached the large floe and stopped to choose the next leg of her route. That was when she heard Vestergaard's voice, and felt a chill greater than the air freezing and pressing at her body.

"Where are you going, Konstabel?" he shouted, his voice reverberating between the icebergs. "There's nowhere to go. You might as well stop, and we can put an end to this." He paused and Fenna assumed he was giving instructions to his men. "You're only making this more difficult on yourself, Konstabel."

Vestergaard's voice echoed once more until it was

replaced by the sound of dogs following Fenna's route. She scanned ahead, quickly, picked her route and jumped on the sledge.

"Let's go," she shouted, and cracked the whip to the right of the team, pushing them left. The lead dog took up the slack as Fenna knew he would, and the team followed. *Tough dog,* Fenna thought. *There's a reason he has those scars. Thank God.* She knelt on the wooden thwarts of the sledge, wishing she had brought a reindeer skin to protect her knees and provide some warmth, but there had been no time. She held her breath to stop it misting in front of her face, just for a moment, to better see her route.

"Shit."

The lead dog pulled them onto a floe that began to wobble. Fenna cracked the whip to the left, urging the team to the right, whistling and clicking to get them to go faster. The route was uneven, the path obscured with ice that trapped the sledge runners. Fenna coiled the whip around an upright, leaped off the sledge and grabbed both uprights in her hands. She pushed, guiding the sledge from the rear, as the dogs pulled from the front.

"Come on," she said, risking a glance behind her and seeing the black muzzles of the dogs leading Vestergaard's team. The bucket seat of the sled was empty, she noted, and there was only one man standing at the rear of the sled. *And it's not him.*

The team behind rallied at the sight of Fenna's dogs. They had been chasing the scent, and now they had them in sight. The man at the rear of the sled tried to slow their speed by stamping down on a metal brake designed for snow on forest trails, not for sea ice. If Fenna had heard it, she would have enjoyed the sound of the metal brake being torn from the sled. She heard only the man's cry of alarm, and mistook it for a challenge, a command for her to stop. She pushed on, driving the team onto another patch of uneven ice where the larger slabs were angled at forty-five degrees. The dogs skittered onto the ice, the sledge slid sideways and Fenna slipped. She fell as the dogs and the sledge slid down the ice floe, the sledge crunching into Fenna's knee and trapping her for a moment against a large boulder of ice.

"Shit." Fenna tried to push at the sledge, but didn't have the angle. She reached instead for the flap of the rifle holster, fumbling at the quick-release knot she had tied that was now frozen. She opened it as the first of the foreign dogs clawed their way over the ice, grasping the butt of the rifle and pulling it free of the holster. Fenna leaned back against the ice, her body twisted and protesting with a sharp pain in her back. She ignored it, chambered a round into the rifle, tugged it into her shoulder and aimed at the spot she imagined the driver of the team would appear. But the foreign dogs, eight or nine of them, were too excited to stop, and the man lost control as the two teams of dogs fought, friend and foe alike, as canine teeth ripped through the fur and flanks closest to them.

The dogs of both teams fought almost silently, the teeth too engaged to allow unnecessary sounds through the mouth. The sled slipped down the ice and crunched into Fenna's sledge, putting more pressure on her knee. Then she saw the driver of the team, as he slipped on the ice, scrambling for a solid grip with his boots, as he aimed the MP5 at Fenna. She shot him through the chest, crying out as the recoil and the combined weight of the sledges and teams jarred her knee. She couldn't move.

The dogs ignored the gunshot and continued to lunge at the throat of the nearest opponent, any opponent. The ganglines stretching from the sledge and sled to the dogs were twisted and knotted and rethreaded as they fought. But as the fight progressed and Vestergaard's team dragged their sled off Fenna's sledge, she felt the weight shift from her knee, and slammed the rifle butt against the ice to push herself free and onto her feet. Fenna slung the rifle across her chest, pulled the knife from the sheath on her belt and hobbled into the mess of lines, teeth, and dogs. She sawed at the ganglines attaching Vestergaard's team to one another, and then severed the gangline from the sled. Once his dogs were free she knew they would have the advantage over her own, but then they could also escape, and she counted on the wild, raw nature of the Greenlandic dogs being more than a match for the Alaskan breed, bred for speed not survival. The dogs took a moment to realise they were free, and then leaped back from the frenzy of the fight. Half of the dogs lingered, looking for another angle of attack, Fenna shooed them away with sharp words and kicks that jarred her knee and brought a tear to her eye. Her tears froze as the dogs ran and she gritted her teeth while pulling the sled off the sledge.

Fenna sorted out her own dogs next, cuffing them with thumps of her fist, and then the butt of the whip when she remembered to use it. The dogs relented, content with a snarl or two before Fenna reminded them again who was boss. She swore as she moved, favouring her good knee and limping around the dogs as she worked her way back to the sledge. She sheathed the knife and scrambled up the floe to scavenge what she could from the dead man's body. The sling of his weapon was trapped beneath him, so she cut it away, and took the submachine gun. She checked the magazine. It was light, only half full. She took it anyway and slid back down the floe, cursing as she crashed into the sledge. Fenna picked herself up and stuffed the MP5 into the sledge bag.

"Okay, boys," she said. "You've had your fun. Let's go."

Fenna pushed at the sledge and the lead dog, blood frozen around its chops, took up the slack and led the team off the floe and onto a stretch of smooth ice, much to Fenna's relief. She squirmed the toe of her boot beneath the sledge bag and leaned over the uprights to let the dogs carry her weight across the ice. She could see at least thirty metres of good ice ahead, and chose to let the dogs run the length of it, before slowing and stopping to pick her route. There was blood on her lip, and she didn't know if it was human or dog. She realised she didn't care. Fenna winced at the pain in her knee, but considered herself lucky.

"Still alive," she said. "Still stubborn." *Burwardsley will be pleased.*

Two black shapes in the distance caught her eye, and she slowed the team with soft commands, using her feet to add more friction until the sledge slowed to a stop. One of the men was Vestergaard. She recognised the shape of the fur hat. *He must have found a better route*, she mused, *for him and his man*. They started to walk toward her, and Fenna decided to wait until they were closer.

She slid the rifle off her chest, worked the bolt and chambered a round. She rested the barrel on top of the sledge bag, changed her stance to ease her knee, and waited. Vestergaard's man chose a position behind a low boulder of ice frozen into place. Fenna watched as he changed magazines, and took aim. His boss continued walking toward Fenna, and she noticed the pistol in his hand. He stopped within ten metres of her, close enough for them to kill one another. Vestergaard was the first to speak.

"You never could stick to a plan, Konstabel," he said. "You always have to make things difficult."

"That's the kind of girl I am," she said. "You should know. You had me trained this way."

"No, that's where you are wrong." Vestergaard's breath steamed around his face as he sighed. "I never wanted you to be like this. It was Jarnvig who said you had potential. He had you trained and this is what I got. I should never have listened to him."

Fenna tapped her fingers on the rifle, aware of the cold cramping her grip, she stuffed her hands in her pockets, choosing warmth over the chance for an impetuous shot. She felt the tupilaq in her pocket and curled her fingers around it, as Vestergaard continued.

"I understand you met my colleague in Canada?"

"Colleague?"

"Meredith. We worked together once. But now, I suppose she is less inclined to cooperate." Vestergaard paused to nod. "Now there's an opportunity, Konstabel. How would you like to make some money?"

"This has never been about money," she said.

"That was your mistake, not mine. But, seriously, we could come to an arrangement." He turned his head at the sound of a helicopter approaching. When he spoke again, Fenna thought she detected a sudden urgency in his voice. "If you were to report a successful mission to my Canadian friend, then you would be in a position to tidy up one more loose end. That's what I have used you for in the past, and, despite the mess, that's one job you have been adequate at performing."

Fenna smoothed her thumb over the bone limbs of the tupilaq. She squeezed it, wondering at the power the shaman had locked within it, wondering if that power was hers, if she could use it, if it would make a difference.

"Well, Konstabel?" Vestergaard tapped the pistol against his leg. "You don't really want to die here, do you? Because that's the alternative, the only alternative." He glanced again in the direction of the settlement as the helicopter approached Nuugaatsiaq.

Fenna lifted her chin and said, "Friends of yours?"

"A nuisance. Nothing more," he said. "Not unlike yourself." Vestergaard raised the pistol and pointed it at Fenna.

She laughed and said, "I think you'll find I can be far more than that." Fenna pulled her hands out of her pockets and grabbed the whip from the sledge.

Chapter 26

The dogs lurched into a run as Fenna cracked the whip on the ice behind them, just before she dived to one side, sliding across the ice to stop behind a boulder. She heard Vestergaard curse and yell a command to his man. *The one with the submachine gun*, Fenna thought, sighing at the fact that all her weapons were on the sledge. *Not all of them*, she remembered and drew the knife from its sheath. She sat up and coiled the dog whip around her chest, it would be useless in a fight. She buried any insecurities she might have about her knife-fighting skills, and chose to remember instead the first man she had killed, with his own knife, in the desert.

"The Arctic is a desert too," she whispered and shifted position to peek around the boulder of ice. The dogs had stopped just beyond Vestergaard. They shifted and fidgeted for lack of purpose and direction in an unfamiliar and intimidating environment. Fenna looked at the leader and whispered, "Just stay there. Just a little longer." The sound of rubber soles slipping on the ice to her left caught her attention, and she turned away from the dogs.

Vestergaard's last man was cautious. He held his MP5 in a tight grip, a textbook position for close-quarter combat. The iron sights of the submachine gun moved in sync with his head. Where he looked, he aimed. *Which is just fine*, Fenna thought, *when you're standing on solid ground. But here…*

Fenna waited until she was sure the man was as close as he dared, before jumping up and throwing the knife at him. She didn't care if it hit him, she just needed a few seconds to vault over the ice boulder and slam her knee into his crotch and her fist into his chest. She was lighter than him, lighter than any of her opponents, but the glassy nature of the ground beneath the man's feet played to her advantage and he slipped onto his back, grunting as a spear of ice punctured his shoulder. He was pinned for a second, and Fenna didn't need much longer than that. She gripped his chin and pushed his head back as she squirmed on top of him, ignoring the pain in her knee, and the burst of bullets he fired from the gun as he tried to blast her off his body. The bullets boomed past her head, leaving a ringing sound in her right ear and the taste of cordite on her tongue. She slapped at the weapon, as she tried to get her knees onto his chest and press his shoulder down on the spear of ice protruding from the jagged shard beneath him. She stopped when she saw the ice pierce his skin and push through his jacket. Fenna shifted her focus to the man's head, slamming the base of her fist into his forehead until she felt and heard his neck snap. The man's head lolled back on the ice and he dropped the MP5. Fenna reached for it, only to be spun onto the ice with two bullets into her right arm. She landed, gasping for air as it was knocked out of her lungs. Vestergaard stepped into view, and aimed the pistol at her head.

"Always so brutal, Konstabel. Why?"

Fenna filled her lungs with icy air as the shock of the bullets piercing her arm, and the impact of landing on the ice subsided. She was about to say something, anything, when she felt the ice move beneath her.

"Never mind," Vestergaard said. "Let's just finish this, shall we?" The sound of the helicopter increased, the *whop whop* of its thick blades beating the Arctic air between the island and the icebergs leading to the glacier. "And quickly, I think."

Fenna caught a glimpse of the helicopter's searchlight as it beamed through the gloom and lit the route she had taken into the ice fjord. She looked at Vestergaard as he twitched at the proximity of the helicopter. The ice shifted again beneath her and she cleared her throat.

"What's that?" Vestergaard said. He bent down over Fenna grabbed the whip looped around her chest and pulled her upward as he pressed the muzzle of the pistol to her head. The tip of the whip wedged between a crack in the ice. "Got something to say?" he said and sneered.

"Yes," she said, and grabbed his wrist and the belt around his waist. Fenna kicked at a solid clump of ice, and took a breath as she felt the small floe upon which she lay shift and topple. She splashed into the water and dragged Vestergaard with her.

Vestergaard cried out and dropped the pistol, as he braced his hands on the solid ice either side of Fenna. His knees slipped into the water, and Fenna tugged at his belt, clawed at his face, and pulled his glasses off. Her teeth chattered as she grabbed at his neck and pulled him down toward her face. The only thing stopping her from slipping under the water and beneath the ice was Vestergaard. She tried to hook her leg through his and pull him down, but again, her weight was against her.

"Too light," she spluttered, as the black icy water lapped at her mouth.

"This is a stalemate, Konstabel," Vestergaard shouted. "Just let go and die."

"Okay," Fenna said. She slipped her hand from his belt and, muscles cramping, she shoved it into her pocket. She pulled the tupilaq out of jacket and pressed it into Vestergaard's face. "Do you recognise this?"

"Hah," he said, as he shifted his grip on the ice, and tried to shake off Fenna's grip. "You believe in magic now? Really, Konstabel, after all we've been through, I thought you would know better."

"But they call you *the Magician*. Don't they?" Fenna's words trembled over her frozen lips. But as the helicopter approached, and before she lost control of her lips, Fenna whistled, long and low, faltering toward the end as Vestergaard laughed.

"*The Magician* is just one of many names, Konstabel. But the last one you will hear," he said, as he pulled his leg free of Fenna's. He turned at the sound of runners grating across the ice and Fenna saw the frown on his brow as the hunter's lead dog clawed across the ice and into view. It sniffed after Fenna, pressing its paws and its weight onto Vestergaard's back. Fenna felt her head dip below the surface of the water, felt the pinch of cold around her forehead, but she smiled at the sight of the dog, all forty kilos of it. She made one last grab at Vestergaard and pulled him under the ice as the dog sprang back from the hole.

Vestergaard's body sank faster than Fenna's as her descent was arrested by the tip of the whip clamped in a crevice of ice on the surface. Fenna still had the tupilaq between her fingers, and she kicked at Vestergaard's body, barely aware of how fast he was sinking as she dragged herself up the whip with frozen fingers. She kicked with what little strength she had left as she broke through the surface, and clawed her way out of the water.

She saw the dogs, saw the sledge, and pulled her way toward it, ignoring the bullet wounds in her arm, ignoring her knee, ignoring the cold. There were spare clothes in the sledge bag, she knew it. There was even food, she could almost taste it, a whole bar of chocolate, already unwrapped, bagged only, waiting to be eaten. The dogs fidgeted as she crawled onto the sledge, her body shivering so hard the sledge shook and creaked. The lead dog mistook the movement for a command and pulled the team and Fenna away from the hole in the ice and back toward the settlement. With no counter-commands, the lead dog trusted to what it knew about ice, and chose only the safe, flat, thick floes locked together between the icebergs.

The helicopter passed to their right, and Fenna watched as it circled around and played the searchlight across the ice until it found the bodies of Vestergaard's men. It couldn't land, she knew, but it hovered long enough to confirm that the men were dead and to document the scene. *They will probably return in the morning*, she thought, *whoever they are.*

A new sound cut through the beat of the helicopter's rotor blades as the pilot switched on the loudspeaker mounted beneath the cockpit. Fenna fumbled the chocolate from the sledge bag into her mouth, chewing through teeth that chattered as she listened to a familiar voice distorted just a little by the noise of the helicopter.

"Konstabel Fenna Brongaard, this is Oversergent Noa Andersen of the Sirius Sledge Patrol. Let us help you. Show us where you are."

CHRISTOFFER PETERSEN

She considered it, for a moment, as the dogs increased speed away from the metallic beast buffeting the air between the icebergs. She imagined being rescued by the Sirius men, the warm blankets, the hot coffee and the interrogation, and a very uncertain life. But it was Andersen's next words that confirmed her decision, as darkness descended on the thin sea ice leading into the fjord.

"Burwardsley is dead. You don't need to die out here. Let us help you."

"Somehow, I knew," she said, as she removed the whip and stripped off her jacket and the sodden icy layers clinging to her upper body. "But I don't have to die out here. He wouldn't want that."

She talked to herself as she dressed, as if the words would make her actions easier. She checked the bullet holes in her arm, grazes really, they stung more than they bled. A bandage could wait, a hat was more important, and she pulled a dry woollen hat over her head. The helicopter began circling the hole in the ice, increasing the diameter of the search with each pass. Fenna willed the dogs onward as she pulled a sleeping bag from the sledge bag and crawled inside it. She stuffed her hands inside the sealskin mittens and shivered as she thought.

The lights of Nuugaatsiaq beckoned and the dogs nosed for home, until Fenna cracked the whip and turned them away from the settlement, and deeper into the fjord. She would avoid the village and sledge straight for the airport at Qaarsuut. *Perhaps everyone would think she was dead?* She smiled at the thought, her feelings buoyed and her body warmed at the idea of being free. The dogs pulled the sledge past the settlement and Fenna closed her eyes, until she was

272

sure they were past the island, swinging wide of the ship, and sledging away from her past and into the future.

Alice is safe, she thought, *and Dina…*

She remembered Burwardsley's words, about saving the living, so that the dead might find peace. He had said something like that, and it sounded good, it sounded right. Fenna smiled as the wind burned at her cheeks and she opened her eyes, staring at the vast expanse of thin ice ahead of her, and a world of opportunities.

LONDON, ENGLAND

It was a terrible connection, and the clatter of mugs, the chatter of customers, and the hiss of the coffee machines, didn't help matters. Fenna pressed the receiver of the payphone closer to her ear and smiled at the familiar voice who answered in Greenlandic. It was late evening in London, but Tulugaq and his family were just sitting down to dinner.

"Hi," Fenna said in Danish. "It's me."

"I know who you are," Tulugaq said, and Fenna could almost see the knowing smile crease his face. "Shall I keep it between us?"

"Yes."

"Good," he said. "It is better this way."

Fenna nodded as she pressed several more coins into the payphone. "Is she alright?"

"Alice? *Aap*, she is fine, although my son is frustrated."

"She is playing hard to get?"

"Very, but the children are happy with their new English teacher."

"That's good," Fenna said. She paused for a

moment before saying, "What about my friend? Did you find him?"

There was a pause and a rattle at the other end of the line, and Fenna imagined the shaman moving to a quieter part of the house. "He is at peace," he said.

"But you never found his body?"

"*Naamik.*"

Fenna let the receiver slide down her cheek as she thought about what to say next. There were no words, only the brief tears she allowed herself before Tulugaq's voice urged her to listen.

"He is at peace, he is with *Sassuma Arnaanut*, the one you call Sedna."

"Beneath the ice?"

"*Aap.*"

Safe, Fenna thought. And then she smiled. He has an eternity to torment Vestergaard. She almost laughed at the thought, and then remembered to thank Tulugaq for everything he had done.

"Be safe," he said, before ending the call.

The connection was severed, and it took a moment for Fenna to realise she was alone, cut off, and removed from the world she once knew, and ready to explore another. *But where?*

Fenna placed the receiver on the hook and ordered a coffee. She found a seat by the window, and enjoyed the warm glow from the Christmas lights that lit the raindrops on the glass. *Too warm for snow*, she mused as she sipped at her coffee. *But perhaps I have seen enough snow for a lifetime.*

She put the mug on the table and studied her hands, ignoring the small scars on her skin, and focusing instead on the length of her nails. No longer were they broken and pitted, scratched or covered in mud, *or worse*. Fenna held them up to the light and imagined, for once in her life, that these were the hands of a lady. She looked at her jeans, the small feminine boots she had picked out in the second-hand store. She smoothed the fabric of her shirt between her fingertips, felt the soft fibres of the cardigan that she wore instead of a fleece. Only the creak of her leather jacket reminded her of her former life, as she imagined the sledge shifting within its bindings.

I probably still smell of dog, she thought, and smiled. She looked up at the sound of someone sitting down at a table near hers. Three people, a couple and a single man. The man smiled at her, and Fenna dared to imagine another future, a possible future, that might one day even include a man. She smiled back and returned to her coffee, more than a little self-conscious all of a sudden, and enjoying the feel of it.

The Christmas lights flickered as a fresh gust of wind played at the cables hung between the shops on the cosy backstreet she had found. The man selling roasted chestnuts grabbed at his hat, and Fenna watched him for a moment, only to be distracted by the sight of another man, a reflection in the window, from inside the coffee shop.

She recognised the face, almost Greenlandic, with a patchwork of ugly scars criss-crossing the man's cheeks. Fenna stared at the man's reflection, putting a name to the face of Yuka, realising at the same time that the life she might have imagined, the life of freedom, was short-lived, and the life she knew only too well, had caught up with her once again.

THE END

ACKNOWLEDGEMENTS

I would like to thank Isabel Dennis-Muir for her invaluable editing skills and feedback on the manuscript.

Once again, while several people have contributed to *The Shaman's House*, the mistakes and inaccuracies are all my own.

Chris

December 2017
Denmark

ABOUT THE AUTHOR

Christoffer Petersen is the author's pen name. Chris lived in Greenland for seven years, and continues to be inspired by the vast icy wilderness of the Arctic. His books share a common setting in the Arctic region, often with a Scandinavian influence.

You can find Chris in Denmark or online here:

www.christoffer-petersen.com

By the same author:

THE GREENLAND TRILOGY
featuring Konstabel Fenna Brongaard

Book 1
THE ICE STAR

Book 2
IN THE SHADOW OF THE MOUNTAIN

Book 3
THE SHAMAN'S HOUSE

and

THE GREENLAND CRIME SERIES
featuring Constable David Maratse

Book 1
SEVEN GRAVES, ONE WINTER

Short stories from the same series
KATABATIC
CONTAINER
TUPILAQ
THE LAST FLIGHT